GO FIGURE

BY

JUD WIDING

AFTER Wally's done runnin his mouth, I ask him what's my cut. He says forty percent. Same as his, on accounta the eggheads get twenty. This is how come I like workin with Wally so much.

Even for Wally, I gotta admit this is a pretty good gag. He's a whaddyacallit when it comes to the scams. Really good at em. But better than that. There's a fuckin word for what'm I tryin to say. I don't get how come words wanna hide from me just when I'm lookin for em. It ain't like they owe me money or nothin. I just wanna talk, honest.

Whatever, I'll be listenin to my programs tonight and that word'll start screamin itself in my ear. What were we talkin about? Wally. Right.

Wally's more than a word. He's just about the brainiest fuckin guy I ever met, only instead of fixin diseases or cancellin poverty he uses his brains to fleece folks. Not just quote bad guys unquote. He ain't one of them green hat types goes around robbin hoods. Wally figures your pockets look heavier than his, you're on the menu. But he'll make ya love him even as he's shakin ya by the ankles. If ya wanted to work out everybody what loves Wally and everybody what hates him, you'd need a fuckin Venn diagram.

The gag Wally's bringin me in on here is, like I just said, a pretty good one. He wants to hit a casino, only instead of guns he's gonna use maths. But he ain't countin cards. That'd be easy. Wally don't go in for easy.

The way he figured, the Sharktooth Casino's got seven roulette wheels. I mean, that ain't the part he was figurin. That's just how many roulette wheels does the Sharktooth Casino got. But his figure was that all of them wheels can't be right alike. They been around the block. They gotta have some wear. So Wally tracks down seven eggheads can remember every fuckin thing they ever heard. Their brains ain't got the same hidin places as mine, I figure. Still don't know what that fuckin word was.

So Wally's got the eggheads, and off they go to the Sharktooth Casino. You might figure callin it a Casino's bein generous on accounta Uncle Sam ain't so hot on the dice-rollin at present. Maybe you're figurin it's gotta be it ain't more'n a few tables got soft green tops stuffed in the back of a fishmongers or some shit. Well, you ain't wrong bout the fishmongers bit, on accounta

Go Figure

Sharktooth's stuffed in the back bit of a warehouse trades in stinky shit comes in leaky boxes. I figure the stink ain't no accident though. I figure it's meant for bein a fuckin discouragement for guys got warrants. On accounta that back bit of the joint? It's a proper casino, lemme tell ya. It's a proper casino on accounta they got machines go bing-bing-bing without there's some dope sittin there pullin a string, and all the dopes they *do* got're wearin the same evenin formals.

Anyway what'm I sayin is, Wally carpools the fuckin eggheads to the Sharktooth. Every egghead takes a wheel, and they play little chips the whole fuckin day, if you wanna call that playin. Just watchin a ball bounce around a wheel. Click click click, maybe you win, maybe you don't. That's what you're payin for, you go to a casino. Payin in pogs. Makes no sense.

Except Wally's figure is that you look real hard, there's sense enough gets you more pogs than how many'd you put down. So he brings the eggheads back to his and cracks em open. They scratch out a fuckin biography for the little ball they was watchin. First spin puts the ball in the red nineteen box. Second is the black thirty-three. Third is you get the idea. The whole fuckin day's spins, they're writin out! Easy like Wally asked em what's your favorite motion picture, or vegetable, whatever shit they know a lot about on accounta it ain't more'n their say so! Only it ain't say so, it's numbers. Fuckin eggheads, I tell ya. Then Wally drives em all to their own, and oh by the way don't he just *love* scootin his spitshine sedan outta the city where some folks're still unhitchin their goddamned horsies, and then anyway next mornin he picks em up again like they're goin to pigskin practice. Only they ain't. Egg-heads goin for sports? Fat fuckin chance.

They're goin back to the wheels. Click click click, all the while they're clockin where does the ball land. Wally takes em back to his. Scribble scribble scratch. Back to theirs.

Again. Again. A week straight, he does this. Then he starts doin his whiz-bang on the scratches. Runnin numbers. Add. Subtract. Long divison. Hey presto. Grease pen shit. Don't ask me. I don't know. All I know is, Wally comes to me and says he knows *this* wheel turns up *these* numbercolors with a quote irregularly high probability unquote, because the wood is all fucked up or something. His figure is, you go in and you play *these* numbercolors on *that* wheel, you can put heavy timber every time and math says you close out smilin.

Sounds loopy to me, but Wally knows his onions. We ain't full-time partners or nothin, but sayin like we was, he's the brains for sure. Where I come in, I'm the other one. That's how come I'm in on this gag, is Wally wants the other thing ain't brains. He wants me to loom.

Sharktooth is a Luciano joint, so we both figure they got a knee-breaker in the basement. Wally wins big one night, odds are he gets a free drink and they say to him come back anytime, on accounta they wanna get that money back and ain't nobody lucky twice. But Wally goes back and wins big a *second* night, people's eyebrows start crawlin around their face. Night three and they're yankin a big chain, pullin that knee-breaker outta whatever fuckin bucket do they keep him in.

What I don't say to Wally is How about you just do it the one night and then relax about it. I don't say that on accounta it's Wally I'm talkin to. He don't need the fuckin money. A hundred gags back, he reads this book by a fella called Dickins, and it's got this scam in it where a guy finds a buncha dupes and say to em Lemme see some cash and I'll give you more back, then he juggles their fuckin funds and sure, some of em get back more just like he says, but most of the dough winds up in the fella's pocket. He says to himself, He bein Wally, he says Why hasn't anybody done this for real? So he does, then a fella called Ponzi ends up gettin his name on it. Wally don't seem too twisted up on that one. He ain't the sorta guy likes his name on much.

Point I'm makin is, Wally don't need the money. He made about a million off that one gag on its lonesome. You hand him a penny, he'll pinch it like he's afraid the other hand's gonna try for it. Which it probably would. So Wally with two and a half million, which I gotta figure is what he's got when ya throw on the between years? How lumpy must his fuckin mattress be? Gettin keepin spendin, in that order. That's what's money good for, if you're Wally.

So anyway, Wally wants to hit Sharktooth night after night after night til somebody in a suit says they wanna talk in private. All I gotta do then, for forty percent, is join the conversation.

You might be wonderin how come Wally cuts me in so generous. It's because I'm real good at my job. And what's my job is whatever you pay me for. Sometimes it's bruisin. Guy says I need you to tune this other guy up, I don't ask questions after How much ya got. Gal says hey you wanna kill my boss for me, I give her the mess rate and the clean rate. Yeah, I get those jobs. Levelin with ya though, more often I get the loom jobs. Somebody's giving you the chagrins, I ring their doorbell. They open the door. I lean in. They gotta take a step back and look up. Next thing they'll be givin you is a real heartfelt sorry.

I'm a tough. A bruiser. I look like my nickname would be Shorts or Tiny on accounta irony. Only I ain't got a nickname. I'm called Samuzzo D'Amato. So you can fuckin say that, because what, you in some kinda hurry? The fuck you gotta do's so fuckin important? Anyway since sayin the full name is weird you can say Samuzzo. Sammy if you're a pal. Wally gets to say Sammy. So I guess I do got a nickname. Whaddyaknow, I got a nickname!

Anyway, Wally mostly pays me the forty percent to loom. Maybe that sounds like my pal ain't got a coconut goes bonk when ya thump it. Head down to the boardwalk, ya might be sayin, there's lots of guys can loom. For much less a cut, too. But you gotta factor in what's loomin behind the loom. Rumpus goes down, bein big just means there's more you to hit. You gotta have the omens too. I got the omens. Big time. Shit goes down, it lands on an uppercut.

Even knee-breakers respect that. They don't, I ring their doorbell. That's how come Wally pays me the forty percent.

So we're at Sharktooth Casino. Fourth night. Wally's hootin and hollerin at the wheel. He's got a crowd of wannabe flappers takin a break from pissin away their daddy's rainy day for a peek at somebody else's streak. The poor kid spinnin the wheel looks like Wally's haul comes outta his hide. Might be it does. Tough luck, kid.

That lunk over there's got the unlit cigar in his mouth, he's back tonight. Got three new pals with him too. All of em bald, like four knuckles. Thumb was out sick, I figure. They're all putterin around on the far side of the craps. Pacin whisperin pointin. Real excited about their ties. Can't stop fiddlefuckin with em. Must be they only just got em. Speakin of gettin, here come the omens.

Knee-breaker and Boss are comin. I know it. No clear how-come. No signs lightin up. Just the omen. Like thunder far away.

I peel off the wall and close distance with Wally, slidin into a seat at the roulette wheel next to his. Back to him. I wanna be able to stand up and turn real slow when Boss says Let's why don't we talk in private. That's one of my whaddyacallem *signature moves*, I figure. The stand and turn. Real slow.

The old timer spinnin *this* wheel is just starin in to space. She waves her hands and says No more bets.

There's just me and one other dope at this table so I guess she was talkin to me. I just hold my counsels.

I take a quick look over my shoulder and spot em. Knee-breaker, Boss and two of the knuckles. Ain't the odds I was expectin. But they ain't expectin me.

The ball's bouncin round the wheel in front of me. The other dope and the old timer, they ain't even lookin at the ball. They look like they're starin down six more years of a twenty-year sentence. Honestwise though, Old Timer's lucky if she manages four. You ask her bout her best qualities, I figure she's liable to say Typhoid.

Behind me I hear somebody say Excuse me sir. They say it in a voice what's been polished too hard, so you can hear what's under the filigree. Yeah I fuckin know that word. Filigree. I'm ain't dumb like I sound. Sort of like this Boss fella here, just in reverse.

I scoot back in my chair. Wally, god bless him, tells Boss to Hold on a minute as the ball starts clickin. Crazy thing is, Wally'd do that even if I wasn't here. That's just what kind of guy he is. I got no fuckin idea how's he still alive.

Boss says to him Sir. I hear Knee-breaker rumblin like old pipes. I put my meathooks on the table in front of me and push up. Real slow.

Wally starts whoopin about red thirty-four.

Boss says Sir, you need to come with me this instant.

Wally says Oh dear, was I making too much noise? I can try to win a bit more quietly.

Then I hear some scufflin. Wally says Hey now, hang

on just a second.

And then I finish standin and turnin.

The two knuckles are starin at me. They get it. Boss and Knee-breaker are late to the show. I'll have to catch em up.

I take a slow step forward. Real gentle, I place a hand on Wally's shoulder and pull him an inch away from Knee-breaker.

I ask Boss What's with the rumpus, I'm tryna watch the ball bounce.

Oh, I forgot to mention. Whatever you figure I look like, I got a voice to match.

Anyway so Boss says Sir I apologize for the distruption, please return to y-

So I says That's fuckin swell of ya, I accept your apologize.

Boss thinks about this a second. He points to Wally and says Do you know this man?

So I says Course I know him, I'm his fuckin translator.

Boss says What do you mean? He just spoke English to me.

I says Not on my watch he didn't.

Knee-breaker gets a bright idea and says Why don't we take this somewhere else?

So Wally suggests why don't we let's take it to the window so's he can trade his pogs for real money. Boss don't like that suggestion. Now of course Wally ain't expectin he's walkin home with cash money. That's how come we got two of the eggheads sittin at the table with him. To scoop up as many pogs as they can while everybody's busy oglin Wally. You can cash those chips whenever, you know that?

Knee-breaker loved his bright idea so much, he tries it out again.

So I says to him Lead the way.

He just stands there. So does Boss. So do the knuckles. Oh shit, Knee-breaker could be the thumb! How come I ain't thought of that first time?!

Anyway, so I says to the knuckles Better yet, go get your two friends. Let's why don't we all go have a chat.

Nobody moves.

So then I ask Boss where's he wanna have the chat. He mumbles about only wantin to chat with Wally. I tell him that hurts my feelins, and also no on accounta I'm the fuckin translator, remember.

I ask him again about where does he wanna have the chat.

Knee-breaker says Alright tough guy, why don't you and I have our *own* little chat?

I says suits me, I'm chompin at the fuckin bit for a chat and don't much care who's it with. Except for are the knuckles coming?

He didn't get my meanin. But they come anyway.

Knee-breaker figures it's gonna be me vs The Fist. The five of em, all at once. Real friendly, we'll all shuffle through the door to the back-outside. Like I walk to one end of the alley, they spread across the other. Like a tumbleweed's gonna be kickin by any second. That's what's he figure.

Either that, or he's a fuckin idiot.

On accounta I open the door to the alley and say to Knee-breaker After you.

And he fuckin walks through!

So of course I follow him fast into the alley, slammin the door behind me. The four knuckles shout somethin, which gets Knee-breaker turnin around. My fist catches him hard under the eye. Just the right angle to keep him spinnin. He stumbles, wavin his arms. Like a dim kid tryin to catch a bubble. I deadleg him with my heel, pop him right behind the left knee. Doesn't sound like a break. Too bad. Woulda been good.

He plops into a puddle. These alleys are always wet, seems like. I punch the back of his head really fuckin hard. He goes down face first. Into the puddle.

The four knuckles finally worked out the door. They hit the alley like a mudslide.

So I says Hang on, I gotta turn the big guy over.

The knuckles start fannin out.

So I sigh real loud on accounta now I gotta deal with these guys quick enough to keep the guy I just slugged from drownin in a fuckin inch of water.

This is a fuckin first.

Let's say I'm the middle of a clock. I'm facin twelve. The knuckles spread to ten, eleven, one and two. Almost like they got a clue what're they doin. Which I know they don't, on accounta One o'clock just pulled a knife.

Now, a knife'll do ya square in a one-on-one. You're the kinda guy wants to pull a knife, I'm gonna respect ya less. But that's your wherefore. I'm only gonna make ya regret it.

But a knife in a four-on-one? Turns it into a one-on-one. See?

Well, look: One o'clock comes runnin at me, screamin and slashin like he got lost in a corn maze. What do the other three do? They sure as shit don't come rushin in with him. That's how do accidents happen.

I make like I'm gonna fall back. One o'clock rushes after me. Only I was just shiftin my weight. Now I'm shiftin the other way. Closin the distance. I weave hard to the right and come up in his personal space. Grab his knife-happy arm. Right hand under his tricep. Left on top of his forearm.

My right hand drives up while the left slams down. One o'clock's elbow cracks. His arm bends right the wrong way. Then it's just spaghetti. I tap his nose hard with my forehead, he falls asleep.

Rookie move number two: they figure I'm gonna make for the knife One o'clock dropped. They're so scared they ain't even looked at my hands. I mean, look at em! The hell do I need with a knife?

No clue, but Ten o'clock sure can't wait to get to the knife. He all but dives at it. I give him a real good look at my boot. Thump. Asleep.

Eleven and Two both rush me at once. Credit where's it due, that was usually the part where guys run away. Boss picked em right. I just hope he's got more for tomor-

WHAM, the door we came through slams open.

I fuckin goose near outta my shoes.

Eleven lands a good one right on my left nipple. No fuckin idea what was he aimin for, unless he figures to milk me to death.

Two comes in fast. Cracks me hard under the jaw.

Eleven shoots for my gut this time. I'm ready. I brace up, let him connect. Then I wrap his fist like it's a little baby bird, and I set it the fuck free. Crank it hard to the right. It twists like a doorknob. Oh, where'd I put my fuckin manners. Knock knock, right between the eyes. Asleep.

Two claps me hard on the ear. I lose my balance a bit. He presses his luck, puts his head down and drives his shoulder at me. More credit where's it due, he shifts me a few steps. Then I dig my heels in. We stop movin. He keeps strainin. Plucky little fuck, I almost feel bad kneein him in the face.

I look up to the door to see Wally and Boss, lookin pleased and ain't so pleased. Respectively. I open my mouth to say somethin, then I remember. I burrow a toe under Knee-breaker's shoulder and flip him over outta the puddle. He starts coughin. He'll be fine.

So I turn back to Wally and says What the fuck, pal? On accounta he knows I goose easy.

Boss figures I was talkin to him though, and he says Listen, I don't want any trouble. Which goes to show what fuckin esteem's he got for his security. Boss keeps talkin, sayin If you leave right now, and never, *ever* return, I will consider this matter closed.

So Wally says to him I don't know, I really think we

might want to call an ambulance, don't you? Or the police? Your men could have seriously hurt my translator, after all.

Boss turns purple, which is an answer.

Here's the best part: Boss lets us cash the chips Wally won, long as we promise to quote never *ever* return unquote. But since the eggheads grabbed a bunch of em when we was kerfufflin, we made Boss comp us for the quote vanished winnings! Unquote!

Like I said, a good gag. I gotta give Wally a bit of shit on slammin the door though. So on the drive back I says to him Why'd you have to go and slam that fuckin door?

He shrugs and says I really wanted to see the action.

So I says Nobody laid a fuckin finger til you goosed me.

Wally says Sorry about that.

And since I can't stay mad at Wally, I says to him Forget about the door already.

So we both forget about it. Just another gag. One out of a hundred.

Didn't figure it for the sort of job to come circlin back on me.

Some smart guy could probably make a thing outta how Godric runs a frame shop.

Oh *shit*, prodigy! That's the word I was tryin to think of earlier, about Wally. Figures. Soon as I stop tryin to think of it, there it is.

Anyway, Godric runs I've Been Framed, which you ain't gotta be a smart guy to make a thing outta, and anyway it ain't a great thing. Godric ain't a prodigy, ya see. He's a...*fuck*. A fuckin whaddyacallit. Not prodigy.

Networker! Gotcha, you little...ah, *heck*.

Somebody says I know a guy who knows a guy, that guy they're talkin about's Godric. And he ain't just for the crimes. Just *mostly* for the crimes. It's how come he runs a frame shop. Perfect front. You know about how frames are so fuckin expensive? They are, and any-body's got a badge pops in on Godric and says to him

Lemme see those books, they're gonna see he flogs a hell of a lot of em. Frames. And when some civvie schmuck comes in lookin for a tasteful mahogany art box, Godric charges em a hundred, goes across town and gets it done for half that. What the hell does he know about frames? Other than they're so fuckin expensive?

Godric needs a front on accounta on his *mostly the crimes* end of the business, he takes cuts. Finder's fees. Just little nibbles off all the shit he sets up. Runnin booze, whackin a guy, loomin, whaddyawant, he'll find the guy can make your fuckin dream a daymare. Problem is, if you wanna figure it for a problem, New York ain't got no ain't-gots, far as the whaddyawants. And when ya get gots for whaddyawants fast as Godric, every week you got a fuckin feast of nibbles.

So this is about three weeks after Wally's Sharktooth gag. I head in to I've Been Framed, only it's just on accounta I wanna shoot some shit with Godric. I made over twenty grand from the roulette gag. I ain't lookin for another job. Just some shit to shoot.

I squeeze down the aisle of his store, on accounta by the way his store is basically just a fuckin hallway. On accounta what's he need uptown real estate for? He just needs a cubby he can clutter up with frames. Only he didn't leave no room for my frame, barely.

I shoulder in and I say Whaddyasay, old timer?

He's sittin at his desk, wearin that little green visor like he's countin votes for Coolidge. No idea how come he wears that. Maybe he just strapped it on one day and forgot.

GO FIGURE

Godric looks up at me and he says I say get outta my store, you lump! He's gotta start with a joke so he can tell you he's just joshin and anyway it's great to see you. Which is what he says to me.

I ask him how's his ailment. You get to be Godric's age, you get ailments. Every week turns out his ailment is fine, only now he's got a *new* ailment frettin him. This week he got right with his osteoporosis, only I don't know he knows what is that. But who am I kickin up trouble's just been kicked down? Anyway, wouldn't wanna pick on a guy got a thyroid near to fallin off.

That's the formalities, so then I figure we can just start shootin the shit like regular when he ain't got a job for me. Only he *do* got a job for me.

Now Wally'n Godric're some kinda separate. I love Wally, but he runs his fuckin mouth. Tellin me every fuckin detail of every fuckin gag. All the shit I don't gotta know. Godric, he gives me the scoop and the take. That's all.

So he says to me It's a loom. Low risk, one night. Two grand.

I tell him Tell em I'm in.

Godric says he will. Then he asks me have I heard about how gingko trees change sex. Only I figured he was sayin sects, like religiouswise. So I figure Gingko Trees is another jobber he's got. Can't figure out where's he headed here. I ask him as much. He tells me it's just a fact he hadn't heard about, he wanted to know if he was the only schmo on the planet didn't know about gingko trees. I says I never heard of him. Good guy? Godric asks who'm I'm talkin about. I says to him Gingko Trees. He says what about em. I says he changed his confessionals. Godric asks what'm I talkin about. I says I figure we're not talkin about the same guy.

This is how come I like shootin the shit with Godric so much. Keeps me on my toes.

I meet Godric's guy under a bridge. Not Gingko Trees, the guy for the job.

The bridge is this guy's let's-go, not mine. I figure the guy seen it in a picture.

He's got one a those cars makes me figure he ain't heard about rain yet. Cleveland fuckin Speedster. No roof. The fuck's up with that, besides no fuckin roof?

He asks me Are you the guy?

I says to him I'm *a* guy, what else ya wanna know?

He unlocks his doors on accounta Godric musta told him about how'm I so personable.

Drivin out, he don't say nothin for a while, so I don't say nothin. Until he says Listen Mr. D'Amato. Then he pauses. Guess he figures I'm gonna tell him to call me Samuzzo.

He finally figures I ain't gonna do that, so he plows on with Listen Mr. D'Amato, I understand you're not especially interested in the specifics of any given job you take. But there is one thing you should know about tonight's engagement.

So I says to him You said to Godric this one's got the quote low risks unquote, so you wanna tell me I'm gonna be engagin at somebody after all, then let's why don't we pull over and say numbers at each other.

The guy, let's call him Cleveland, he shakes his head and says No that's not...no, this is going to be a perfectly civil conference. It's just that, my business associate with whom we will be meeting...he's going to be bringing some backup of his own.

Cleveland keeps pausin like he figures I got somethin to say as yet. I don't say nothin on accounta that's what I got to say.

He keeps yappin, sayin My associate's bodyguard is attempting to create something of a reputation for himself. He means to paint himself as unpredictable, a loose cannon, that sort of nonsense. The joke of it is that his unpredictability is itself highly predictable. So my associate has warned me, in advance, that his bodyguard will be attempting to...oh, what's the best word for it. To startle you.

So now I'm not not sayin nothin on accounta not bein interested. Now I'm not not sayin nothin on accounta not bein *not* interested.

I figure Cleveland sees the difference. He smiles a little bit and says to me It seems that there is a rumor going around, that you have a propensity to start at loud noises. Perfectly reasonably, but I'm afraid it leaves you open to just this sort of exploitation.

So I break my vow of fuckin silence and says Why would your quote associate unquote tell you about his own guy tryin to goose me?

Cleveland says He told me because he doesn't want things getting out of hand. His bodyguard feels confident that your professionalism will keep you from assaulting him after the, as you would say, goosing. This would in turn further bolster *his* reputation. He would become the wildman who got the legendary Samuzzo D'Amato to jump, and lived to tell the tale.

So I says to him Whaddyamean, legendary?

This ain't good news to me, I got a legend. My whole thing is that I'm strictly off the books. Kinda like Wally.

Cleveland waves that away. He says Word gets around, you know. Ours is an industry of reputations, and yours happens to be exceptional. Minus the goosing, I hesitate to add.

So I says That didn't sound like fuckin hesitation to me.

Rest of the way to the meet, Cleveland's hesitatin properwise.

The meet happens in a field in Jersey. It's got the full moon over it and everything. These fuckin guys. Real dramatic.

As promised, it's Cleveland and me walkin in on Associate and the wildman. They parked their jalopies at opposite ends of the space, lights on. It's a real breathtakin fuckin landscape of light and shadow, is how I might describe it. Sometimes I get the poetries, yeah.

So I stand a step behind Cleveland, off to his right. Pretty fuckin standard loomin technique. Only nobody told the wildman, Tommy fuckin Toothpick over there, who's bouncin from toe to toe, hair floppin around like it can't get comfortable. He sees me starin and he gives it right back. Then he leans on the lever, like. Gets real still.

I got his number.

Here's the part ya might say's sticky. When's he gonna pop? He's gonna wait til I'm close, I figure.

So *now* I gotta figure, what's my what's-next? Keepin my distance ain't gonna do much for bolsterin my quote reputation unquote. Lookin mean ain't hard, standin here and bein the biggest guy in the county. Harder to look mean when you're backpedalin from a guy's so small the doctor's still givin him lollipops. So it ain't a matter of if, talkin along whether's he gonna come at me or not. Meet breaks, he's gonna walk up like we're old chums. Then he'll get his big idea. Unless maybe I beat him to it. Jump at *him*. See who gooses.

That's the move. It's a thought's got a smile in it. So I let my muscles take a load off and I wait for when's the meetin gonna break.

I start listenin to Cleveland and Associate. They ain't talkin about fuckin nothin. Um uh um so the prices are and the shipments um uh, fuckin boilerplate.

So I turn my head to look at Cleveland. Only I'm tryin to keep my eye on Tommy Toothpick in the same peep. So I turn real slow.

I guess Tommy Toothpick was bankin on a faster turn. I catch his eyes dartin to Cleveland. They got a look in em. Then he's lookin em back to me.

Ah, shit.

By the time I'm swingin a punch at Cleveland, he's fumblin for his gun.

Now, I ain't got much lovey-stuff for guns. Or knives, like I already said. Time you spend learnin to use a weapon is time you ain't turnin yourself into one. Your gun gets snatched, whaddya got? Whereas I got tree branch arms, the kind you build the damn treehouse on. Pull em outta their sockets, see if I care. Even limp, I can swing em from the trunk.

Havin said so, I can't say I ain't got *no* lovey-stuff for em. See, the reason I don't use guns is just the how-come I love when other chumps use em.

I spin out in front of Cleveland, straight on. Still movin, I use one mitt to snatch his bean shooter. The other bunches into a fist. And since my arm ain't outta it's socket, there's a lotta muscle drivin it into his face, one, two, three times. Somethin snaps and he falls asleep.

I keep whirlin til I'm back facin front. Associate's scrabblin for a gun of his own. Toothpick's lookin like he just figured he's the one that fucked the jump. So I shoot em both between the eyes. Try to, anyway. Guess it's only fair to say that time you spend turnin yourself into a weapon's time not learnin to use other ones.

My shots go straight through the space fillin up these guys' in-between. Associate's got his popper out, got it pointed right at my head. So I flick on the safety on Cleveland's gun on accounta safety first, and I chuck it at Associate. Smacks him right where I meant to put the bullet. He's reelin for a sec, and Tommy Toothpick's still just tryin not to shit himself, so I charge Associate. On the way I snap up Cleveland's gun from at Associate's feet. Put it to his temple. Pull the trigger.

Click.

The fuckin safety.

I flick it off, but now Associate's recovered. And I'm half-sure Tommy Toothpick just fuckin stabbed me in the shoulder. I got a sharp pain, and somethin warm makin my shirt all soggy.

Tommy Toothpick's tryin to get a piggyback ride. Associate starts shoutin about a clean shot, can't get a clean shot. He's right fuckin in front of me. Of course he's got a clean shot.

So I says Don't worry, I got one, and I show him how to do it. Jam the gun up under his chin, pull the trigger. The top of his head blows off. Like he had his first bright idea and couldn't handle it.

That leaves Tommy Toothpick, who's twistin the knife around in my shoulder now. I scream at him, point the gun back over my shoulder and pull the trigger. He decides he don't want a piggyback ride no more. I spin around and catch him runnin hell for leather back to Associate's car. I shoot at him once, twice, three times, four. The fourth finally lands. Right in the low back. He falls flat on his face.

Fuck, my *ear*. I mean, my shoulder too. But my *ear*. That over-the-shoulder shot, I squeezed it off right next to my ear. Now all I can hear is beeeeeeeeeeeee, like I got a tiny fire engine's mad at me. My seein's all blurry. Is this how come eggheads need glasses? Hearin damage?

I shake it off, walk over to Tommy Toothpick. Still

alive. Good news. I flip him over, not half as gentle as I did the Knee-breaker at Sharktooth.

Tommy Toothpick don't look so good. I kneel down and ask him Who told you I goose easy?

He says somethin I can't understand, on accounta my right ear's screamin at me. I turn my leftside at him and ask again.

He says to me Fuck you.

So I says Pal, you're comin up on last words. You make em count, I'll make what comes next real easy.

He spits blood at me. He ain't got the energy to get it up to my face. It splats back down on his.

I ask him does he see how it don't pay to be nasty.

He says Go to hell, you fucking goose.

So I pause on accounta I can't figure do I wanna tell him a zinger like Save me a seat, or maybe do I wanna just say somethin's got more zip similarwise to You first. Only then I realize I waited too long, so now its gonna sound dumb if I try to tell him a zinger, no matter how much fuckin zip's it got. So I says to him Toodle-oo, dipshit. Then I give him a face massage and he's done sayin shit.

But then *I* say Shit, first on accounta tough guys ain't supposed to say Toodle-oo, second on accounta I didn't get my answer. I figure he knew callin me goose would get me endin him quicker'n I could pose a fuckin follow-up.

I wipe down the gun and the car, on accounta this real fuckin fascinatin tidbit Wally told me. He tells me, just this fuckin year, Congress signs this piece of paper.

GO FIGURE

Who gives a shit, right? Congress Signs Piece of Paper's news like Chaplin's Havin A Rough Go Of Somethin Ain't That Fuckin Hard. Only this piece of paper's a piece of paper says now the FBI's got a thing calls itself the Identification Division. What do they do? All sorts of shit, but one of em's slurpin up every rascal's fingertip prints anybody's got on file. Everybody's got their own fingertip print, you believe that? You callin me a liar? It's fuckin true. Look at your finger. Closer. Stick your fingers in your eyes, see if I fuckin care. That's for callin me a liar, when I'm just tellin you what'd Wally tell me. And what'd he tell me is, every time you put your filthy mitts on somethin, it leaves a fingertip print. Somebody gets a look at that, they use dust or some shit, and but anyway now somebody's got a look-see there, then sees you got another one in a file, and they got twelve points where the two fingertip prints're likewise, uh oh, now you're a jailbird.

I don't figure I'm explainin it right. Point is, they can do ya for fuckin touchin stuff. World's gettin tough for a bruiser, lemme tell ya. Somebody tells me there's a thing called knuckletip prints, I'm headin for an early fuckin retirement.

Anyway. I wipe down the gun and the car. Then I walk home.

The whole walk I'm thinkin about Sharktooth. Must be one of those fuckers there is tellin people about me goosin easy. That fuckin door.

Soon as I can hear again, I'm gonna have to go knock on it.

FIRST thing's first though.

I push through I've Been Framed and ask Godric What the fuck?

He swings that little leprechaun visor my way and says How'd the job go?

I tell him It was a fuckin hook!

Godric looks real surprised, which gives me the very-glads. Never thought for a second Godric was involved in the setup. Figured he might laugh about it, though.

Instead just makes a fish face.

So I ask him How'd you not catch onto this guy? Somebody vouch for him?

Godric starts lookin like the bear what caught the fish what was makin the fish face. He says to me Yeah.

I ask him Who was it, on accounta I wanna get to know em.

He just looks at me real steady, only his eyes ain't so steady. I know that look. It's his hard-thinkin look. Ain't a face I see him makin all so commonwise.

So I says to him I ain't sure what you gotta think so hard about. I been fuckin hooked, you know who's the guy vouched for the thing. Just

Then he cuts me off and says Ok. Right. Ok. Then gets a piece of paper, starts scribblin a name and address.

I ask him about pronouncin this guy's last name.

Godric tells me you say it like Puh-ZAY. Then he says I'm just asking you, as a friend, please at least *start* with a conversation. Paul and I are old friends. I'm sure whatever this is, it's a big misunderstanding.

I nod like I'm thinkin how civil's my chat gonna be. Paul Pezet's name and address go into my pocket. Another door to knock on. I say thanks to Godric and ask him how's his thyroid holdin up, still attached or what? He says it's great now, only he don't sound like it. And instead of pickin a new ailment, he points to mine.

He says to me Your shoulder looks like hell, Sammy. Godric gets to call me Sammy too, you probably figured that on account he did and I ain't recedin what's he got left of a hairline.

I grab at my shirt and yank it for a look-see. I ain't had time to change my vestments yet, so yeah, it does look like hell.

I says to him I'll level, it feels like it looks.

He asks do I need a hand stitchin it up.

I says Nah, you already stitched me up once.

That's another thing he ain't laughin at. He just nods and tells me about how his ankles're made of gout this week.

I walk into the Sharktooth Casino and ain't nobody happy to see me. And meantimes Knee-breaker and Boss ain't nowhere to be seen. Figures. But I read Mr. One o'clock straight away. Hell of a cast he's sportin. He spots me. Don't look like he's fixin to be a good sport bout the cast.

He tells his shoulder a secret as I'm makin my way over. The shadows behind One o'clock make up two more knuckles, Ten and Two. They still look like shit. Pool their wraps, you could dress a mummy.

Everybody gets a hard stare from me. I figure, odds are one outta two I got the source of the goosin rumor in front of me. Only other ones it could be are Eleven o'clock, Boss or Knee-breaker.

I march right up. Try to suss out who's lookin more goggle-wowed. All of em're lookin pissed. But all of em're lookin like they been expectin me, too.

Stands to reason, I figure. Whoever tried to hook me probably figured it didn't take when Cleveland ain't called back lookin for pay. So all three knuckles in fronta me are still on the table, far as who's the fuckin blabberboy goes.

So I ask em do they got insurance covers accidents been done to em on purpose.

Don't look like they do.

So I tell em to call their boss outta what cupboard's

he hidin in, call Knee-breaker and Ten o'clock while you're at it. They don't get it so I says to em Get everybody from the alley, we gotta have words.

Boss is on the floor even though nobody went and got him. Guess he made me from a window. Knee-breaker's close behind, only he don't look half as mad as Boss.

He says to me, Boss does, he says We agreed that you would never darken my doorstep again.

I shrug and say Your doorstep ain't so great I'd be darkenin it without a why. Let's talk somewhere quiet.

Everybody flinches a bit.

I shake my head. No, I says to em. I ain't lookin for another chat like the last. I point to Boss and Knee-breaker. I says to em You and you first.

Boss says I'll call the police if you don't leave here at once. You are trespassing on

So I says to him Suits me up and down. Call the cops to your fuckin fishhouse what's got card crimes in the back. What happens first, they show up and collar me prior to the vice squad comes swingin in, or I put your nose through the back of your head and walk out the door?

Boss starts to say something. He looks at his crack team of muscleboys. All of em got more cracks than a second-stringer on Vaudeville. Even Knee-breaker's still workin off a shiner.

I remind em that I only came to have a gab, and I'm talkin about a real yap-around, not another fake one actually means nose-boppin. So let's why don't we not put me off conversation. You and you, I says to em again with another point and a point. Then the rest after, I says to em furthermore, if I ain't satisfied.

So Boss shrugs and says Come on then.

He's got one of them oh-look-at-me-lookin-at-you offices. No windows to the great outdoors. Just a big window lookin at the casino floor opposite. Looks like a pretty fuckin borin job to me.

Plaque on his desk says Max Rachel. He tells me Go on, ask.

I ask what does he want me to ask.

He says Ask if you can call me Mr. Rachel. That's what all the macho lunkheads do. It's a feminine name, I know, very funny.

I tell him I was just gonna call him Max from go. No sense keepin it formal.

Max sits in his chair the way wrestlers sit on the guy from the far corner. Knee-breaker takes up behind him. There's a chair across the desk from Max. I sit in it like a regular fuckin person.

Max asks me Why did you come back here? I consider our business closed.

I says to him So did I, til recent. I give him the hook's generals.

He says You got crossed. I can't *imagine* why anybody would want to eliminate you.

He's got this tone really wants me to know he *can* imagine.

So I says to him he might wanna smarten up his

tone, on accounta he's on my list.

He asks what list that is.

So I explain it to him, how when he and my guy slammed the door open, it mighta *looked* like I jumped a bit. And somebody mighta seen that happen, and if that somebody's got a design on me gettin done in, rubbed out and such, that somebody mighta gone and told somebody else. That somebody else might know a guy what knows a guy what knows me, and that guy mighta been my guy what knows guys, and I'm talkin bout *me* if that ain't crystal-like. And that's how'd they do it.

Max says Well, you can take me off the list. It wasn't me.

So I says That's just what'd I figure on hearin from the guy who it was.

Then he says That's also what you'd hear from the guy who it *wasn't.*

I got nothin to say to that.

I ain't a detective. Max ain't a real crook. I can't speculate on *his* fuckin dance card, but it don't seem like neither of us could figure which way do we jump next.

Fact is, this ain't how I do business. Usually I got a real easy question I'm askin to somebody's for sure got the answer. I ask, they answer. Or I break a finger, ask again, they answer. Or I break a second finger. You get it. It ain't often I ain't even sure what's the question, or am I even askin the person can gimme the whats-up.

So I says Huh, on accounta I got no more clues.

Then I says Well, shit.

What am I gonna ask they can't just throw shoulders

up about? This ain't my forte. Got half a mind to just kill em all and be done with it. Only that ain't ethical.

So I says to em Goddamnit.

Then I get an idea. Only it ain't an idea's gonna bring me much sunshine in this room ain't got no fuckin windows. So I stand up and walk out the door.

The four knuckles are waitin for me on the casino floor. Two makes a crack about What, are you scared to talk to us?

So I says Sorry, I can't hear you on accounta your nose is all fucked up.

Which is sorta true. But mostly I can't hear him on accounta my ear is still all fucked up.

I'm headin to my car when somebody shouts Hey! loud enough I can hear it.

I turn around. Knee-breaker's comin for me. Not at a run. At a trot, like I dropped my pocketbook and he's bringin it to me. So I just turn around and wait for him. Square my shoulders. Get ready for a dust-up, one I'm pretty sure ain't comin but not *too* sure.

He says to me I've been looking for you. Since the alley.

I says to him You'da kept lookin if I hadn't shown up.

He nods like he knows it, from havin hit a load of dead ends. Looks at me real hard. Rubs his nose a bit. Then he says That was a real decent thing you did for me, flipping me over. You could have let me drown.

I tell him I got no problem killin a guy rubs me wrong, but I get no kicks from it. If I ain't gotta off somebody, I don't.

He says to me There's a difference between not killing and *saving*.

I ask him if he's about to tell me about Jesus Christ now.

He smiles at that, puts out his hand and says Hatch Adler.

I ask him if that's a kinda tree. He don't know Godric so he don't get the joke.

So I take his hand and say Samuzzo D'Amato. I don't tell him it was a pleasure to meet him, on accounta it wasn't. But on second blush, he seems a decent kinda guy. I don't buy he's the one ratted on my goosin. So that's one suspect down. Maybe I ain't so bad at detectin after all!

Hatch says to me how I shouldn't be caught hangin around, on accounta if Max tells him to cream me then he will. I'm wavin at a memory when I tell him he'll *try*. He smiles. Says he owes me one.

I don't get why people love owin ones. Owin ones is how the fuckin world war happened.

Which brings me back to my idea. On how to get even better at detectin than I already am: take a page from Cleveland's book of fuckin dramatics.

WHEN the book's over, I close it up and look at Daff so she knows to explain it to me.

She asks me what didn't I get. It's pretty clear.

I ask her How would he have solved it if he didn't get the letter?

She says he wouldn't have.

So I says Awful convenient he did, then.

She says M-hm.

I fuckin elaborate and says Almost like cheating.

She shrugs and tells me to call upon the author.

Don't get me wrong, it was a good yarn. It even had some guys with bad attitudes meetin in a field at night. With the moon and everything. Maybe Cleveland read the same yarn. Guess he missed the part where the good guy wins.

I figure if it's allowed that they get ideas from the

39

paperbacks, so can I. But all the books Daff's got me hittin got a letter in em. Or a piece of paper under a box. Or a brick got a piece of hair inside it. Some bullshit clue like that solves the whole damn mystery in one go.

I ask Daff Where's *my* bullshit clue?

She says I don't think you're going to get one.

Some fuckin help these dimers are. She asks me if I at least enjoyed any of them.

I throw the one I just read across the room where I got a whole pile of the fuckin things, and fold my arms and tell her Yeah I did. But I got no fuckin ideas from em.

She pats my arms what I just mentioned I got all folded and says Well maybe they'd apply if you were solving a murder. That's what those are all about. But you're trying to track a rumor. Then her face lights up like she just got hit on the head by an apple. She says I know! I've had you reading the wrong things. She runs into the room where we got all her books, and come back with one's real long and all about rich ladies talkin shit about each other.

A groan just on accounta I figure it's expected. Then I read. And goddamnit if I don't learn.

When the book's over in the pile, on accounta old habits, I don't look at Daff. I'm just starin straight ahead. Gears are turnin. Rumor, yeah, Daff's right. I was treatin this like I'm tryin to find any old whosit, like Where's The Money or Who Sent You. Somethin you just break fingers over. But maybe I gotta think about this like...a rumor. Like some high society whosaidit. More'n that, like a fuckin disease or something. You can't break influenza's fingers. You gotta be smarter.

No clue how long'm I gawkin at my belt buckle, but when I'm done I look at Daff and I tell her It can't have been one of the Sharktooth guys what told about my goosin easy.

Daff smiles. She says Why not?

I smile back and call her out for pretendin she don't already know the answer.

She says Maybe we have different answers. Even though she knows we don't.

That's how come I love Daff. She don't try to pretend she ain't smarter'n me. But she don't rub my face in it neither. Not less we're havin a night in, hubbah hubbah.

So I says to her my answer, which is Hatch said he was lookin for me but couldn't find me, on accounta he didn't know my name or who's in my socials. So, if that's how is it, how are they gonna muster up the hook and get the guy *doin* the hook to distract me with sayin somebody's gonna goose me?

Daff starts battin for the other team, she says Well they could have found you through Wally, couldn't they?

I shake my head. I tell her I don't buy it. Wally's too crafty. No way they track him down fast as they'd have had to.

So she says Maybe they got their own bullshit clue.

41

Maybe one of them saw Wally at the deli or something.

I just shrug on accounta I can't say that ain't possible. It just don't make a click noise in my head.

So I says I'll ask Wally, but good odds're he didn't say bubkis to nobody. Therefore, I says to impress her, I *deduce* that in that for instance, the goose rumor didn't start at Sharktooth.

Daff nods. All proud and shit. Like I'm the kid ain't neither of us wanna have. But then she says If that's the case, then where did it start?

I think for a second.

I'd be real sad if Wally told somebody where to find me. But I kinda hope he did.

On accounta if the source ain't from Sharktooth...I just gotta wait for a bullshit clue.

Halfway through the night I wake up and say Bullshit.

Daff takes a deep breath in and says Hmlrpa?

I tell her I already got my fuckin bullshit clue. Godric gave it to me!

Now my eyes're are adjustin, I can see Daff scootin back, half-sittin up against the pillow. She says How's that?

I says He gave me a name and address, the guy what connected Cleveland with Godric in the first place. That's my bullshit clue!

Daff nods. Like the universe owes everybody a bullshit clue, and she's the one makes sure it pays up.

Hey, maybe she is. Daff, Daphne Carr to folks ain't

got the fortunes good enough for callin her Daff, I figure she's got a line on what most people pretend they got. If she's pretendin too, she's fuckin Mae Marsh.

I give her a kiss on the cheek and I says to her Goodnight, Daff.

She shimmies down to the bed again. Makes a happy little cat sound.

No clue what do I sound like sleepin.

GO FIGURE

PAUL Pezet's got the kinda big glass house you ain't gonna get without throwin a few stones. Forgot to ask Godric what's Paul's vocational. If booze ain't involved, then I'm a librarian.

Lights inside are off. Lights *outside* are on. He's got big ones on poles, like on Broadway. No chance of goosin *him*, then. Any way I make for a door, he sees me comin a mile away. Then again, I ain't any kind of sneaky. Ain't many situations call for it.

This one does. Now, if I fixed Paul as a stinker for sure, if I knew it was him settin Cleveland up with Godric, for Godric to set up with me, only Godric didn't know what Paul was after, but anyway if I knew Paul was the rotten egg for sure I'd be seein how good his big fuckin palace windows are for stoppin sledgehammers. But I ain't sure. Could be Cleveland duped Paul same as he duped Godric. Gotta make sure before I get architectural on him.

Gotta ask.

Which means I gotta get in, real sneaky.

I just sit here in nighttime for a bit. Lookin at the big fuckin lawn, lit up by big fuckin lights look like they got constructive criticism for the sun.

Around the back of the house, same deal. Already checked. Glass castle in a fuckin sunshine moat.

Now, I ain't good at sneakin on accounta I'm so big. Same reason says I ain't never gonna be runnin a five minute mile. I figure it for about a hundred feet of green between the black I'm in and the black I want on me. I can take my chances, maybe. Back up, get a runnin start. Sprint to the house fast as suits my stumps. Hope Paul ain't fixin a midnight snack durin the time I'm outta dark.

That's gamblin though. I don't hold with chance. Not as fit as certainty. Usually. Depends.

But how else am I gettin there? Either I roll the dice, spin the wheel, shuffle the deck, other shit that'd set Max Rachel's frontispiece…or I keep runnin slow shadow laps. On accounta I ain't got any better ideas.

I figure Daff would. Ain't often I wanna pack it in even as I got feet on the jobsite. When I do, it's always on accounta I wanna talk to Daff.

Ah, fuck it. Sometimes ya gotta bet the horse, flip the coin, peel the banana.

I walk around so's I'm right in fronta the back door.

Go Figure

At least I think it's the back door. Whole fuckin thing's just glass and some art deco-lookin bullshit between, got two identical doors on either side. Only this one ain't got a walkway with stones and rose petals or what the fuck, it's too dark for me to see what's there. All I can figure is, this must be the fuckin back.

I take ten big steps to my rearwards. My heel bonks into a little rock, so I gotta shift aside a bit. Just gotta hope my foot don't catch somethin mid-step just prior to I hit exposure, go down flat on my face. At least nobody'd see it if I did. Unless I caught it right prior to light. Flopped out like a sprinter's dick at the Olympics. Hello, world.

Ain't worth the chagrin, makin meditations about it. Just gotta punch it and see what's what.

Helps to think of it like a punch.

I press off hard, slicin the air with my hands like I'm fixin to put it on a sandwich. I make it onto the yard with no slips. Pound pound pound I'm hustlin hard. Feels like the house is fuckin runnin away. Yard seems so much bigger when I'm on it. Anybody's lookin out a window or door or wall or whatever, they'd gotta work hard to *not* see me.

Somethin insults my left toe. My whole leg takes fuckin umbrage. I go down hard, rollin onto the shoulder I only just fuckin got stitched. By Daff. She ain't gonna be so pleased about redoin her needlepoint masterpiece. Ah well, that ain't this. I just gotta keep my fuckin philosophizin down to a grunt, I can't start shoutin on top of everythin else.

I aim to keep on rollin and kinda succeed. Stumble a bit gettin back up. Then I'm movin again, though I got a toe and shoulder on my fuckin back now.

House still seems far, so I'm runnin with my head down. Only I guess it ain't as far as I'd figured, on accounta I hit a rock ain't where it oughta be less it's fuckin aesthetic. I take to the skies and go straight through a window. It shatters, and it ain't quiet about it. All the little shards are clappin for me as they settle to ground. Good fuckin job, they say.

Well, I'm in Paul's house now. He's got a real dark livin room, but I figure it ain't so dark at daytimes. Or with lights. Really the dark ain't so endemic to his design. Yeah, that's another word I know.

Real slow, so I ain't gotta palm the glass in the rug, I work up to my feet. Shakin little crystals off all the way. Brushin em outta my hair. I do a quick spot check. Shitload of scratches, skin and clothes both. Nothin serious though. Lucky break. Get it?

I crunch off the carpet and head to the kitchen. Real sleek, marbletop that shines in the dark. I'm listenin for…anythin. Ain't many people you can't rouse by takin away what's basically a whole damn wall.

No footsteps. No alarms. No voices. Not nothin but nothin.

If I proved one thing, it's that I ain't made strides in sneakery. So I give myself a tour like I'm shoppin to buy.

Turns out Paul's upstairs. Only I can't be sure it's Paul, on accounta I got no clue what does Paul look like. Not that knowin his face'd do much good. Ain't nobody's makin an I.D. here less they got patience and a strong stomach.

Poor guy didn't go easy. Teeth and fingernails pulled, set in a neat little pile to one side. Face caved in. Wrists tied with barbwire. More little slashes on his chest than I got soarin through his window. Most of em deep, from the look. Dollars to donuts the guy's tongue ain't in the same hole where'd it start the day.

He's still leakin a bit. Fresh. I musta missed the guys done this by an hour. Too bad. Now I can't ask Pezet nothin.

I hate these freak jobs like the sort musta done this. Guys who smile bout the wrong stuff. You wanna off a guy, just fuckin do it! Why you wanna carve him like a pumpkin? What fuckin grade are you in?

No way to know did Paul have it comin or not. But ain't many people got *this* comin.

Most nights previous, I'd see Paul's dead and make trails. But I read too many detective stories now. Well, I read about three. Four only on a technical. That one had ghosts and shit, so I don't figure it for a proper detective story.

So my point is, I'm thinkin in connectionals now. And what I got here ain't just a guy looks like he lost a fight with a lawnmower. What I got here is Paul Pezet, who told Cleveland to talk to Godric about findin me, so Cleveland could hook me. Key link in the chain. One

I was hopin could clue me in on who's got it out for me and why. On accounta now I'm feelin like there's more goin on here than I figured. Somebody's tryin to fuckin smoke me, and they're breakin bits in the chain might help me figure out who are *they*.

Even worse, they're tellin everybody I fuckin goose easy.

Previous nights Samuzzo, he'd say to himself Fuck this and go home. Fuckin dead end, that's what this is.

Only I ain't that Samuzzo. I'm *this* Samuzzo. Current night Samuzzo.

I'm gonna case the joint. Get a clue.

Paul, may he rest in fuckin peace, figured himself for a modern man. And for some fuckin reason, the whole thing with modern is hidin shit. Drawers got no handles, closets got no knobs. Home furnishin for folks wanna make sure their keys *stay* lost.

And me here, stumblin around in the dark. I gotta do it like this, though. I got the experience lets me have a say-so, from the outside you can't see shit in this house with those yard lights blazin. Say somebody's stuck around after slicin Paul up like salami, and somehow ain't seen nor heard my dramatic entrance, I ain't lookin to give em another shot at spottin me. It's just givin my headache a headache, on accounta I gotta feel every single fuckin surface in the house so's I don't miss a trick.

When I'm not busy feelin shit, I clock a couple whaddyacallems. Abberances? Things the gumshoe says about right prior to it's Chapter Next.

One is, puttin to one side the livin room wall I crashed through, I can't spot no signs of foul enterins. No other smashes or cracks anywhere. Front door's got a jam made of, I don't know, somethin weren't never a tree. Whatever it is, it ain't the least bit stressed. Not that it would be. Not the kinda door you can kick twice, you see what I'm sayin?

Two is, Paul's house's got security. There's a dog in the front hall. I learned about the dog when he came runnin at me sayin Who the fuck're you? I ain't never bonked a dog yet, only he don't know that, so I just lifted up my arms and yelled at him You wanna know what's it feel like to have a flat face?! He ain't figured that for persuasive so I grabbed him by the neck scruff and threw him into the basement. Soft-like, though, on accounta I got a big heart over animals. Point is, the dog weren't perturbed til I came down smellin like his buddy's insides.

Third is, and really three's got a size oughta make it One, I see the table's set for three. Two plates been licked clean. One of the guys wasn't so hungry. Now, I didn't see no fuckin ring on Paul's finger. And there weren't no kids room upstairs.

So here's my a-ha: Paul got done by two folks he says Come on over for. He lets em in himself, his dog ain't got no objections to em. Hi, how are ya. Let's have a dinner. They musta planned the dinner ahead of time. Only maybe not. I check his desk, flip open a little planner he's got and have a look-see for DINNER WITH

SUCH AND SO. But no. His planner ain't got nothin's gonna illuminate, less it's gonna matter where's he been havin liasons with his secretarial.

But here's my *real* a-ha, the one I'm feelin all big-chested about. Two of the plates in the kitchen been licked clean, remember when I said that? One of em, the guy hardly touched his food. So I fuckin *deduce* that we got three guys sittin down to dinner. Two of em are cool as can be. The third? Quakin. Tummy gettin toss-ed. Can't get down half his meal.

That sounds important, I figure. Whether one of the guys did Paul was sweatin before things went south…or if Paul mighta known what was comin, even as he's in-vitin em in.

That's the kinda thing might make a difference. I fig-ure Godric's got a good bead on Paul's socials. That's my clue. And it ain't a bullshit one neither. Only thing that's bullshit is, how I'm gonna find out if Paul was the dinner picker-at-er.

Remember when I was sayin about the patience and the stomach?

OK so I'm lookin at pots and pans, I'm sniffin plates, and I'm seein what'd somebody forget to eat. They all three of em had steaks been sizzled in a skittle. Plus a bowl of leafygreens with some vinegar and ketchup or some shit. I rustle through the trash til I find butcher's paper. With the label still on. Good shit.

Me findin the label and the label itself, I'm sayin. Two and a half pounds of high-grade boneless. You wouldn't fuckin believe about the price he paid! On the meat, I mean. The steak.

Two and a half pounds for three heads, figure it's spread even…about three quarters a pound per body. Right? I figure my mathematics ain't fuckin astray there.

I head back to the table and pick up the uneaten cut. Red juices run out. Looks good. I take a bite. Still good.

Bit cold, but good shit ain't good shit on accounta the how-hot.

So add back on the bite I just ate. And that second bite. Not as good as the first bite, I gotta say. Anyway, add back on the three bites I took out and you've got at least a half a pound of heifer ain't stinkin up somebody's gut.

I wager it's Paul's gut's got a beef deficit.

But I already told ya, I ain't so big on wagers and chances. I done my night's worth of roll-the-dice, and don't ask again. I'm a man likes some muscle behind the punch. You catch my meanin.

I got a moment of pause on accounta Paul's already been through a lot tonight. But seein as he's *through*, I figure he ain't gonna mind. Plus, I'm gettin anatomical on him so's I can catch who dealt him crosswise.

So I pull Paul outta what I sure hope wasn't once-upon his most favorite chair and lay him on the bed. On his side, right up to the edge, facin me. He's on his left flank. Right up to the edge. Facin straight at me. He keeps fallin on accounta I guess he ain't heard about fuckin rigor mortis yet.

Once I got him near balanced, I stuff his cuttin block's biggest knife into his belly and unzip him.

First thing comes out is all kindsa blood. No stomach though. I sorta figured everything'd come rollin out at once. Guess I missed.

I reach in, grab a holda somethin soft and pull. It comes out. Some of it, anyway. So I pull. More comes out. Ain't all of it though. So I pull and pull and pull like a pokey-hocus on a hankey.

Now I got a big long sausage ain't got no links. I'm figurin I ain't got the tummy.

Is the tummy above or below the intestines?

Jesus, the fuckin stink! My body starts coughin and I can't make it shut up already. I thump myself hard in the chest, but that don't do much save scare up an itty burp. I wanna crack a window but the whole fuckin house is a window. I don't see where's a handle or no-thin. I ain't lookin to leap through another pane, neith-er. So I lift my shirt over my nose and paint my knees red. I grab holda the hole I opened and start carvin upwards. I know not to push too hard, on accounta one time Daff tells me open this box of laundry powder, so I grab a knife and pop it in, only nobody told me there's a fuckin bag in the box, what's up with that? Turns out I rend the fuckin parcel. Which I get that I fucked up, but also, who's fuckin packin your powder?

I don't know who fuckin packed this Pezet, so I split his tits gentle as I can. Gotta apply a bit more pressure when I hit breastbone. Oh hell, a little more.

Now I got him good and perforated, so I tear along the dotted line. Pull his chest back like sideways curtains.

Hoo, boy! What a fuckin mess. Everybody's got in-side like this, then? Like fuckin Scottish cuisine? Kinda turns my stomach, figurin on it, only now my stomachs turnin and I'm figurin on *that*. Other stuff starts turnin, so I gotta turn my figurin off my icky bits and back at

Paul's.

Ok, so I figure the stomach is one of the calzones in the middle. The twisty bits down towards his feet and floppin on the floor a bit, my bad, those are the gutty-works. Up top we got the two balloons in a box what gotta be the lungs.

I give the lungs and ribs a pull, see if I can't get em out for a quote clearer bead on the suspects unquote. No dice, and not in the way's my preferred. His bird-cage is packed in tight. Christ, this is what I always figured a raccoon's house'd look like. Shit stuffed where it don't fit, all stinky and wet.

Forget it. I slice open the first calzone.

I says FUCK ME and jump back. My shirt's doin fuck all for my nose. Whatever's in that stockin's worse than mustard gas, lemme tell ya.

I step outta the room. Take a deep breath. Another. One more. Suddenly I'm havin a think on those three steakbites I cadged, I nearly ralph. Deep breath. Tough guys ain't meant to goose, and they *definitely* ain't meant to ralph.

Calm and fuckin collected, I give my knees another coat of red.

Pretty sure what I popped was his tummy. Only there ain't no chunks of steak in there. Just slop. Plop-pin out onto the carpet one glob at a time. Plop. Plop.

Paul's got a look on his not-so-face, like Get on with it already.

I says to him What's the rush, you got a bus to catch?

GO FIGURE

Only I figure it's me's got the rush, on accounta daytime's makin overtures.

Ok. So. I reach in. Thumb open the stomach. Ain't no way to get a fingertip print offa somebody's icky bits, I figure. Nothin else to do, anyways. I pull the lips open and yank.

Paul figures I want all of him to turn, and turns out he's a fuckin people pleaser. He starts rollin forward. Nearly falls on me with his whole fuckin gut flappin in the breeze.

I catch him with one hand and pull the stomach til it rips out. Trails all sortsa shit with it. But whatever about that shit. I push Paul back onto the bed. Turn the stomach upside down and shake the insides out. Like emptyin a pencil case fulla mashed potatoes.

So now I got a pile on my hands. Not literally. Not yet.

Now I gotta get my hands in the pile.

Here's some screwball shit: I'm already gettin accustomatized to the stink. The things a guy can get accustomatized to, huh? I look at Paul and he ain't half as amazed by it as me. Fair play to ya, Paul.

I reach into the pile and start siftin. I was really hopin I'd just see some chunks. Real obvious. Like a shark what ate a license plate.

No luck. So I gotta dig. Mosta the slop is orange. Further down's some of the leafygreens. Sound my rootin makes's like two kids just discovered kissin and they ain't minded on who knows it. I try not to have another think on that steak I ate. So of course now I'm havin a think on just such a subject. I feel it comin up.

Then I find it in Paul.

A grey chunk. I wipe it off best I can. Give it a real good study.

Fuckin steak.

I keep siftin. I only find two more chunks. Rest is green and orange.

Three fuckin chunks of steak.

Just like I had.

I get real real *real* close to ralphin just then. But I don't.

On accounta I'm too happy. I just used my clues to find a new clue! Like a real fuckin detective! Old Samuzzo would nevera known that Paul got killed by two guys what'd he invite into his home, rustled up some expensive steak for, but was so fuckin afeared of he couldn't even eat it past one two three bites!

That ain't just a clue. It's a goddamn lead! Fuck me, I can hardly keep from clickin my goddamned heels as I'm jumpin back out through the window what I flew through comin in.

GO FIGURE

IF I'd known he was gonna be on the dial, yeah, I mighta done things different.

Turns out Paul Pezet was some kinda deal. The rat-a-tat son of a bitch on the radio's sayin Paul was a quote entrepreneur unquote. Which don't mean much on accounta so am I. Just that they wouldn't be callin a spade a spade if *I* got on the news, lemme tell ya.

Anyway, they sure got some wacky theorizins on what's old Paulie boy been up to. Rat-a-tat says the cops're tryin to figure does he got ties to crime, and that's a fuckin laugh, they oughta be askin which and who and how many. Instead they're just throwin darts, talkin about racketeers'n union disputes'n satanic screwballs, probably fuckin outerspace aliens. They're all buggin out about he was sliced open. Fair play to em, I guess. That sure is a quote salient detail unquote.

I ain't worried is this gonna blow back on me. Let

em grab all the fingertip prints, let em put em in a big book Coolidge can sit on so's he can reach the dinner table. Maybe they find my fingertip prints been other places. I got no clue how long have they been collectin these, in *actuals*. Let em put pins on a map. Get the whole bullpen in, they can point at it and try'n figure on who's the guy fingertip printin on all kindsa crime pies. Long as they ain't never taken my fingertip print right off my goddamned fingertip, they got no way of knowin who's this fingertip print belong to. Pretty big fuckin flaw in the system, I figure. Just shows ya, they ain't so fuckin smart.

Still, it's a little bit embarrassin, twicewise. I oughta thought on scrubbin off my fingertip prints when I was otherwise occupied clickin my fuckin heels, there's first. Second's that I went and opened Paul like a newspaper when I coulda used what Daff's callin quote context clues unquote. All in everythin, not a night I'm gonna be tootin about. No way. But Daff knows, and Godric's gonna know when I tell him what'd I detect.

Speakin of Daff, when I told her what I done she didn't seem too impressed.

She just kept shakin her head, sayin Sammy Sammy Sammy. Real disappointed.

That makes me sad on accounta I never wanna disappoint Daff. So I says to her It ain't like I was smilin wide while I'm makin his belly grin. You know I don't reach for cutlery less I got a good reason.

She sighs and says I know.

I says to her What else was I supposed to do? Take

him to the doctor?

Now I think I'm readin her right. She's feelin a bit sick on what I done. Only she can't think of how else I shoulda played things. She says about the quote context clues unquote, then I remind her on I already done my night's roll-the-dice.

She don't say nothin against that. I guess she figures I got her number. She just looks at me and says Next time, see if there's another option.

I says I ain't bankin on another situation where I gotta weigh do I wanna carve a turkey's got a history of entrepreneurin.

Daff don't say nothin to that. Knows me well, Daff does.

Godric, though, he gets all kindsa slapstick when I tell him. But he knew the guy, so I figure that ain't outta line.

He starts flappin his arms and askin about how's the world gotten crazy, did the war poison everybody's brain or what. Gets so worked up he didn't even mention no ailments. Finally he settles down and I says to him the full scoop. How I found Paul, what I done.

I finish real quick, on accounta I ain't a fella holds with embellishments. Godric just sits real quiet. Hangs his head. Visor turns his whole face green.

I ask him how far back do he and Paul go anyway.

Godric tells his bellybutton Fifteen years.

There's another thing mighta made me do things different. If I'd known. Kinda glad I didn't.

I tell him I'm real sorry. Then I tell him what I got for slimmin Paul down. Paul, he lets in two guys for a pricey dinner. Too scared to eat much. I ask Godric Do you know two guys Paul's afraid of might fit that bill?

Godric has a good long think on it. Tick tock tick tock, then he looks up at me and throws my question back at me.

I tell him Close as Paul and me got at the end, I'd fuckin pause to call us pals.

He waves that away and says It sounds like whoever is responsible, they're after *you*, yes? They cultivated a relationship with Paul, knowing he was connected to me. They used him to get to me, and they used me to get to you. That didn't work, so now they're trying to cover their tracks, to keep you from coming after them. That seems a fair assessment, wouldn't you say?

So I tell him I can't find fault with your reasonin, old timer. But then why're you still suckin air?

He shrugs and says to me I don't know enough about Paul's acquaintances to be of much danger to them, I suppose. Whereas some of *my* acquaintances would pose a considerable danger to *them*, were *they* to harm *me*.

I says to him Like me.

Godric nods and smiles real small. Then he says Unfortunately, the lapse in knowledge that likely protects me also prevents me from being of much help to you. But maybe the thing to do here is to look at *your* acquaintances.

I give him what I figure is a funny look and say Whaddyamean, call up my buddies and ask do they knew a guy called Paul Pezet?

Godric frowns and says No. Obviously not. Look at the papers. Keep an eye out for new disclosures about his underworld connections. I can help you out with those, too. See if you can find any overlap between his circle and yours.

I says Like a Venn diagram.

He says Exactly.

Now I'm figurin on Venn diagrams...and I just about slap my own head.

Musta made a face to match. Godric says to me Looks like you've got something there.

I tell him, I got a fuckin loose end.

WALLY comes back from the bathroom with wet money in his fist. He loves this gag; go to some speakeasy ain't in your own neighborhood, order drinks, pay with wet money. If the bar's somethin ain't a total dive, maybe they ain't never been handed wet tender before. Maybe they figure the risk to reward ain't tippin their way. Maybe they'll say This round's on the house.

I seen Wally try this gag, god, maybe a hundred times now. I seen it work four times. But Wally's a fuckin optimist. So here he comes with the wet tender.

He tells the bartender Two whiskeys on the rocks.

The bartender snatches the bill like it's always irked him, how's most money so damn dry.

Wally sulks a bit til the drinks come.

I ain't gonna grill him just yet. Wanna get his defenses down. So we shoot the shit til the glasses run dry. I pay with a bone-dry paper note and get some coins back for it.

Halfway into round two, I change our fuckin track.

I lay out what've I been up to lately. Hittin the fact that somebody out there's got it in for me, *and* they heard some rumors about I goose easy.

I says to him I know you'd never do nothin crosswise at me, but I also know you got a restless jaw. So I'm askin, did you mention me goosin out behind Sharktooth to anybody?

Wally's eyes get real big. He says to me Oh god! Not in a million years!

So I says I know you wouldn't in a way you meant to. But you ain't always got a tight lid, see what I'm sayin? I'm askin if, *maybe*, whoops, by *accident*, you mighta let somethin slip ya didn't mean for.

For a minute Wally's just rubbin his chin, starin at his drink. I think maybe I gotta call him back to now, when he finds it.

He says to me I might have.

I should have fuckin known. I ask him Who'd you say it to?

He says to me Somebody I really trust.

I ask him Who's that?

He says I mean, I really, *really* trust them.

I says Who is it.

He says You're going to get upset, so, um, please don't get upset.

I tell him to spit it out already.

He says My lawyer.

I look at him for a long time. Then I says Wally.

Wally waves his hands and says No no, she's not that kind of a lawyer.

I says to him Wally.

So Wally spins on his stool to face me. He says She's on the up and up, believe me. With us, I mean. So I guess, she's on the down and down.

I says Wally, I don't see what my name's doin crossin a lawyer's path.

He says She was just asking about the Sharktooth gag! So I told it to her! *Yes* she's my lawyer, but we also happen to be friends. Is that against the law now?

I says to him If it is, good news is you got representation zipped up.

Wally gives his lap a disapprovin look. He says She just does some work for me. Then he lowers his voice and he says Patent litigation, dummy management for the pyramid gag, real estate contacts, things like that. No criminal prosecution, not once.

I say *Wally*.

He says I'm sorry.

So I ask him You got patents? What'd you invent, a wet wallet?

He says to me No no no, I didn't invent anything. You can get a patent on something without ever actually making it. Then he gets real excited and leans forward and he says So I just file every stupid idea for a product I have, then Janis keeps her eyes peeled for infringements. Somebody comes along with an idea that looks just a little bit too similar to mine…lawsuit! Then Wally leans back and just about claps his hands and says Do you have one of those potato mashers in your house? If you do, guess what: I get a royalty from that. And I didn't have to do diddly!

So I ask him Ain't you always stuck in court then?

He laughs and says to me They always settle! Lump sum or a tiny royalty. I love the royalties. I'm telling you, I've never been to court with Janis in my life before. That's something of a specialty of hers.

I says Duckin the judge.

He nods. Got his smile back. I figure I wanna see that big fuckin mouth in a frown once more before I call it settled.

I says to him So when're we goin to meet Janis?

There's the frown.

Janis's got a classy office. Or I figure as much, if I can judge from the waitin room.

Wally's been all nervous about me meetin his counsel. Says he don't like quote cross-pollinating unquote. I ask him what the hell's that supposed to mean. He mumbles somethin about Janis runs a legitimate business. I remind him So does Godric. He stops runnin his mouth so much after that.

Our appointment's closin out Janis' day. Fella behind reception takes us back to her office. Kinda wild, lady lawyer's got a fella on the desk. Lady lawyer at all's wild to me. Wally tells me just last year lawyers started bein ladies. And there ain't never been a law says a fella can't run a desk, I figure. Still. Wild.

Only this boy ain't so wild. He's too fuckin…city. Struttin all important like the pigeon knows the way into the bakery. Like Wally ain't never fuckin been here before. Kids this kid's age shouldn't be allowed to walk like they know so fuckin much. There oughta be a law on *that*.

He swings open the big door to Janis' lair. First thing you spot's her desk. Second thing's the desk again. Then the third. I'll tell ya, the desk is so fuckin big I can't figure out there's room enough for the rest of the room. Barely enough floor for the chairs.

She leans back in her buttoned fuckin throne and says You must be Mr. D'Amato!

I ask her Or what?

She looks at Wally like I guess he fuckin told her I'd try to crack wise. I figure crackin wise is a good way to lay the ice when I'm acquaintin somebody. Never saw sense in tryin to break the ice. Why you wanna walk on broken ice? You fall in, turn into a popsicle, drown. You're goin out on the lake, you want thick, sturdy ice.

So I crack wise sometimes.

Only Wally gave her my number.

So I turn around real fast and frown at the kid runs the desk. I tell him How about you close the door or else I rearrange your priorities.

He closes the door.

So I turn back around to Janis, slower this time. Ain't no rush. I tell her Yeah I'm Mr. D'Amato. You can call me Samuzzo. You ain't gonna call me Sammy, but Wally can call me Sammy. So you hear him call me Sammy, you don't get no familiarwise designs. I'm Samuzzo. Got it?

She throws her hands in the air and says Clear as crystal! Why did you want to see me so urgently, Mr. D'Amato?

Mr. D'Amato? That ain't...Well, I can't really take a tone for her bein *over*formal, so I gotta let it slide. I shoulda figured Wally's friends'd be sharp.

I cock a thumb at Wally and say This guy here told you about the Sharktooth gag.

Janis nods.

I go on and says As he's lost in his fuckin recollect-ions, it seems he mighta said somethin to you ain't the sorta somethin he oughta mighta said. Somethin that I got it in my head you mighta said to somebody else, on accounta now it's makin trouble for me and it hadta come from *somebody*. It ain't the sorta thing you have a lucky guess on.

Janis touches all her fingers together, real soft. Tap tap tap, she taps the meat of her prints together. Then she says Well Mr. D'Amato, that's a very serious accus-ation you're making against me. You see, your friend Mr. Zwillbin is not only my friend, he is my client. And as I consider discretion to be the greatest of the unsung virtues, I am honor bound, twice over, to hold his peace as I do my own.

She looks thoughtful for a second. Swings out of her seat. Starts scootin out from behind her desk. As she's scootin she says I can only assume the detail to which you elliptically refer is your being startled by the slamming of the door in the rear alley of the casino. Wally himself gave this only passing mention. A bit of texture in the overall tapestry.

I tell her I get the feelin you figure you can talk circles like I ain't gonna watch my fuckin perimeter.

Wally nudges me and says That's just how she talks.

Janis finally finds her way around the desk. She stands up right in fronta me. Studies me hard. She says to me Mr. D'Amato, as one professional safeguarding a reputation to another, I tell you that I spoke not one word of Mr. Zwillbin's tale, to anyone.

I study her right back.

And I says to her Well shit lady, I buy that. Only that means I'm back to I got no fuckin clue who's tellin people I goose easy.

Wally reminds me how it's maybe more important that I got no fuckin clue who's tryin to off me. I just shrug about that. I find out who's after me, I says to him, I kill em. Killin a guy's easy. Killin a rumor?

But one thing at a time, how about.

So I ask Janis what's her hourly rate.

She smiles like she knew I'd be askin her a favor before long. She says How about a quid pro quo?

GO FIGURE

So here's my ask for Janis, was I was seein can she get me a who's who of everybody Paul Pezet ever ran with. Yeah, I coulda done it myself. But I got no interest in that part of the detectin. What, am I callin up cops and pretendin to be from some other precinct, lemme see your fuckin documents? I got a small heart for documents. I respect em, but I got no heartspace for em. Janis loves em, and more important, she's got that shitsmear behind reception can't get *enough* of em. So Janis not only says she's gonna quote collate unquote Pezet's socials, she's gonna do her own diggin, make a few calls, see if she can't pull up somethin the cops missed.

I hope she makes Reception do the most borin bits. I hope it ruins his fuckin day.

That's my quid. Or maybe it's my quo. I ain't got a lick of language ain't English, and ya mighta noticed, I ain't got a grip on that's gonna bear my weight. I know it ain't my pro. It's quid or quo. Just forget about the foreign stuff already.

What I'm tryna say is, for all this, all I gotta do is help Janis out with this thing: Janis' mom is havin a yard sale, only she's basically just a pile of sticks in a wheelchair. And I guess her yard is fuckin big. So Janis needs some muscle there, make sure nobody gets any notions about grabbin some antiques and leggin it while granny's still tryna get her specs on. I tell Janis, just make sure Wally ain't invited and it'll all be fine. Janis laughs. Wally don't. Just looks pissed I showed his hand.

Day of, I show up at Janis' mom's house. Big fuckin yard, like she told me and then I told you. And here comes Janis' mom Agnes, rollin down the drive. Wheelchair's as promised, only she don't look so dusty to me.

She rolls right up to me and then some. I gotta take a step back so she don't roll over my foot.

I wanna say somethin draws blood but Janis told me Be nice. So I says to Agnes Show me where's your shit.

She flaps her lips at me. It's like starin down a camel. She wheels herself around and pumps back up towards the house.

I ask her You need a push?

She stops. Wheels herself back to face me. Stops. Shows me her middlemost fingers. Wheels back around. Gets back to pumpin.

Steely old broad. I like her.

She sure does have a lot of shit though. I tell her as much. She says Well that was the last box. You wanna set it all up on the tables, asshole? Or do you wanna borrow my fucking wheelchair, and I can go find an eight-year-old who's out of his crying phase?

I laugh at that and I says Fair play, ya fuckin dinosaur. Tell me what'm I puttin where.

So I drag a few big tables onto the lawn and heave out some cushytush ottomans while I'm at it. Next hour or so, Agnes' shoutin at me from the drive. Sayin What are you, touched? The tucker stays together! or Is that the best you can come up with? You gotta put the carolers into a fucking scenario!

I give it back a couple times. She says to me Do I have to hold your hand or something? And so I say to her Yeah, why don't you come take my hand and fuckin *walk* me through it.

Some people'd get mad you remind em about their fucked up appendages. Agnes, she just sorta titters. A good egg, she is.

I'm just about done with the spread when folks start arrivin. All of em look loaded like Agnes. Moneywise, I mean, only while we're on the subject they don't seem the sorts of folks Prohibition done much to keep from goin flush in the mug.

Agnes makes this loud spittin noise. I look over, she's tappin her fingers together just like Janis. Runs in the family, I figure.

She says to me Vultures. Every last one of them. Fucking buzzards.

I tell her You point me out your least favorites, I'll give em a tour of the basement.

She laughs and taps her fingers harder. But she don't sayin nothin to that. I figure I maybe oughta make clear I was kiddin. But the vulture's're in earshot, and they ain't gotta know that.

They grab stuff from the tables and take it to the drive. Agnes wheels up to em and starts dickerin straight away. I don't know she gets the concept. She starts by sayin I'll not take a red fuckin cent below thirty. Then the kid goes and gets his mom, and she says to Agnes What about twenty, and also please don't swear at my son. Agnes says to her Tell you what, if that's your son I'll call you a charity case and drop to twenty-nine, and I wanna hear you say yes or I'm saying no, got it? So the Mom says twenty-five and Agnes says Deal.

That plays out a buncha times. Lotta people give me worried looks as they're fishin through the shit. Makes me figure more'n a few had designs. But none of em got the nerve to follow through while I'm standin there. None that I see, anyway. Closest thing to trouble is a guy rolls up I guess got history with Agnes. And I don't mean that just on accounta they were both already about a hundred when Napoleon was havin a rough hike.

Agnes sees him comin and she says Oh Jesus Christ. Alan's here!

I catch her tone and ask her What's Alan thinkin, comin around here?

She says to me I bet he wants to buy the Murano vase back.

I ask her which one's that.

She mumbles I'm keeping it.

So I says to her You wanna tell Alan that, or you want me to?

She thinks about that real hard. Alan's close enough he just about made the decision for us when she says Get rid of him.

So I square my shoulders and walk right at Alan, fast. I say to him Fancy seein you here, Alan.

He got the message.

Alan aside, I gotta say, it was a good day. We shifted about half of Agnes' shit.

I start packin up the rest. I ask her if she's mothballin all this or what.

She looks at me like I'm a mustard stain. She says It's going up on the estate sale.

I give her the once over and ask her You dead all of a sudden?

She shakes her head and tells me her house got snatched away.

I says to her Don't that mean you gotta leave your shit there on accounta it don't belong to you no more?

She smiles and starts tappin her fingers. Only it's a real thin smile, like it's draped over *somethin else*. You can sorta see the *somethin else*'s shape under it.

I look at her big old house. Somethin you might call a Manor. I bet, ha, listen to this, I bet when she had Alan over, she probably met him in the foyer. Only she said it foy-yuh. Like, Meet me in the foyer. That's where I'll wait foy-yuh. Ha!

Anyways, I ask her Who took your house? You want I go pay em a visit?

She says And give them a tour of the basement?

I says If they ain't got one, I'll dig em one.

So she pats me on the arm and says Tell you what, if one night you lose interest in the keys your wife's gotta jangle in your face to keep you focused, you look up Bullington Realty. Ask them how the fucking bed and breakfast is working out for them.

I point at her house and I say That's gonna be a bed and breakfast? Must be some fuckin breakfast they're gonna give!

She starts tappin her fingers again. She says You'll have to ask Bullington about that.

And goddamnitall if I don't say to her I'll tell ya what they say.

Go Figure

look up Bullington Realty in the phone book. Give em a call. I talk to a lady seems nice enough, only she can't wait to get me outta her ear. I call back and the damn thing rings forever. I don't see no address. Nothin I can knock on. I didn't know you're allowed to not have an address. I wish I'd fuckin known that.

Daff sips her coffee at me in a way says to me I'm losin the thread.

So I says to her Listen, this was a steely old broad got some tricks up her sleeve. She don't deserve what's she bein served.

Another loud sip. Daff reminds me I got some person or persons unknown lookin to dig *me* a basement, so what am I doin tryin to muscle some brokers for an old lady I don't know well enough for sayin Hi at the grocery.

I tell her I know Agnes plenty well. I know about

Alan. Her fuckin nemesis or some shit. And anyway, she knows about you.

Daff says to me Did you tell her or did she just see your ring?

So I says Well I know about Alan.

She asks me What's Agnes' last name?

I fold my arms and say I'm gonna call Janis, see does she got a clue who was Pezet pallin around with prior to he got popped.

We still got one of them candlestick ringers. Some folks, they got the phones're just a box with a dial and a funny hat. I ain't got nothin against that sorta somethin, only the candlestick suits me fine. That ain't related to anythin, I'm just givin you my preference. That gonna be a problem, I wanna give you my preference?

Anyway. Got the candlestick at the side of my face. Couple minutes later I got Reception on the phone.

He says to me Thank you for calling the offices of Janis Kidderminster, this is

And I says to him Reception. It's me. Lemme talk to Janis.

He says I don't know who *me* is.

I says to him Well see a fuckin therapist then, why are you wastin my time with your existentials?

He says nothin for a second. Then he tells me Please hold on accounta I guess his memory's refreshed now.

Then Janis comes on and she says Hello, Mr. D'Amato.

I ask her if her mom's got the same last name as her.

She says yes.

So I says to her Your mom's called Agnes Kidder-minster?

She says yes.

So I says Thanks and I hang up.

I go back into the other room and I say to Daff The steely old broad's called Kidderminster. Agnes Kidderminster. Then I say Damn it all. On accounta I just remembered that wasn't why'd I call Janis to begin with.

I ring her back and get Reception. He says Thank you for

And I says Me again. I figure Janis is expectin my dialback.

She is.

She says Mom tells me you two hit it off. I certainly can't claim to have expected that.

So I tell her Yeah, you got a real fuckin sweetheart of a ma.

Janis don't say nothin til she says Are you calling for an update about Pezet?

I tell her Yeah I am.

She tells me she got a list of names. Pezet's pals. Most of em she just lifted from the cops, but a few she rustled up on her own. She put em in different columns, she tells me.

I say You got em in fuckin columns? No shit! Then I grab a pen and tell her Ok shoot.

She asks me what I mean.

I say Gimme the names, I got a pen.

She says to me It's really quite a few names. I expected you would come by and I could just give you the paper I wrote them on.

I says to her Well if I'da known that I'da put my fuckin shoes on. You ever heard of the postal service?

She tells me of course she has, and does she want me to mail it.

So I says To me? Fuck no. But I got a whaddyacallit, a courier, if you see what I mean.

She says she don't.

I tell her to send it to Godric. Only I give her his business address.

She tells me she don't feel comfortable sendin it to a guy she's never met.

I says to her Listen, he's good people.

She asks me Well what if it winds up in somebody else's hands?

I ask her How's that gonna happen? You write the wrong address?

She explains Or I was *given* the wrong address.

So I says to her You think I ain't sure of the address of the buddy who runs my courier if you see what I mean?

She says I'm just presenting it as a possibility. It could also get lost. That's not exactly unheard of.

So I says to her Alright already, just fuckin have it ready and I'll be around.

I figure I can hear her fingers tappin over the phone.

Go Figure

I always figure Godric's shop's just a fuckin mess. Turns out he's got himself a system. I come walkin in with the folder from Janis, I hardly squeezed my way back to him prior to he's fishin a corkboard out from behind a pile of frames and shit.

There's part a me wants to tell him we don't need that fuckin thing. Then there's the part a me always wanted to tack some shit on a board so's I can stand back and say Hmmm.

So I say Whaddyasay, old timer?

And what he says is Have you read through them yet?

I plop the folder on his little table and tell him They're comin to ya fresh. I ain't laid an eye on em.

Godric's jaw gets restless. I ask him has he got a new ailment or does he just got somethin sparklin on his tongue.

He says You haven't looked them over yet? Just once?

I tell him I didn't wanna miss anythin.

He says to me You won't. We were always going to review them together. A preliminary survey might have saved us some time, though.

I ask him You got plans tonight? Cause I figured this was your plans.

He breathes real loud and adjusts his little green visor and says Let's see what we've got, then.

So we start siftin through papers. Janis wasn't lyin. She gave us fuckin columns. Loads of names. People names. Business names. Even some animal names. Everybody but everybody Paul Pezet ever got paper with, and a bunch besides. Some info on how'd they do their dallyin. Jesus, how'd she find all this? I can't hardly keep it all straight. That's how come I brought it to Godric.

Godric's my whaddyacallit. When he's not findin me jobs, he's bein my fuckin whatstheword.

I says to Godric What are you, old timer?

He looks up from whatever name he's been givin scrutiny. Now he's givin *me* scrutiny.

I explain how I mean what are you relativized to me?

So he scrutes at me a bit more and says This feels like it's going to be one of your little jokes at my expense.

I tell him No no no, I'm just tryna remember the word for somethin that helps you remember all the stuff you couldn't never remember otherwise.

He says A note?

84

I say Kinda, but only this is a thing's got a memory so it can find stuff too.

He says …? And then he says Like an automaton?

I say I don't know nothin about that, but I figure it for a word.

So he says Sammy, I know it annoys you to keep hearing it, but I really think you should let my friend look at you.

That ain't even close to what word was I lookin for, so I says Unless me sittin on a couch and talkin about what'd my dad say made me sad back yesteryear's gonna help *here*, I can't even figure why're you tryin this shit again.

So he says He's not that kind of doctor.

So I says I ain't lookin to have chopsticks stuck in my ears neither.

Godric breaths loud and says I don't know the word you're looking for. Then he starts readin the pages again.

So whatever the fuckin word I was tryin to think of is, that's what Godric is. He's that fuckin word. We been workin together so long, he knows just about every job I ever done, every mug I ever talked at. I'm tryna remember a thing I done and I hit a wall, I just head on over to Godric and I say Whaddyasay old timer? Then he tells me about his ailments. Then I ask him the thing. Then he tells me about it. Sometimes he even remember shit I done better than I do!

That's how come I gotta bring all this to Godric. How'm I gonna look at everybody Paul Pezet's ever met, make a single lick of goddamned sense out of it, then *also* remember every fuckin guy *I* ever met, and see where's the overlap between me and Paul? No way am I gonna ever do that. Godric's the guy for that.

Also seems respectful to bring it to him on accounta he and Pezet go way back. And now whoever killed his one buddy's tryin to off his other buddy. So Godric's pretty down about the whole thing.

The door to the shop says Ding. Which if you translate it from Door to English it means Cover your fuckin indiscretions, we got a live one here.

So Godric throws his blanket, what's covered a lot of indiscretions, and I'm only countin the ones I know about or fuckin *wanna* know about, over the board.

The lady who comes in, she's at least got the decency to see she's interruptin somethin. She says I'm sorry, the sign said open but, um, are you closed?

Godric gives her an old timer smile and says Well I'd hoped I was, but I can't argue with the sign. So what can I do you for?

She's got this picture of her dipshit kid she wants framed. So Godric's gotta run down all the options with her, like he's gonna do it himself. I get outta his way. But I wanna keep workin. So I lift up the blanket over the board, duck under and drop the blanket. They stop talkin out there for a second, so I guess I look pretty fuckin stupid. Whatever, I ain't given much thought on my how-do-I-look. Anyway, they start up yakkin again. I figure I came out on top there.

Except for I'm on bottom of the blanket, and the

blanket's for keepin people from peepin through. And in this instance, I'm countin light as people. So what I'm sayin is, I can't really see nothin.

I just stand under the blanket and I wait for em to finish.

After the lady goes away, Godric says to me You can come out now. He's takin a real high tone with me. He's gonna ask me to get fuckin checked again.

So I throw the blanket off me and the board and tell him Time to get back to deducin.

He's scrutin me again. He starts punchin in the air and he says You know…people with physically demanding careers, like football players or boxers, uh…well, sometimes, if they sustain too many hits to the head, it starts to take a toll. Factor in your tour in France, it's not

I cut him off and tell him I ain't been hit in the head that much.

He says I've been doing some research. People are starting to understand what happens in the brain when

I interrupt him and say You like the research, huh?

He sighs and starts lookin at the Pezet papers again, on accounta he knows what was I gonna say.

I ain't dumb. Maybe my memory's got more hidin places now, but I ain't an idiot. Or I ain't so much more an idiot than I used to be.

I ain't fuckin dumb.

Later Godric wakes me up and he says I think I found something.

I tell him Let's hear it.

So he pulls a piece of paper off the end of the table, on accounta he ain't fuckin usin the board no more. That makes me a little sad. No clue how come.

Anyway Godric points at the paper and says This guy? He's connected to UFGW.

I ask him Is that like women's UFG?

He asks me What the hell's UFG?

I tell him I got no fuckin clue, but I figure the W is for ladies.

Godric looks at the paper like he's gotta make sure. He says No Sammy. It's the United Food and Grocery Workers. It's a union.

I says to him Jesus, I thought unions went out with Gompers.

Godric don't respond to that. Maybe he ain't heard about Gompers croaked. Anyway, he says And *this* guy, Denver Eustis, Janis has him listed here as a lobbyist with Working for the Country America Institute.

I says to him *Now* who sounds like he got hit in the head too much?

Only he don't think that's as sharp as I do. So he just keeps talkin, and he says about how Pezet was in semi-regular contact with Eustis. Buncha letters the cops found in his house from Eustis. Janis don't know what did the letters say, since the cops only wrote about they exist on a report. But they're letters from Eustis at Pez-et's place, ain't no question on that.

GO FIGURE

I reach for the page and I says Great, where am I findin this Eustis fella?

Godric pulls the paper into his chest and says to me Now hang on a minute. Eustis is the point of contact for the Rockefellers and the Bostwicks of the world, but I don't think he's the one *you* want necessarily. Besides, he works for a congressional lobbying group. Ties to the railroad. It's a prickly time for all of them. Not the sort of doors you want to be knocking on without a firm plan of action.

I feel my eyebrows foldin their arms, so I says to him I thought you said he was Union. I can do Union.

So he says I know you can. And have. That's the connection. Eustis works for...

He stops and grabs a pen. Guess he figures I'm too fuckin dumb to follow along without he draws me a picture. I wanna say another somethin sharp, only I know he ain't gonna give it the appreciation he oughta.

So anyway Godric writes *Denver Eustis* on the paper. He draws a little umbrella over that name and writes *WCAI* above that. Then he says to me Eustis is a lobbyist with Working for the Country America Institute. The WCAI originated as an arm of, and remains allied with, the AFL-CIG, or American Federation of Labor and Congress of Industrial Groups.

Then he draws a little umbrella over *WCAI* and writes *AFL-CIG* a bit bigger above that.

And then he says The AFL-CIG is a union federation, under which the United Food and Grocery Workers operates.

He draws a little sideways arrow and writes *UFGW*. Then he says The UFGW is *the* union for food production in this country. Farmers, shelf stockers, chicken choppers, if they're a part of getting food on to your table, and they pay union dues, they're probably sending those dues care of UFGW.

So I just stare at the paper. I really wanna say somethin smart. Godric thinks I'm a fuckin idiot but I ain't. I just can't think straight when I got him on deck. It's like I let him do my rememberin for me, then I just forget to do it myself.

I really wanna say somethin smart on accounta he just did some real egghead shit and I'm bringin shit's got a normal-shape head.

I got nothin so I just say Sounds good so far.

Godric ain't even focused enough to look at me like I can't catch a ball, which I know he'd be doin if he'd got himself focus enough. He's fucked off wherever eggheads go when they're seein cursive. He says to me Do you remember, gosh, this was about ten years ago, not long after Ferdinand, when you and a bunch of other big guys got called in to break the union strike in California?

I says to him Yeah, yeah! I fuckin remember that! The scab job! The guys who'd work the store are feelin crosswise with the honchos, so the honchos call in some muscle don't scare easy to keep things movin!

So he taps the paper with the pen and says Precisely! And he looks at me like the only reason I didn't catch the ball is on accounta I hit a fuckin homer.

GO FIGURE

So I stare at the page and I says to him Is this the only commons I got with Paul?

Godric nods and says M-hm.

I walk through it again with my finger and I says to him Alright. So your thinkin is, the…UFGW, they're still smartin over I scabbed em ten years ago. So they're lookin lookin lookin for me all this time, til somehow Denver Eustis figures his buddy Paul Pezet knows a guy, and the guy he knows is *you*, and you know *me*. And then the union, they send word *all the way up* to Denver that *he's* gonna tell *Paul* to talk to *you* to get *me* usin *Cleveland,* and

Godric asks me Who's Cleveland?

I says to him The guy drove the Cleveland.

Godric just nods about that.

I says to him The guy did the hook on me.

Godric says I'm with you now.

I says Swell and then I says to him So yeah the job turns out to be a hook. Only the hook don't go so well, so they figure they gotta cover their asses. So they kill Pezet, only they're gonna make him real uncomfortable first. And they're doin all this on accounta I was baggin some highly fuckin controversial groceries ten years back.

Now Godric's the one lookin at the paper like he can't shake sense outta it. He says to me Well, when you put it that way, it does sound a bit dumb.

And I smile on accounta now I'm makin *him* feel dumb. But I ain't the kind to rub a man's face in his less-thans. So I clap him on the back and I tell him Hell of a fine job though. I never coulda come up with that.

Godric smiles and pats my hand. Kinda thing only old timers can get away with without I give em a talk on personal space. He says to me It's a lead, anyway. Do you want me to see if I can get you an address on this Eustis character? To rule the UFGW theory out, if nothing else.

I say Sure, I'd fuckin appreciate that. And while you're at it, see if can you find me those other toughs the store brought in for packin groceries. On accounta I figure if this is the thing, probably the other guys are gettin hassled too, right? Or dead?

Godric tells me That's a really great idea. Only he says it in a tone of voice like he can't fuckin believe his ears. Like an iguana just walked in and said my idea. So that don't make me feel so great.

GO FIGURE

GOTTA figure yellow journalism ain't dead like everybody says. On accounta that's how do I find out about the cops found my fingertip prints.

I'm grabbin a bite at a deli, extra bread so I get some fuckin fiber. All the best delis, they got little newspapers on the counter. Daily rags, the ones got exclamation points after all the headlines. This one's screamin about a break in the Pezet case. They lifted some fingertip prints in the kitchen don't match what they were figurin to find. I'm wrackin my brains on why the hell they were dustin the kitchen, til I remember the knife. I just sorta dropped it and made trails. So they figure they're gonna find fingertip prints in the kitchen. They figured right on accounta I had to touch near every fuckin inch in the no-handle dark there.

So now they're crowin about this fuckin profile, this fingertip print profile. The fingertip prints they got, they sent em over to this fresh-paint room in the FBI, and they already got some matches tie the Pezet crime to a few other crimes around New York and Jersey. Some of those crimes got fingertip prints, some of em they got other shit links no-fingertip print crimes to fingertip print crimes. Modus operandi, technique signatures, the fuck do I know, not much more'n these clowns. Anyway, readin about all the cases my fingertip prints point at, I get heartburn. The good kind. Whaddyacallit. I'm comin down with nostaglias.

This ain't the sorta thing gets me quakin, even if they were sayin the whole FBI's on it, which they are. They're sayin this is gonna be the case proves the fresh-paint fingertip boys're worth their paychecks. Whatever about that. Like I was sayin before, they ain't got my fingertip prints off my pointers, and I ain't got no papers I ain't paid Odette for the privilege of holdin em. And those papers sure as hell ain't in my name, cept for when I'm tellin folks I'm called Michael Berns. And good fuckin luck to the genius tries to catch me like I'm some fuckin straight-on crime guy does the same crimes for the same guys. I do jobs for all sorts, so there ain't no motive to suss out. Not unless they got somebody strong on socials like Godric. But I figure anybody strong on socials as Godric ain't runnin around with a badge, see what I mean?

Granted, I ain't never had my CV reachin such a

large audience before. But you know what, I say Good luck to em. Good luck to who'sever lookin. They're gonna need a *lotta* luck, in case they ever find me.

Daff ain't happy about it though.

She says to me Just because you aren't on the radar now doesn't mean you can be reckless. All it takes is one slip-up, one little trip down to the station. They print you, you're done.

I says to her Sorry, I didn't think of the kitchen.

She asks me Well, what else didn't you think of?

I tell her I ain't in a position to know.

Maybe that don't make her happy but she ain't up in arms no more. She tells me Godric called, Janis called, and Agnes called. I'm real glad about Daff for a whole lotta reasons, but one is she's real good with the phone.

I says to her Agnes called? She leave a number?

Daff says to me Yeah, she did, but you should probably call Godric back first out of any of them, right?

I tell her Godric ain't goin nowhere, cept across town to pick up a framed picture of a dipshit kid. Where's Agnes' number?

She makes her lips go flat and says I put a note on the counter.

I ask her What'd Agnes say she wanted?

Daff's lips get even smaller and she says She didn't say, but Janis called to warn you that her mother's a bit fond of you, and she got your number out of her daughter's receptionist.

So I tell her That shitsmear's givin out my personals? That pinchfaced so-and-so? Well, I'm easy with it this time on accounta I'm fuckin fond of her too, but

She says to me Think about it. You told me the receptionist doesn't like you. He gave your number to Agnes. To *get* you. Janis didn't make it sound like her mother's fondness is something most people find especially rewarding.

I point out to her how people probably say the same about me. She don't say otherwise. I was kinda figurin she would.

After dinner I go get my candlestick and I spin in Agnes' digits. She picks up and asks me hello. I says to her Whaddyasay, ya old battleship? She asks me Where'd you learn phone etiquette, the back of a cereal box? I says to her Good for you stayin current, on accounta the only cereal you ate growin up you had to harvest and fuckin grind.

So we got the pleasantries outta the way. Agnes tells me somebody stole a load of her shit. I say I can't fuckin believe it. Then she starts to tell me how she can't believe some of the stuff they knicked. She's describin clocks and silver and all sorts. She's doin a real good job, givin me all kinds of detail.

It's on accounta the details that I then says to her What the hell are you talkin about? That's the shit you sold!

I figure Agnes is havin a good old think about that. She's all quiet.

Til she says What the hell are *you* talking about?

I explain to her how she had a big old fuckin yard sale the other day on accounta she's sellin her house.

She says I'm not selling my fucking house!

I says to her I'm just tellin you what you told me, is they're buyin you out for a bread and breakfast.

She asks me See, you're chewing shit and telling me to spit. Who's buying me out? Who's building a bread, fucking *bed* and breakfast in my castle?

So I says You told me it was…ah, shit. I call to Daff Hey Daff?

She asks me Yeah?

I shout at her Do you remember what I told you the company's buyin Agnes' house was called?

Agnes' little voice on the phone is sayin about Is this some kind of fucking joke, you pervert?

Daff comes walkin into the hall. She says Why don't you ask Agnes?

I tell her Agnes don't remember probably on accounta an ailment I ain't qualified to figure about.

Daff makes a face like she's lookin at a bird got a fucked up wing. She says Bullington.

I tell her thanks and then I tell Agnes Bullington Realty. Then I remember about how I gave em a call and got just about hung up at, which means it ain't like Agnes just fuckin made em up, and I relay that rememberage and my deduceage. I ask her Where'd you pull Bullington from if they ain't buyin you out, huh? Lucky guess?

She tells me I ain't had luck in fifty years and look at me now!

I ask her where's she callin from, these digits for the mansion or are they for the funeral home where she lives.

She tells me It's a electrical telephone, you bitch. I can call you from anywhere I want.

I tell her congratulations and ask where's she callin me from *now*.

She tells me Wherever I am, I don't have to be. Then she hangs up.

I look at the phone like it's gonna talk more sense now that it ain't gotta sound like Agnes. In the hall there, Daff's got some definition on her mouth now. Like an umbrella. Like Godric's gonna write *CHIN* under it and *NOSE* over top and call it a lead.

I tell Daff Poor Agnes's got her eggs all scrambled or somethin.

Daff says I have a feeling she'll be calling back, at *least* once. You should share your diagnosis with her.

Feels kinda rotten, but I ain't excited to talk to Agnes no more. She's a sweet old cow. It ain't her fault she's a few jingle bells short of a, uh, that fuckin stick you put jingle bells on and shake around. It ain't her fault she's gone daffy, is what'm I sayin.

But I still don't wanna talk to her no more.

So I says Lemme call Godric, maybe he's got some doors I gotta knock on. Then *you* can talk to Agnes, since we're figurin she's callin back.

I wanna keep a straight face so Daff thinks I ain't bein a jokester, only I can't hold it. I smile a bit.

Daff's umbrella goes upside down a touch. But not a whole lot.

Then we both got the flat mouths.

GO FIGURE

GODRIC tells me he's got an address for Denver Eustis. It ain't a home address though. Eustis's takin a trip to D.C. for some lobbyin shit. Somethin about they want some new better ways to wave at trains as they go zippin by. Ain't my business. Point is, I got the skinny tells me he's gonna be in *this* buildin at *this* time. How'm I gonna get him alone, how'm I gonna lean on him about ancient groceries, I got no clue. But I know how'm I gonna find him. And when.

I ask Godric about the other guys scabbed with me back in the ancient grocery age, he says he's got two of em, figures he can track the last. I tell him good, and let's bring em here. Tell em it's a job. Offer em pay. I'm good for it, or I figure I can get Wally to pony up. Just gotta point out I need a hand dupin folks. He'll love it.

So anyway I pack a bag. I give Daff a fuckin kiss on the cheek, tell her Don't say nothin to Agnes ain't civil. Then I pile into the car and make for Denver.

I'm drivin hard 'til night. Forty miles an hour I'm talkin. Then now it's night so I pull over to some motel ain't fleabag but they ain't exactly got mints on the pillows neither. I get a room with a great big bed on accounta I like to fuckin treat myself sometimes. The bed ain't so comfy but it's big. Bein fair though, it ain't like I asked about comfy, and they sure didn't offer nothin neither.

I go back down to the lobby and give Daff a ring. I tell her I figure I can make it in three, four more days I keep peelin tar like I am.

She asks me What?

I tell her again, slow and loud.

She asks me Are you not there?

I says Hello?

She says Hello?

So I ask her Can you hear me?

She says I can hear you! Can you hear me?

I says to her Of course I can hear you, I ain't got the bum hookup!

So she says to me What are you talking about?

I says to her You asked me ain't I there. You forget already?

She says I wasn't talking about the connection, Sammy. I'm talking about you!

So I ask her Huh?

She tells me I was asking if you're not there yet?

I says What, did I fly? How'm I gonna be in Denver already?

She don't say nothin.

I have a real good think. Then I says What kind of a fuckin name for a human is Denver anyway?

I'm back in the car haulin ass east. It's two in the fuckin A.M. This Eustis fucker named Denver by his parents, he's got his fuckin pocketwatch-wearin maga-zine-subscribin news-understandin big shot meetin in five hours. Then he goes away, and who knows when's Godric gonna nail him down next. Meanwhile I got guys takin potshots at me. *And* they're fuckin tellin who knows how many fuckin people that I fuckin goose. So I got five hours to make up a whole fuckin day's happy trails, and then some more on toppa that.

Good thing is the roads I'm on are pretty much paved'n dead. I can stand on the pedal.

Bad thing is I got a shit car. Tops off at just over forty-two.

I ain't about to do math, but I figure that ain't gonna be fast enough.

I wanna head into one of them towns sometimes twinkle over the fuckin hills and cruise for a new ride. Not lookin to buy, you see what I'm sayin. Only with my luck I figure I'm goin nowhere but the middle of fuckin nowhere. And even if I find a ride, I never stole a car I ain't got the keys for from a sleepin guy's pocket.

So I just keep standin on the pedal.

My eyes get kinda heavy.

Fuckin bullshit. Tough guys don't fuckin zonk behind the wheel.

Tough guys ain't supposed to sleep *ever*, now that I'm thinkin on it. When's the last time you heard a tough guy sayin Sorry boys, can't play another hand, I gotta get a solid six hours? It ain't done. Less they got one eye open. Then that's alright.

Why the fuck did I splash out for a big bed at a fuckin fleabag? What, am I gonna roll around like I finally got a date for prom?

I don't notice my eyes fell shut til I'm pryin em open. I'm sorta between lanes. I straighten it out quick.

The little red needle is laughin about 42. Car's got numbers goin up to 100, but the needle ain't budgin. Real fuckin pleased with itself, that needle.

I punch the dash. It breaks. That's what I fuckin thought.

The wheels of the car start laughin too. Turns out I'm partway drivin on somebody's croppage.

I crank the wheel hard. Back in the lane. Now I'm all kindsa awake. Partly on accounta the fuckin agrarian giggles.

Mostly on accounta the cop car runnin its gumdrop behind me.

Go Figure

FIRST thought is I fuckin gun it. Leave this cop in the dust. Only then I remember I *am* gunnin it. And anyway, I'm the Runaway fuckin Match all of a sudden? I'm racin my car around town? No fuckin way.

So what'm I gonna do? I gotta pull over. Which I do. Then I'm just sittin there. I got a little red bubble blowin up and burstin over my shoulder. I don't hear nobody get outta the cop car. He's just sittin there. What if this ain't a cop? What if Big Grocery's got a price on my head, and it's an even better fuckin price if you got the Club Card?

Or also but then what if it *is* a fuckin cop? Daff's right. I get fingertip printed, they're gonna be full-timin it just to stamp my name on half their fuckin catalog of cold cases. Suddenly all of those cases're hot again, and boom. I'm cooked.

Holy shit! I just thoughta somethin. When I find the guy's been spreadin the goosin rumors about me, I'm gonna look him in the eye and I'm gonna say Your goose is cooked. And then I'll throw him into a fuckin volcano or some shit. Your goose is cooked. That's so fuckin good.

So I gotta make sure this cop don't send my fingertip prints to some federal wants to show how good he is at lookielikies, on accounta I gotta tell somebody their goose is cooked.

So ok, so. Ok. What do I got? I got whatever's the reverse of the charismaticals. I ain't gonna be sweet talkin nobody no time soon. Don't matter what kinda cop shows up figurin what kinda sex for fairer, I bat my eyes at em and they collar me for assaultin an officer. But I ain't in any position to be loomin at present neither. I'm big. My car's medium. I could stick my legs through the floor and wear it like the weirdest fuckin lederhosen you ever saw. Sittin inside though, I gotta hunch and crunch. Not nobody but nobody ever got rattled by a guy hunched and crunched into a box half his size.

Ok, so. Ok. I got no idea what I got.

Nobody's gettin out of that fuckin car back there.

Ah, hell. I just figured a thing I can do. Ain't a thing I'm clickin heels for, but a things a thing, and that puts me out ahead of havin no thing, I think.

Here the thing: I can make the cop zonk out.

Go Figure

I don't like fuckin with law directly, as such. Turns up the heat too much. And anyway, they're just doin a job of work, same as me. The way I figure, if a cop's squarin up against me on accounta I infracted one of their fuckin statutes, we're in the same boat seein as ain't neither of us are any kind of sunny on the law just then.

So it ain't choice number first, zonkin a cop. But I could do it. If I gotta.

Knock knock knock. Cop's knockin on my window. Didn't even see em showin up.

Em on accounta there's two of em. The other one's creepin around the passenger side, blastin the backseat with the kinda sunshine ain't nobody about to be feelin real soon.

I thumb the little nub on the door to lock. Then I crank the little handle under my window, rr-rr-rr-rr, and then it's down. I point across my lap to the guy's got the torch and say to the cop on my side, I says to him I ain't never seen a flashlight that small til now.

Driverside's got a script he favors over my howsit-goin, so he just says Sir, do you have the slightest idea how fast you were going?

I says to him forty-two.

He asks me Why in goodness gracious are you flying down the road at a forty-two miles an hour tonight?

I tell him On accounta my car don't go any faster.

He twists his face up at me and asks for License and Registration. He don't say please.

I pop open the glovebox and pull out some papers

Odette says to me are as good as the real deal. So far they dealt me straight. Me, buttoned-up Michael Berns. Real fuckin respectable name, on accounta I'm a real fuckin respectable guy.

Cops might not agree though. Might not figure Michael Berns to be a real guy at all. Then they're gonna say Hey Mike who ain't Mike, you wanna stick your digits in some ink?

Driverside hands my License and Registration over the hood of my car to Passengerside. He starts wavin his flashlight around over em. Then Driverside leans back down and just stares at me.

He asks me Have you ever been pulled over before?

I ask him This gonna go easier dependin on the answer?

He smiles and says Most people are nervous when they get pulled over. A little shaky, or way too tense. You don't seem like either.

I tell him it's on accounta I'm a model citizen.

He leans back and looks at Passengerside. His face turns red and blue and red and blue and then white when Passengerside's light is pointin towards him. Driverside squints and waves his hand in front of his eyes and asks his partner How many times do I have to tell you?

Passengerside says somethin to Driverside. I can't hear on accounta that window's closed.

Turns out I ain't gotta hear. Driverside's hand goes to his belt. The gun hangin on it, to paint a better picture.

Go Figure

He asks me if I wouldn't mind steppin outta the car, real slow.

I ask him What's the problem, officer?

He tells me to Step out of the car, Mr. Berns. The way he says that name, I know he knows it ain't real.

Hell.

Driverside figures I'm up to mischief, so he tells me put my hands where he can see em. I lift em up right in fronta my eyes.

Passengerside's kinda crouchin over, shinin his light through the window.

I ain't gettin in their car. That's for fuckin certain. So all I gotta figure now is, do I put em to sleep or do I kill em?

Let's say I kill em, leave em on the road and hit it, the road I'm sayin. I do that, other cops turn the heat up, but at least they ain't got a fake name for stickin their most favorite fingertip prints on. I gotta figure they'll find em here, but it'll just be one more fuckin mystery.

Zonk em, though, and they go find somebody's a grade-A scribbler and say Now see here, this Berns fella looks a little like this…

Ah, hell. I never been the sort kills a person ain't got it comin. Try for that, anyway. These two ain't done nothin earns em a hole in the ground, and if I ain't got some sorta code, then, I don't know, what the fuck?

So I leave em breathin, then. But that don't mean I gotta make the sketch job easy.

So I make a fuckin face.

I ain't the kinda guy makes weird faces in the mirror. So I got no clue how weird's my face look right now. But it sure feels like I got my eyes bugged wide. I'm stretchin my lips like this guy I saw what lived through a bullet flyin so near his face it kissed his lips and missed his teeth. Curlin em back so my pearlywhites're sayin harya.

So I'm sittin there lookin at the door of my car and I says to em How you want me to open the door if I got my hands in the air?

Driverside steps forward and tries the handle.

Locked.

I says to him Force of fuckin habit, I'm drivin through country. Never know who're you gonna run into.

He says Unlock your door, sir.

I tell him I gotta hit a little switch right under the window. You're gonna miss my hand for a second.

He says Just do it and then put your hand back up.

So real slow, I reach down and press the little switch. I put my hand back up.

Then he pops the door open and skitters some steps back. Still got his hand on the gun. He says to me Please step out of the vehicle.

So I step outta the vehicle, only its more like climbin. Takes a few seconds to get all of me out. I figure he didn't figure my size right on accounta he's got his eyes buggin out almost as big as mine.

He flicks the little leather strap holds the gun in the holster.

I ask him Why're you flickin the little leather strap

holds your gun in the holster?

He just tells me Turn around and face the vehicle, sir.

So I turn around the face the vehicle.

He tells me Put your hands on the vehicle.

So I put my hands on the vehicle. Passengerside's still just standin over there lookin simple. I ain't worried on Driverside. He gets in my personal space, he's good as sleepin. It's Passengerside I'm worried on. We got this fuckin car between us, and I ain't the type slides over hoods.

Driverside says to me I'm going to search you now, sir. Do you have any weapons on your person?

I tell him No. Which is true on accounta he didn't ask me is my *person* a weapon.

Instead he asks me Anything sharp? Knives, needles, that sort of thing?

I says to him No, officer. Since I'm still tryin to stretch my lips to the side it comes out like *no aw-i-shur*.

He tells me Don't move. I'm beginning the search.

I say *OK aw-i-shur*. Then I says to Passengerside, Hey you.

Apparently he don't just *look* simple, seein as he points his fuckin torch right at me. Which is also right at Driverside.

Driverside starts vocalizin his displeasure. He don't get so far on accounta the back of my head crunches him in the teeth. He takes a fuckin chomp into my noggin. Don't think he really meant to. I don't figure he was expectin the opportunity.

Anyway, I spin around and give him a left right left in the head stomach chin. Zonk. Feel better in the fuckin mornin.

Then I drop fast as I can.

I hear Passengerside blubberin. I figured on accounta Driverside's got him holdin the torch, he's gotta be green. Sounds like I figured right.

Only he ain't so green he don't know how to draw his fuckin firearm.

Only he's just the *right* amounta green for sayin some stupid shit like Sir, I'm drawing my firearm! Put your hands up, I'm going to approach!

Thing is, there ain't much room either of us got for maneuverin here. Ain't no good way to sneak up on the other guy, on accounta the other guy can just have a fuckin peek at your footwear under the carriage.

Passengerside's finally catchin on here, on accounta he tells me Back up! Walk down the road a bit, away from the vehicle! Hands behind your head! I'll follow you!

I ask him How far'm I goin?

So while he's ponderin that I steady up alongside the car. Keepin my head down, I bend my knees so I'm in a real deep squat. I says to him Hey, how about you just fuckin show me? Then I stick my hands under the car and stand up.

Now, I don't figure I can flip the car by myself. Never tried. But Passengerside's real panicked, and I figure he don't figure what I do figure. Turns out I'm right, which I know on accounta he stops squawkin about what's his fuckin five year plan to me and starts backpedalin. I can hear him scuffin his shoes on the road.

Ah, hell again. Maybe the five year plan ain't such a bad how-about, on accounta I ain't thought this through much past havin a fuckin quip says Hey, how about you just fuckin show me. Now I catch on how fixin one problem made another. I gotta keep him from puttin distance between us. I got a long reach. Bullet's got me beat.

But one thing at a time on accounta holy shit, I'm flippin the car! I oughta just drop it back down, only I wanna see can I do this or what. So I keep standin standin standin til I can walk under it. I'm pushin it with my shoulder now. I got it licked!

The side mirror says to me Crunch as the car flops on its side. Then the whole thing keeps on rollin. It flops down on its back and says Crash. It clears its throat then shuts up.

I don't see Passengerside nowhere. Fuck. Where'd he scamper to with his fuckin firearm? I can't even enjoy a little victory without somebody's gotta spoil it.

I put my fuckin head on a swivel. Nowhere. Nobody pops outta cover squeezin off rounds. I don't hear nobody tryin to flank me. Just quiet.

Til I'm movin towards the vehicle, all hunched. Then my shoe says to me Squish.

I look down and you know what I fuckin see? A pool of fuckin blood.

I walk around the car's other side. Passengerside's

passengerside is stickin out from under. I ask it What the fuck? Only it ain't in much condition to explain.

Not much to explain anyway. Looks like actually neither of us figured I could lift the car. I wonder who was more surprised about bein wrong.

Woulda sworn up and down I heard him scuffin his way backwards.

Ah, hell. I lost count of how many fuckin hells happened just tonight. I was considerin either I zonk both cops, or I kill em both. Zonkin one and killin the other ain't much of a how-about. That's whaddyacallit, both world's worst. I got the heat up, *and* the face and fake name on my fuckin fingertip prints.

This is fuckin bullshit! Now it's in for a penny, ya know? Actually I ain't so clear on what's that mean. I figure it's a thing people say just right prior to doin somethin like shootin a sleepin police officer once between the eyes and twice in the heart with his buddy's gun. Just to change up the M.O., I figure. Maybe they're sweatin that more'n the fingertip prints.

Godfuckinshit, I'm all kinda unsunny on this! I ain't the kind of guy brains people ain't got it comin! These two fellas, they probably got a fuckin quota. Gotta write some such number of fuckin citations. Just a job. Then I go and brain em.

Ah, *fuck*. I got another fuckin issue. I can't flip the fuckin car rightside back. Heat of the moment, I musta got a boost of fuckin muscle. Moment's gone snowy now. Car's stayin on its upside-wrong. Which means it's stayin here. And the car's registered to Michael fuckin

Berns. Which means the three bullets ain't gonna way-lay the cops hardly a bit. They're gonna get the prints, call up whoever down at the courthouse's got the vehicle registers, and now they got a name for the prints anyway. Still ain't got a sketch, I got that goin for me, but now every fuckin thing I got under the Michael Berns name, it's fuckin cooked.

I'm kickin myself the whole while I'm fishin my shit outta the back of the car. I hoof it til the sun comes up, on accounta it ain't til then I find a gas station's got a phone for me.

I ring up Daff. Boy, she's gonna be in a crosswise way on this.

She says to me Hey! She sounds real happy. I hate makin her not happy when she's happy. But, I mean, I figure that's kinda by necessary the only time I can *make* her not happy.

I says to her Michael Berns died.

She don't say nothin for a while. Til she asks How bad?

I lift my hand off the top of the phone. Covered in dust. The phone is. I'll tell ya, they let their gas stations go to shit out here.

I tell Daff Pretty bad.

She tells me Goddamnit Sammy, I'm in the middle of something. When she says somethin like *I'm in the middle of something*, she's talkin a goddamned composition. She makes music on the piano, I forgot to mention. We got a piano she plays. She's real good.

So I says to her Well it's fuckin lucky you ain't carvin

those notes in a fuckin sandbox, right?

Daff hangs up. I shouldn'ta said that last thing.

I hang around askin folks comin for gas can they give me a ride to the Big Apple or what. One of the guys workin the pumps tells me take a hike. I start to tell him somethin, only then I figure I oughta keep my profile low as it's likely to get. So I start walkin. Only I ain't lookin to stick to roads, so I heave my bag up and trudge through a fuckin field. Is it corn or rice or wheat, I don't fuckin know. What state am I in?

Don't matter. What matters is I ain't got a car. And this ain't the worst thing, but I ain't fond on how heavy's this bag I only brought on accounta I thought I was goin to fuckin Colorado. My arms're all sore from liftin the car. That was pretty fuckin impressive, huh? Too bad about Passengerside.

It ain't til I been walkin about an hour that I fuckin think about what I just done.

Or, uh, what I *didn't* just done.

I find another phone I ain't gotta put coins in and give Daff another ring.

She says to me I'm working on it. This time she don't sound happy. I ain't gotta wonder how come. If my crackin wise weren't enough, there she is havin to pack up and get outta the house we been livin in as Mr. and Mrs. Michael fuckin Berns. I got a feelin she's gonna quote forget unquote to pack a lotta my shit.

I tell her I'm real sorry about what I said earlier, and on toppa that I'm real sorry about how I fucked this all up big time. But, uh, Michael Berns just smoked two cops, and if one of these cowpunchers figures on gettin out a bag of dust and a little brush, it's gonna turn out Michael Berns smoked Paul Pezet and did a whole lotta other shit besides.

She don't say nothin.

I says On accounta fingertip prints.

She don't say nothin, only louder.

So I says to her Real sorry Daff. You might wanna be just gettin outta there on more a straight-away basis. Today, like.

Daff says to me Jesus Christ. I've got some questions I can't *wait* to hear you try to get out of answering. Then she hangs up again.

I just hope she ain't gotta lose her fuckin muse on that music.

GO FIGURE

TURNS out I'm in Ohio for some fuckin reason. Which is wild on accounta I can't dream up any reason for bein in Ohio. Only here I am. My fuckin luck, lemme tell ya.

First thing I do is keep walkin til I'm somewhere humans're supposed to be. I find a little rest area's got pretentions to callin itself a town. Head into the even littler truckstop's only a diner on accounta the sign outside.

Rear booth, away from the windows. Back against a wall. Clear line on the door. Me and my luggage settle in and I have a go on makin myself look small, on accounta I hear a guy at the bar sayin the words Flipped A Goddamned Car. So if *somebody flipped a goddamned car* hit the airwaves already, they probably got the A.P.B.s on big S.O.B.s. I got no clue what the fuckin law in Ohio is. Maybe they can tell me takin up so much space's the probable cause. Then I'm *really* biffed.

Soggy old waitress asks me what do I want. I tell her French toast and coffee. She asks me do I want cream and sugar. I tell her Extra and more besides. She nods and walks away. Never wrote nothin down. It ain't much to remember, but still I'm some sorta impression-ed. Put it this way, there's a half good chance she puts my French toast down and I'm thinkin How did she know?

I still got a lotta cash on me. Lucky. Do I have another I.D. on me? I pat my pockets on accounta I already know the answer's no. Some bus stations, don't they wanna check your I.D. prior to you gettin on? Fuck if I know. Only it ain't worth riskin the exposure of a fuckin bus stop if it ain't even for certain I'm gettin on the damn thing.

Call somebody to pick me up? Like I'm in fuckin middle school? What kinda tough guy calls somebody to pick him up? How's *that* rumor gonna play? No. I gotta get my own dumb ass home.

I can't fuckin believe this. Denver fuckin Eustis is havin his meetup now. Lobbyin so's they got brighter lights for wavin down trains, I figure. Ah shit, could I take a train? Nah, same problem the buses probably got. Oh well. Denver, though. Few hours from now he'll be scuttlin back into the woodwork. Who knows when Godric peeps him next?

Gotta hope he found somethin on those other gro-cery baggers then. Boy, but I could use a fuckin win right now.

The lady puts my French toast down. I tell her Shit, that was fast. How long's that been sittin around back there?

She says to me Eat it or not, bucko. You think I care?

I tell her Maybe I don't eat it, you guys save some money puttin it back in the deep freeze for some other schmuck.

So she says You wanna send it back? I'll let the chef know it's not up to snuff, huh? How's that, asshole?

So I says You know, you put me in mind of a dear old friend.

She tells me she's sorry for whoever's got the business end of my affections. I ask her if her surname ain't Kidderminster, or if she never knew anybody by that name.

She says Are you kiddin, mister?

Then we both laugh on accounta that sounds like Kidderminster.

I says I'm serious though.

She says No I don't fucking know anybody by that name.

I tell her Thanks and hurry up with the coffee.

Then I have a real hard think.

My brain don't remember the phone number, but I figure my finger will. So I slide away from my French Toast before I've laid even one chomp on it and use the phone what's close enough to the kitchen I maybe ain't meant to use it, only I don't see a sign says I can't. Sure enough, I turn off the brain and give the finger a long leash, here's the number gettin dialed in like it's Daff's.

The phone says Ring ring then it says Hah? in Agnes' voice.

I say Howdy Agnes, you remember your old pal Samuzzo?

She says Of course I remember you, you're the whore's son who helped me move house.

I tell her I'm real glad to hear you got your sea legs back. Listen, you don't talk to your daughter at all, do ya?

She asks me What kind of a question is that?

I says One's got an easy answer.

So she tells me No, Janet stopped returning my calls quite some time ago.

I ask her Jan*et?* You got two daughters and no knack for namin?

She tells me no she don't, and she's got a refrain on her question.

So I ask her You got any other buddies I oughta know about? You talk to anybody? Or are you one of them hermit types?

She says to me I pretty much keep myself to myself and that's just the way I like it.

So I tell her Great. You think you can keep your head screwed on long enough to drive to Ohio?

Bit of a fuckin production, gettin her here. I go find the kinda fleabag motel I was avoidin before, one you can't even *ask* for a big bed. But that's alright, I ain't plannin on stayin the night.

I call Agnes back with the address and she remembers I asked her to come pick me up. She don't remember that she said she wasn't gonna do that though. So I feel kinda bad about it, but I says to her Listen here lady, you made me a solemn fuckin promise you were comin to pick me up.

She tells me I don't recall saying any such thing, asshole.

So I says to her You feel like recall's your strong suit, huh?

She says fair enough and I tell her where's this fleabag palace at. Then she's on the road. I make double sure she's got the number of this fleabag, and that I got an atlas at the ready.

Do I feel like a fuckin skunk for playin this lady's mental problems like a fiddle? Eh, sure. Only not so much it ain't a relief I don't gotta show my face and shoulders and chest and arms and legs at a bus station.

I tell her Give me a ring every hour. So's I can keep informed on where's she at, does she remember where she's goin. Most hours on the hour the phone rings, I pick it up and a toadvoice calls me asshole, so I know she's got it handled. One time she calls late and cloudy, so I tell her to tell me where's she at and what signs she's passin. Run my finger around the atlas til I got it square where's she at and where's she gotta go, then I tell her. She says to me Thanks a lot, and then she calls me a name.

Round about nighttime she pulls in to the motel

drive. I pop outta the room, draggin my stupid fuckin bag behind me. I open the passengerside door and she asks me What the fuck are you doing?

I says to her Christ, your memory on the fritz again? You're givin me a ride!

She says to me And I'm driving home as well, am I?

I explain to her Course. Otherwise I'm givin *you* a ride.

She asks me After I drove all the way up by myself, is that right?

I says What's wrong, you gettin cranky it's past naptime?

She spits at my feet and says Always, and you're welcome, you soiled bicycle seat. I imagined *you* were driving home.

I tell her My license ain't in great standin.

She says to me Then drive carefully. And she shifts over. Pretty nimble move for a lady got such advanced years. Makes her look like her years is only intermediate.

I wanna argue but I feel rotten about not havin said thanks straight away. And I ain't about to sacrifice her to the fuckin bedbug temple.

So I guess I'm gonna drive careful.

I figure Agnes is gonna sleep the whole ride back. Just goes to show how much I know about old halberds like her.

She stares out the window at the nighttime flyin by, then sometimes she'll say somethin to me makes me wonder does she got some chickens flown the coop.

Like one time she turns to me and she says I agree with her. Clothes are for everyone. I agree with her.

So I ask Agnes Who the hell's *her*?

To that, she's got nothin.

Then another time she turns to me and says Do I have to sit here listening to you breathe through your mouth all night, or are you gonna sing me a song?

I tell her My voice ain't got much music in it.

She just spits at my feet again.

After we're far enough along the stars ain't the same, I ask her So what's goin down about your house, huh?

She asks me What about it?

I ask her Bullington buyin it or what?

She says to me Plech. Like she's tryin to make the sound of a bug splattin on the windshield. Then she says I don't know anything about that. My daughter handles all that shit.

I says to her You don't sound so happy about that.

She don't say nothin for a long time. Just like Janis when I start pokin her about her ma. So I says to her You guys don't get along, huh?

Agnes looks out the window again. I can tell she's wearin a big old frown, even from just seein the back of her skull. She says to me She works with some unsavory characters.

I says to Agnes You gotta figure who's your company in the car here.

She starts tappin her fingers.

I ask her You ever met a fella named Wally?

She says Plech again, so I know for sure she's met

Wally.

I says to her I don't figure we're all that bad.

Tap tap tap, she don't say nothin.

Well, she ain't gotta believe me. All that matters is I gotta believe me. We ain't all that bad, me and my buddies. We really ain't.

Go Figure

And see, this is the kinda thing I'm talkin about. Wally, sittin on top of his mountain of fuckin money, went out a while back and bought me a fuckin safe house. He finds em faster'n I could ever need em on accounta he's got his foot in pies most people only stick their thumbs in. Remember in '20, how the whole world fell down a flight of stairs? On accounta we forgot how do ya run a bank when there ain't a war on? How much you wanna bet Wally was one of the guys jumpin ship from the top and landin on a little guy?

I never fuckin asked, and I ain't about to. Ain't my business. What is my business is Wally's good at findin me safehouses. This one here, he just buys it, cha-ching, now it's mine. On accounta we're such fuckin buddies. So he ain't so bad, see?

The plan's been, an I.D. gets burned, Daff and I regroup at the safe house. So I drive back to Agnes' place, which I figure she still owns but for all I fuckin know Wally or Janis or Woodrow fuckin Wilson's got a name on the deed, and but so anyway she don't ask me to drop her anywhere else. So I leave her and the car there and get to walkin. Lucky for me, but also Wally planned it this way so it ain't really luck, well anyway the safe house is a ways away from the house we got under the Michael Berns name. I'm just now realizin its pretty funny, or at least kinda funny, that the I.D. just got burned is called Berns. What a world, huh?

But yeah so it's a good job the safe house ain't near Berns' house, on accounta sometime ain't too far from nowtime, there's gonna be all kindsa law lookin that fuckin place up and down. We got all sortsa whaddya-callems in place, plans you make when you're plannin things won't go accordin to plan. Things like when you're keepin all your paperworks in tubs, so's you can just burn em up easy. Maybe Daff just burned the whole house down, too. That woulda been good.

So I feel pretty covered hittin the bricks to the safe-house. Ain't worried about a dragnet this far out. And besides, I don't want people spottin me in Agnes' jal-opy. I get caught, all of a suddenly Agnes is gettin drag-ged into it, then maybe Janis and Wally and all sortsa other people ain't interested in gettin any kinda audit. Safer for everybody I hit the bricks, draggin my trusty fucking luggage behind.

Sun's poppin up by the time I see the house. I rem-embered it bein bigger. The house, I mean. Real small little one-story thing. Only I figure it's got a basement, on accounta the backyard takes a real hard dip down. If it ain't got a basement, it might as well be a breadbox on a big fuckin plinth.

Contingency! That's the word I was searchin for just a little ways ago.

I pull out my keys and pick the one I ain't never used before. Moment's pause prior to I put it in the lock, on accounta I gotta envision there might be spiders in here. The idea was Wally's got a guy or a gal comes and cleans the place once a month, just so it don't get repoed by creepycrawlers. But he told me that way back aways. Who knows did he kept payin that bill or what.

Anyway, key goes in the lock and the lock says Click. I pop the door open with my hip and throw my long sufferin suitcase inside.

Nobody shoots it, which is nice on accounta that's basically all the clothes I got at the moment. I peek inside and say Hey Daff?

She pokes her head out from around the corner.

I says How's it goin? You lose your music or what?

She taps the side of her head and says to me No, I got it.

I tell her I'm real glad to hear that, and just as much I'm real sorry about fuckin things up.

She suggests I quit standin half in half out and just come in.

So I do.

I bring her all up to speed on what happened, how I got home, all that.

Daff puts her hands on mine and looks at my eyeballs. She asks me Why did you shoot the other cop? I get that the first was an accident, but why do the second?

I tell her I was tryin to stop the sketch prior to it got to the scribble-stage. I done it the way I did on account-a I wanted to throw off the M.O., only I forgot about the prints and the car bein upside down.

Then my eyes got all squashed.

Daff asks me Are you alright?

I says to her Yeah I'm alright, I'm just tellin you bout the cops who'd I make into pancakes and waffles.

Daff says to me Oh, Sammy.

Now my eyes start leakin. I ain't sure how come, til I figure shit, this ain't leakin! It's *weepin!*

I says to her Holy Christ! Am I cryin right now or what?

She shakes her head and grabs my hand and says Oh, baby.

I point to my face and I says What's goin on here? This ain't never happened before!

She says I know, I know.

I just can't get over it. I says You feel it more in the shoulders than I figured! It's like laughin in reverse! Would you get a loada this?

She leans forward and gives me a big hug. I still can't figure what the fuck is happenin to me. Tough guys don't fuckin weep, ya know what I'm sayin? I ain't never weeped prior to now. Even when I'm a baby, my ma always said to me I weren't no frivolous infant. I only ever said Boo Hoo like I meant business.

So I says to Daff He coulda done a sketch of me. But like I'm sayin, if I'd been thinkin of the prints I woulda done stuff different, no doubt.

She's talkin soft now, only she ain't lettin me off the hook only on accounta I'm washin her fuckin blouse. She says to me But it sounds like you were aware of the registration of your car becoming an issue, right? So best case scenario, the I.D. was compromised whether or not you killed the other cop.

I kinda push her away a little bit and I says to her No, I wasn't thinkin on the fuckin registration til I already shot the second. Like I said, I woulda done it different if I'd thought. Look! I'm fuckin weepin! I ain't clickin my fuckin heels, and I can't call a fuckin do-over. So how about lay off for a fuckin second, maybe!

Daff squeezes my hand and shakes her head. She says I'm just…

Daff don't usually pause this much when she's talkin. Pauses ain't a good sign.

She keeps talkin by sayin I just, killing an unconscious police officer, you know…that's not the sort of thing I ever expected you to do. Godric and I were

I interrupt her by sayin Not now, Daff. I ain't jokin. I don't wanna hear this Godric and Me shit right now, this ain't the fuckin time.

She gets quieter but she don't quit talkin. She says Sammy, this is precisely the time.

My voice gets louder'n I want it to, but I says to her The fuck, Daff? I'm sicka this shit, this Godric and You *shit!* What'd he tell you, tell me go see a doctor can tell me I got punched too hard? That bein in a big war scrambled me? No shit. There, two fuckin bills we ain't gotta pay.

She asks me Why are you so resistant to getting help?

I tell her On accounta I'm a fuckin bruiser, and bruisers don't need no fuckin help!

She says to me Bruisers also don't cry or goose, but here we

I interrupt her and I punch my own titty and I says I'm a fuckin bruiser! I don't need fuckin help! Only I says it so loud it's more like I'm yellin it.

So she goes quiet as much as I went otherwise, and she says Sammy. Listen to yourself.

So I suggests why don't *she* start listenin to myself.

To that she pulls her hands back and starts choppin em on the table like a law grad turned hibachi chef. She says You get help all the time. What do you call Agnes picking you up in Ohio? What do you call Janis assembling Pezet's contacts for you? What do you call Godric poring over them and making connections you'd have missed? What do you call Wally buying us this safe house, and paying to have it maintained for *years* before we ever set foot in it? What do you call me ripping up our entire fucking lives by the root when you give me a single phone call? You're big and you're tough, but you're not an island. And that's alright! It's not a bad thing to let other people contribute to your success, just like you contribute to other people's success!

I'm tryin to think of a really sharp thing to say back at her, but I can't think of one. So I says to her This ain't what I fuckin need right now, is to be arguin with you.

She says to me It doesn't have to *be* an argument. I want it to be a conversation.

So I says Yeah, well I want it to be over. I need to go to fuckin sleep, I wanna get a solid s…I got a lotta shit to do today.

I start tryin to walk towards where I think I remember they keep the bedroom in this joint. Daff steps in fronta me. She says Godric and I aren't attacking you. We're worried about you because we love you.

So I throw my hands up and say Jesus, is this when the banners roll down? I'm tired Daff, lemme sleep already!

She sighs and steps outta the way. I stomp back to the bedroom, only it turns out I didn't remember the layout right and now I'm in the mudroom. So I stomp across the hall to a room where Daff's stuffed all the shit she salvaged from our house.

It's a *lot*.

I see some of my clothes pokin out of a box in the corner. I wanna ask how she managed to squirrel all this out, but I know she's just gonna say she had *help*. I ain't lookin to give her the satisfaction.

So I stomp back out into the kitchen and I ask her How the fuck do I get to the bedroom?

She tells me It's in the basement.

I ask her What the fuck kinda design is that?

She shrugs. Her head moves and I can see her face is kinda wet. I feel pretty rotten about that, but she's also on my fuckin case when *I* got a wet face, so I guess if she feels rotten about *that* then we're even.

I go downstairs and fall onto the bed. Takes me a fuckin hour to get to sleep, it feels like.

FIRST call I gotta make is to Wally.

Let him know he don't gotta send the housecleanin around no more. Also to say thanks for the fuckin hermitage.

He says to me No sweat at all, my friend. You get any further *vis a vis* who's got designs on you?

I tell him I got a few leads. Might have to do with grocery stores.

He asks me How's that?

So I says to him That's a real good question.

Next call I'm makin is to Godric. Only insteada on the phone, I'm gonna see him at his shop.

He asks me What the hell happened? So I gotta break it all down. I think about I might try sugar coatin it, make myself look a bit less of a fuckin dunce. On accounta I know if I come all out with it, Godric's gonna give me the same shit Daff gave me. But I end up tellin Godric what's true on accounta I can't come up with enough fake to gussy it.

After I'm done he just tuts and says to me You know what I'm going to say next, right?

I says to him Well since you and Daff are talkin so much, I'da figured you know she already said it at me.

Godric just shrugs and blows some air outta his nose. Then he says Alright, well, you'll be wanting some new papers from Odette I imagine.

I nod.

So he says to me I'll make you an appointment.

I tell him You're a pal, Godric. Even if sometimes you wanna give me some shit, you're a real pal to me.

He just nods and says I only ever give you shit *because* I'm your friend. I hope you feel that.

So I says to him Don't get soft on me. Let's hear what's up with my dear old scabs.

Godric looks at me for a second too long. Then he says *Oh.* Right. Then he starts shufflin around papers on his desk. Finally he finds what's he after and hands it at me. It's got three meaty faces got names and all sorts besides next to em. Godric tells me these are the three guys I scabbed with way back, but he don't gotta. I remember em. He does gotta tell me that they're all in town figurin Wally's got a job for em. Plannin on meetin in three days.

I ask him Why so many days away?

He says Because they've all got their own schedules, Sammy.

To that I says Oh. On accounta for some reason I just assumed none of em was busy like I am. I'd sorta imagined I was gonna be the only one still big and strong as a decade back.

I ask Godric How old're these pictures here?

He says to me They were all taken post-war.

I say Shit. On accounta they're all lookin pretty fuckin tough still. I ain't goin in there makin accusations, I just wanna know are they gettin dealt dirty like I am. But…what if one of em's the one squealed about me goosin? What if one of em's started scabbin *for* the, uh, whatever that fuckin union's called? What if that one's got a buddy? What if they're all buddies and I'm the fuckin odd man out?

All of a sudden I'm feelin kinda uneasy about this thing I never had a stray thought for. Three on one, that's nothin. I done more. But three on one where the other three's all my size? That, I ain't so sunny about.

But when Godric asks me what'm I sayin Shit about, I tell him Nothin.

Odette, I been mentionin her. She's a fuckin wizard. Paperwise, I'm sayin. I got no clue how does she do what she does, but she does it so I figure she's got a clue on how. Good wizard never spills their how, anywise.

Spot her from a distance and you'd make her for six feet tall. She's lanky like that. But get close and you'd wonder does she make it up to how tall the cardboard clown says you gotta be the ride the ride.

I don't know how the hell'd Godric find her to begin with. She started doin papers for me when she was still in fuckin school. That was the year I got back, '19. Don't know why she was still showin up for her tests and shit. The amount she charges for papers, she don't fuckin need to.

Fact is, her papers are the best. Hold em up, check the stamp or whatever. Can't tell it from genuine. She's so fuckin confident she dresses em all with her quote distress signature unquote. Little scuff on the bottom right looks like her initials, OM. I tell her that ain't such a swell idea, but she calls it her satisfaction guarantee. Ain't nobody been dissatisfied yet, I figure.

Havin said all that, her stuff didn't do so hot under Passengerside's flashlight, that's true. But that ain't a knock on her. Like I said, I've taken out fuckin loans on her I.D.s. Fuckin wizard. Like I said.

But I gotta figure it ain't so easy for her to get all that lined up, on accounta she ain't hardly ever happy to see me. It always goes like this, she tells me she ain't happy. So I tells her I ain't happy either. Then she calms down and says fair enough and sees about makin me a new person. Like a fuckin stage drama. Just watch.

I clomp into her buildin and get a dirty look from the doorman. Course, she lives in a place's got a doorman. Anyway, he gives me his dirty look, I give him a dirtier look and he looks at his pants. Up up up to the penthouse fuckin floor, elevator kid knows to keep his mouth shut and eyes down. Early twenties, this kid is. Odette, not the elevator kid. Penthouse fuckin floor.

Go Figure

My knuckle's just about to tap her door when I hear her call It's open! So I walk right in. Odette's just standin there, waitin for me.

I asks her You always leave your door unlocked?

She asks me What the fuck happened to Michael Berns?

I tell her He got what he deserved on accounta he was a bad egg.

So she says That one took me a long time. I'm not happy to see it melt away like that.

So I says And it cost me a lot of fuckin money, the gettin and especially the losin. You see me singin a ditty about it?

She bites the inside of her cheek and says That's true. Sorry. Then she gestures like she wants me to come sit at her workdesk.

See? Told ya.

So she's makin sure all my personals hold, height weight and all that. After a while I tell her Hey, I got a question for ya.

She says to me Shoot.

I ask her Say I got somebody's out to get me, not a fake name looks like me but *me*, Samuzzo D'Amato, how'm I gonna get rid of em? What's a good way to lose em, I mean?

Odette says to the desk The best thing to do is run everything through the new you...Frank Patricks, how's that for unassuming? The fewer things you do as Samuzzo, the fewer opportunities they have to catch you out. Better yet...you know what, I'm gonna set you up with a second one. It won't be quite as nuanced, but it doesn't need to be if you're smart about how you use it. All the big stuff, you run through Frank Patricks. All the little stuff, you run through, uh, let's say Douglas Barker. That way, you can minimize being Samuzzo without turning Frank Patricks or Douglas Barker into a second Samuzzo that'd lead the law to you when you inevitably burn them both.

I ask her about that tone she got at the end there.

She smiles and says If you find somebody else who can do what I do, I'll start watching my tone.

I tell her Fair enough. I ain't totally at peace with her answer, on accounta these guys found me as Samuzzo through people don't use my other names. Can't hurt to have a little extra lookout though.

So I ask her how much extra Douglas Barker is gonna cost me.

She tells me Not as much as Frank Patricks.

I tell her Fair enough.

Then she tells me Smile, on accounta she's got her very own camera.

More I'm thinkin on it, more I'm thinkin bringin just Wally to the scab meet ain't such a hot idea. Most times I wouldn'ta had him there anyways, but for this time he's the moneybags of this gag, so he's gotta tag. These guys put their palms out and don't get em full of fuckin specie, there's gonna be ruckus on accounta nobody used to flat rates likes havin their time taken for free. So long as they get paid, there ain't gonna be trouble. I don't figure there'll be, I oughta say. But I can't figure for *certain.*

So maybe I need some…I maybe might *want* a big buddy in this one.

I figure I got just the one in mind.

Nobody at Sharktooth Casino looks too happy to see me. Still'n again. Christ, but they can hold a grudge here, huh? I'm hardly through the door when I got all four knuckles closin in on me. I ask em don't they ever clock out. They don't say nothin to that.

I don't gotta wait but a minute before Max and Hatch come stormin into view. Max's got his hands wavin above his head like he just walked through a spiderweb.

So I says to him Relax. I'm here for the big guy. And I point to Hatch.

Max figures I mean to rough his muscle up, I figure. He says to me I am going to give you this one final warning, despite the fact that I've already given you more than enough.

But he don't get no further on accounta Hatch tells him It's alright. He walks up to me and says If you wanted to talk, you should have caught me outside of business hours.

I says to him Casino's don't hardly ever close, right? So I got no clue when're you workin or not.

Hatch nods his head at the door. We step outside. Max and the knuckles're makin seagull noises. Hatch just gives em a palm like he's sayin Hold your horses, ya fuckin seagulls.

So we get fuckin conspiratorial right out in the fishmongers. I says to him I'm reconnectin with some old chums maybe ain't so chummy anymore. I ain't figurin anythin's goin sidewise, but I ain't such a fuckin sunnyside kinda guy I ain't preppin for it does. You wanna pick up some cash loomin for a night or what?

He says to me My limit is usually two *ain'ts* per job.

I laugh and I says to him You don't want the money,

I'll find somebody ain't such a fuckin stickler for diction.

He nods and says How much?

I tell him Well since I figure I got the saved-your-fuckin-life discount, I could rent ya for three fifty.

He has a real good think about it. Then tells me Ok. Which is a welcome fuckin whatsit. I figured he was gonna dicker with me a bit. Guess he's all sortsa grateful then.

So I says to him You're alright, ya know?

And he says to me Right back at you.

Now I guess we're fuckin buddies.

Godric figures we gotta do the meetin somewhere sneaky, on accounta four big guys, five now that I got Hatch on board, all makin serious faces at each other's gonna turn some heads. Only we don't wanna do the meet at a place we eat or even shit, just for in case if one of these guys is crooked.

So we gotta find a public spot's no stranger to big fellas. I suggest How about a speakeasy, howzat for a fuckin brainstorm? Godric says to me Depending on where the bar is, that's actually a great idea. So I ask him What the hell ya mean by *actually?* He just looks at his visor the way he does when he knows I'm givin him shit. Cept I don't figure I was *only* givin shit with that one.

Anyway, he sniffs out this uptown dive called The Tusk. Kinda place they gotta work hard to keep it lookin so scuzzy, on accounta they got so much money comin in. And I figure only half's from bartabs, you see what I'm sayin.

Then it's the night and Wally's pickin me up from the safe house. Frank Patricks' still huntin for a place to call his own, ya see. Oh, and Frank Patricks ended up costin me a grand. One with four fuckin zeroes. You believe that shit?

Anyway Wally asks me How are things with the Mrs.?

I tell him She's still bangin on Godric's fuckin drum.

Wally don't say nothin to that.

So I ask him You wanna fuckin start on me too?

He says to me No, no way man. Only I don't buy it and I don't figure he said the words figurin I would.

It ain't a long ride to Hatch's place but leave it to Wally to pack as many fuckin words as possible into it. He's runnin his mouth about a new gag he's dreamin up, he's figurin he's gonna go to some real high-class dry cleaners, get his best suit scrub-a-dubbed. Then he's gonna take the receipt and forge a billion fuckin copies, mail em out to every restaurant he can find. Tell em, guess what, one of your servers spilled some fuckin merlot on my suit. So I had to go get it scrub-a-dubbed, and here's what did it cost. You wanna make this right or do I gotta start makin a stink on it, ha ha, see what I mean. Wally figures some folks'll pay up on accounta it ain't so much what's he askin for. What's the clever bit is, he's asking for ain't-so-much a billion times over.

Once I figure there ain't a slot in this one for me, I sorta zone out. My mind just starts wanderin. Thinkin about the meet. How'm I gonna sound out the scabs? I gotta figure they're gonna see us all together, us old-time scab buddies, and work out why've I got em here. Do I just ask em if I goosed, maybe they saw it and told somebody? I ain't lookin for hard feelins, but suppose one of em's harborin some? Some fuckin ill will?

Or also, ya know, did somebody kill *them* or somethin, take their place or somethin. I figure that oughta be a fuckin consideration. Or somethin.

Anyway Wally's done now and waitin for me to pat him on the head. All I can think to ask him is You figure to make enough money's gonna cover the postage? But I know Wally. It ain't about that. So instead of askin a dumb question I already know the answer about, I just tell him That's real clever.

Then he starts runnin his mouth *again*. And this time my mind ain't gotta wander too far to start wonderin. So I cut Wally off and I says to him You're real generous with tellin about your gags, huh?

Wally says Not always, but sometimes. Depends who I'm cavorting about with at the moment. With you, for sure I am.

I turn to look him right in the eye, only he's a real careful driver so I'm scoldin his profile. I says to the side of his face Gets me wonderin. How sure are you you didn't say nothin about me goosin to nobody wasn't Janis?

Wally squints at the windshield. He says to me A hundred percent. I don't tell tales out of school. I'm really discrete, especially if we're talking about somebody I don't trust. I only trust the most trustworthy people. That's a pretty short list of people, I might add, just the trustworthy ones. I trust you guys. You, Janis, maybe one or two others.

So I ask him Who're those one or two others?

He shakes his head and tells me Nobody I've spoken to for, oh, half a year at least. It wasn't them, and it wasn't me.

I just sorta look at him. Well, I don't *sorta* look at him. I look at him.

Wally turns and sees me lookin, and not just *sorta* lookin, and he makes a sad face. He asks me You seriously don't believe me?

I get the kinda heartburn ain't got nothin to do with eatin too much meat before bedtime. I'm hurtin Wally's feelins, not believin him. But...well, I says to him what'm I thinkin, I says I got no reason for not believin ya, only I got no reason for *not* not believin ya neither.

Wally takes a hand off the wheel and flaps it like he's tryina buck a bug off it. He says to me I'm *helping* you, for God's sake. I'm paying for three guys I don't know to come in, including travel expenses, and I'm not complaining, but I'm not even sure what they're here for. You wanted them here, but I'm just not sure why. You're going to ask them if they spread some stories? If they're in cahoots with an evil grocery union? I personally would be going after the lobbyist if I were you, but I'm not. You asked me, one friend to another, for help. And I'm

144

I cut him off and say Help? It ain't like I'm fuckin beggin on my hands and knees!

He says to me I never said you were.

So I tell him I asked you to do me a kindwise is all.

He looks real disappointed at the steerin wheel and says Whatever you want to call it. I'm doing you a kindness, even if I think it's a pretty dumb kindness to want to have done, but whatever, it's your kindness, and I'm doing it because we're buddies, and because I trust you. So it'd be pretty swell if you started trusting *me*, yeah?

I says to him You gotta see why's it kinda hard to trust a guy gets his jollies from scammin folks. Like, implicitwise.

Wally's got nothin to say to that.

So I says to him I'm sorry I went and said that thing. I know you're straight with me. I'm just fuckin unnerved by I got somebody startin rumors about me, and then on toppa that tryin to fuckin rub me out. And here I gotta play fuckin detective. It ain't my fuckin purview, Wally. But it ain't fair makin like it's your fault. I'm sorry I spoke at ya crosswise.

The side of Wally's face gets kinda dreamy. He says Don't worry about it. We'll figure it out.

So I says to him I'm real fuckin touched about you sayin *we* just there.

He turns and gives me his whole face for a second. He says Of course it's *we*. You think I want to waste my time trying to find new muscle? You're my best investment, Sammy.

So I laugh and tell him I can't be a good one, on accounta when you're runnin your mouth I ain't got much interest.

He kinda chuckles but he don't laugh like I was figurin. I'm prouda that one though. Investment. Interest. Ah fuck you, that's a good one.

Just when's Hatch gettin into the car, I got a fuckin lightbulb flashin in my head. I wanna tell Wally, only I ain't lookin to get into the whole thing with Hatch here listenin on accounta I feel more at my easy keepin him in the dark. So I just gotta sit with it.

What I wanna tell Wally is, why's somebody gonna be goin around spreadin word that I goose easy, then turnin around and tryin to wipe me out? Why waste time fuckin with my reputation if you got them other designs? If this was one of them revenge stories like that one's got a fun prison breakout at the start then it's just a bunch of fuckin rich folks havin dinner for a thousand pages, it'd be on accounta the bad guy's razzin the good guy. But I never, ever heard of nobody runs in my circles razzin as foreplay to deep sixin. First time for everythin I guess, but I ain't convinced.

So I gotta figure, maybe it's a fuckin coincidence. Maybe they ain't connected. I mean, obviously people what got it out for me hear the rumor about I got a weak spot, they're gonna adjust their fuckin approach. But I gotta figure, makes more sense the person started yappin about I goose probably never fuckin met the person tryin to smoke me.

Which ain't a happy figure. On accounta now I gotta

be a detective twice the fuck over. It's a figure puts me in a pretty lousy way.

I ain't in a talkin mood. Don't seem like Hatch is neither. So Wally's pluggin the hole. Not talkin about gags now that we got an interloper. Just runnin his mouth. Talk so small some brainbox over in Europe's wonderin how many angels can dance on it.

Too bad things ain't gonna stay just like now. Me not talkin, Wally for white noise. Great for stewin in thoughts.

Only stewin makes my way I'm feelin feel fuckin lousier. And lousy ain't a great way to feel, for meetin old friends.

GO FIGURE

THE Tusk is a workers bar full of big guys, but only one or two's bigger'n me. And ya know, now that I'm thinkin on it, maybe it ain't such a swell place for havin a how-are-ya for fuckin strikebreakers. Seems some kinda disrespectful.

Whatever about that though. I walk in first. Hatch comes in second, Wally's in back.

Looks like everybody here's double cheesed on acc-outna unions ain't what the used to be, and they gotta break the law they want a drink with their pals. Good luck to the G man wants to storm this fuckin joint and start lockin people up for bein fuckin bibulous. Everybody's got ugly facial hair what looks like they just got done cleanin the tub with it. Apparently it's fuckin dress code. Guy with a big scar on his face comes saunterin up. I got a feelin he ain't gonna ask us do we want a table for three.

He says to us I've never seen you before.

I tell him They got a word for that. It's hello.

He leans back a bit and tells me I better not have come here lookin for trouble.

I tell him I agree, on accounta I can't spot anythin looks like trouble to me.

He looks at me, then Hatch, then Wally. He sticks with Wally. Then he points to him and opens his mouth like he's gonna say somethin. Probably about how Wally's a pretty fuckin big outlier here, by way of bein so fuckin small. I figure Wally saw it comin too, on accounta he says to the guy Sorry, do we need to toss a nickel in there to hear the next song?

Scar's lookin kinda sad now. He tells us to just fuckin leave him alone.

So I gotta remind him I ain't the one came floppin up to him sayin I don't know his face.

He says You guys are jerks. I was trying to give you an amiably churlish welcome and you just started being…fucking…uh, jerks. Fuck you guys. We got a beer and shot deal tonight. I hope you all get totally drunk and say hurtful things to people you care about!

Then he just wanders back to the bar. I guess that was kinda fair for him to say. I jumped to a fuckin conclusion. I ask Wally If I look at a guy and figure I know what's on his mind just on accounta how does he look, ain't that a prejudice?

Wally says I guess so.

So I says Damnit, was it just me figured he was comin over to give us some shit?

Wally tells me he thought the same. Hatch won't admit it but I fuckin know he did. So I says to Wally Hell, I ain't happy about I've got a prejudice.

Hatch says to me Everybody's got them.

So I ask him Why didn't you cop to it then?

He tells me Because I don't have them about the proletariat. My uncle's a proletariat, he's really nice.

I says to him You tryin to say I got a problem with the fuckin workin class?

He says No. I just couldn't think of another way to describe that guy.

I says to him I ain't got a problem with nobody cept the people look like I oughta have a problem with.

Wally says Yeah, that sounds like prejudice.

Boy, not only do I got a case twice as hard as I figured to crack, now it turns out I'm a fuckin...prejudice guy! Guy who's got a fuckin prejudice! That puts my way even more towards lousy. I just wanna go home now. Read a book with Daff or some shit. Only I've gotta meet three fuckin lunkheads. So I says to Wally and Hatch Why don't you two go find us a fuckin booth to sit in. Or a corner we can stand in. Whatever.

They look at the rest of the bar, which if you got rid of all the funny angles still ain't much bigger'n one of them cheapo Pullmans. There ain't a place to sit. But Wally's got a good bead on my moods I figure. He tells Hatch Let's see if there's an outdoor section maybe, then off they go lookin for a fuckin patio. Like this is the kinda place's got a fuckin patio!

I turn and wait. Check the pictures of the guys Godric gave me. Turn again and look down the bar. One of em's here already, slouchin over whiskey. Fella named Harris. Got a face like a horse's first stab at sculpture. I remember him from the scab job. He smoked a lot, but never let it burn past the halfway. After it did, he tossed it. Got real popular on accounta it was easy to bum off him.

So I walk up to him and I say How are ya, Harris?

He looks at me like he don't know me. Which I guess he don't for a second. Then he looks at me like he *do* know me. Pretty fuckin crazy, watchin somebody's face turn you from stranger into the opposite. He says to me I'm wondering what the fuck I'm doing here. How about you?

I tell him It's gonna make sense in a bit. I got two associates over... Then I gotta look around the room on accounta where the hell did they go?

Harris says to me Maybe they went to the outdoor section.

So I says They got a fuckin outdoor section here?

He says Yeah, it looked pretty nice. But I figured I wouldn't see you back there. So...

Then he knocks on the bar.

Scar comes over, he says Yeah?

Harris tells him I was just knocking.

Scar says to him Why?

Harris says For emphasis. I don't want anything.

So Scar says Well, don't do that. Then he looks at me. He asks me Why are you just standing around? Should I kick you out for loitering?

Go Figure

I tell him Try it, I'll give ya somethin worse to kick me out about.

Scar points to me and asks Harris What's his fucking problem?

Harris shrugs and tells his drink he ain't qualified to speculate.

So I tell Scar Lemme get the beer and shot thing. Light beer, dark shot. You spit in either of em, I'm gonna put the

He cuts me off and says to Harris See? He's threatening me and I didn't even *do* anything! I just tried to give him an amiably churlish welcome!

Harris keeps starin at his drink, mumblin about how he's just tryin to drink that drink.

I says Just get me the fuckin booze.

Scar goes and does that.

I tell Harris Anyway, I got some buddies somewhere around here. One guy a bit bigger than the rest, the other a *lot* smaller. Little guy's the one's got your money.

Harris asks me What's the job, exactly?

I tell him to ask the little guy called Wally. So Harris grabs his drink and goes and does that.

Scar comes back with my drinks. He asks me again why'm I just standin around. I figure I wanna try bein nice to him so I says to him I'm waitin for some buddies of mine.

He says to me I thought you came *in* with friends.

I says to him I got more comin. You wanna somethin like how you can't believe I got friends?

And he says No, because I'm not a fucking mean

153

person. Why don't you go hang with your friends in the back, away from the bar? Why don't you write down the names of the other two on a note telling them to go meet you back there and I'll give it to them?

So I explain to him On accounta I ain't twelve fuckin years old. I said to my friends I'm gonna meet em at the bar. So I'm gonna meet em *at the bar.*

Then I spot the other two scabs walk in.

Together.

Hm.

They're called Mash and Childs. Childs is his name, but it's also irony now on accounta he's old. Older'n I remember, which I figure is fair enough on accounta linear time. But older'n his picture too. Looks older'n pictures *period.*

Mash's lookin fit as ever though. He's beefy, but cut. Like somebody stuck my muscles onto Wally's body.

I wave to em and I say Didn't realize you two came as a pair. I say it tryin to make my voice not sound suspicious. I don't even know why'm I fuckin suspicious. I just ain't keen on they came in together.

Childs says to me We're staying at the same hotel, if you can believe it.

I tell him No, I can't believe it.

Childs laughs.

Mash says to me That's not true. We just work tog-ether a lot now. Didn't take long for us to figure out we both got the same call. How come you didn't tell any of us about the others?

Childs asks me How many others, by the way?

Go Figure

I stare at em for a bit on accounta I guess I buy the story. Lotta tough guys like tough buddies. Especially seein as they got different whaddyacallems. They ain't the same type. Childs's rickety but wise, probably got a million connections. He starts slippin, maybe he wants a guy he knows pickin up his slack. Mash's still prime. He and Childs cut a deal, that's easy money. Safer too.

Still. Puts me off my easy a little.

Anyway, I tell em One more. Harris.

Childs laughs again. I don't remember him bein so full of fuckin cheer last time. He asks if we're gonna take a trip to the local grocer, start baggin shit. I tell him no, but that's a hell of a memory.

Then I tell em to grab some juice and meet me in the outdoors. I feel kinda weird sayin it on accounta I still ain't seen the outdoors so maybe it don't actually exist. But if that's how's it gonna be, then did all my buddies round the corner and fall into a fuckin sinkhole or what?

I throw back my shot and slam it on the bar. Only I accidentally hit it so hard the glass blows up. The whole bar goes kinda quiet for a second. A few people shout shit like Mazel Tov and Heyo. Then it goes loud again. I thought that lookieloo shit only happened at quote family establishments unquote.

Big surprise, Scar comes stormin over in a fuckin mood. He asks me What's your fucking problem, dude?

I think, I ain't got a fuckin problem. Only I don't say that, I just say nothin. No clue how come. Instead I just take my beer and look for this fuckin sinkhole.

155

BRINGIN Hatch mighta been a bad idea. These scabs seemed real fuckin sociable with me, but now that I got this lunkhead they ain't never met loomin next to me their sociables got a whaddyacallit. Somethin stinks but you put it in a pretty wrapper. That sorta whaddyacallit.

So I figure it's time I oughta lighten the mood. So I says to em You all acquainted to Hatch here? I brought him on accounta I was worried one of ya might be figurin to cause trouble. One or maybe more'n one. I says that last part with a real crosswise look at Mash and Childs.

They look back at me more straight-like. Childs asks me Like what?

I says to him Trouble.

Mash asks me Right, but what kind of trouble?

I says to him Kinda trouble gets met with more of

157

the same.

Harris chimes in, sayin Did you think one of us would be attacking you or something?

I says Or maybe more'n one. I throw my crosswise look at Harris in case he ain't seen it from the first time.

Harris asks me Why the hell would any of us want to start trouble with you?

Then I says Oh right, on accounta I forgot that I ain't explained nothin to any of em yet. So I lay it all out, from the hook with Cleveland to Pezet bein offed even though or maybe on accounta he set up the hook to Godric figurin Pezet links to me through some fuckin grocery union that might not think I'm so swell on accounta this job what I did ten years ago with these three guys at the table.

They nod the whole time. Not askin questions. That don't mean they ain't got em. They're just fuckin professional, they know you don't cut off the setup.

So anyway I get to the end and I look em all straight in their eyes. Well, I look em all straight in their eyes one at a time, on accounta they're sittin too far apart to get em all in one. Anyways I'm sorta gettin a glimpse of their eyeballs and I ask em Whaddya thinka that? Any of you guys get jumped lately by some guys wearin green aprons? Or maybe one of you didn't figure the scab pay was sweet enough, so now you got a green apron hangin up in your closet?

They're all just sittin there still, only they ain't noddin no more. I can't figure what's runnin through their heads. But nobody looks *got*, you know what I mean.

158

Hatch says to em Answer the man!

I gotta tell Hatch Take it down a titch. Real swell of ya to take the initiative but that ain't the tone at present.

Hatch shrugs and makes an earthquake noise in his tummy.

Finally Mash says to me Um…well, I don't want to speak for Childs, and I certainly don't mean to stuff any words into Harris' mouth, but just for me…no. The answer is no.

Mash sounds real fuckin agitated. Good thing Wally's a fuckin social thermometer. He leans in and tells em Just to be perfectly clear, you were invited here under false pretenses, but the money is still real. We're paying you for your time.

They look all kindsa relieved about that.

Childs starts laughin. He says to me Why the hell didn't you just call us up and ask us if we're dead or not? Or if we're in the pocket of Big Grocery?

I tell him I like to look a man in the eyes when I ask him a question.

He says to me No, yeah, I get that. But still. That's a lot of money for a long shot.

I says to him I didn't figure the shot for bein so long.

Harris is watchin me through his eyebrows. He takes a little sip of his booze.

Now I ain't Wally when's it come to readin folks, but I also ain't Hatch. So I says to Harris You look like a man's got somethin cookin.

He says to his drink I'm just a little bit surprised you felt the need to buy our time. Or lie to us about why you wanted it in the first place.

Mash and Childs nod and go Mm m-hm.

I tell him On accounta if one of ya was lookin to do me crooked, I gotta get that upper hand.

So he asks me But why just assume one of us wanted to hurt you? Why *start* there? We all got along really well on that gig. And also it was *a decade ago*. I don't mean this as an insult, but I really don't think about that job, and consequently, you. Ever, really.

Mash and Childs are up to their old tricks.

I gotta admit, I'm at a bit of a fuckin loss here. I ain't thought about that job in ages either, not til Godric brought it back to me. And even after, he tells me I done the job…all I can remember is that I done the job. I ain't got a single fuckin anecdote provin I was the one bagged them groceries, instead of a guy just looks like me. I mean, ain't nobody looks like me, but you take my fuckin meanin.

So I ask em Well, gettin chummy on a job ten years back ain't cause enough for me to call ya up and tell ya hop on the first choo-choo gets ya to my neighborhood.

Mash asks me Why not? I would have. I had a great time with you guys. Work all day, play all night.

Childs says to him I bet they've still got your photo behind the counter at that one shithole. What was that one called?

Mash says Oh yeah! It was… Then his face gets heavy and he mumbles Fuck, they might have a picture of me. What *was* that shithole called?

Harris says I can picture the sign out front.

Childs says Yeah! The big alligator…

Mash says to him Crocodile.

Childs rolls his eyes like he and Mash've had the fuckin alligator crocodile argument a million times already.

I ask em So we were all some fuckin hellraisers, huh?

Harris takes a bigger swig and says Only off the clock.

I says to em So we were all joshin around, yeah?

Mash and Childs look at each other. They pick the faces they wanna show me and then they show em to me. Childs says You could say that. Joshing. You could definitely say that if that's the word you want to use. Then he starts gigglin.

So I says I'm only sayin, like I was sayin earlier, that fuckin hook I walked into almost worked on accounta they knew I got a fuckin heel like the guy in the long fuckin poem. I goose easy. So *I'm* sayin, maybe one night we're all joshin around, somethin gooses me. I goose. And on accounta we're all buddies, we have a big fuckin laugh about it. And maybe I don't make it crystal, that's the kinda heel ain't supposed to be gettin direct sun, you know what I'm sayin. So maybe you go home and you're tellin your buddies about the grand fuckin time you had scabbin in Cali. And maybe you tell em about the goosin bruiser called Samuzzo. On accounta it's a quality fuckin anecdote. I get it, I ain't afraid to look in the mirror and bust a fuckin gut when's it called for. But I'm askin you guys, have a good fuckin think about if any of that's got you recollectin.

So I guess we're back to them just fuckin sittin there. They don't look like they're havin any kinda fuckin think, good or otherwise.

I elbow Hatch.

He shakes his head real fast and goes Huh?

I tell him Fuckin nevermind. I look over at Wally. If he's out explorin the farthest fuckin reaches, at least he knows how to make pretend he's payin attention.

So I ask the three guys in fronta me Well?

Harris says I get the feeling you're not going to like the answer. And just being totally honest, you don't seem super, um

Childs cuts him off and says Stable enough to hear it.

Mash nods and says Mhm.

I squint so hard my eyes are just about closed. I growls at em, I growls I don't know what kinda fuckin conspirament you motherfucks got

Hatch finally remembers why's he here and says Should I punch someone?

I elbow him and I says Stuff it!

Hatch rumbles.

Harris points at me and he says Ok, so I'm going to use that. That? Elbowing a friendly like that? That's not something I could ever have imagined you doing.

I ask him What the fuck'm I takin from that?

Mash says to me And, I mean, if we're being completely candid...last time I saw you, you were a little more...um...well, you always had a very unique way of speaking. It's just gotten *more* unique since we last met.

They all three start noddin.

I ask em Are we havin a fuckin intervention? I'm sure you're all real fuckin different for havin ten more birthdays in the rearview, but

Harris cuts me off and says I don't think you are. Sure, I mean. I doubt you remember anything about us.

I put my fists on the table and says to em Skip to the fuckin what-are-ya-sayin.

Childs waves his hands in the air and says Samuzzo. We never saw you *goose*, if that's your stand-in for *startle* or something. We only ever heard about it.

I lean on my knuckles and asks em Who from?!

They all look at each other like one of em farted and they all know who. Then Childs turns at me and says From you. *You* told us about it.

GO FIGURE

I can't figure what kinda fuckin mind game is this. And I don't get no room for figurin. Childs just keeps goin by sayin Shit, if we're all just coming out with it...I assumed you were insecure about being easily startled and you were trying to own it.

Mash says You told us about trying to use your toaster as practice, leaning on the lever and bracing yourself for when it popped back up.

Harris says You had anecdotes. Times you got startled on jobs.

Childs says Honestly, by the end of it we were all kind of like, maybe we should tell him it's not a big deal? Because it seemed like it really bothered you.

Now I figure I'm the one's just sittin there lookin.

I can't...I got no fuckin recollection of ever tellin that to anybody. Cept maybe Daff.

But I also ain't got no fuckin recollection of baggin groceries with these guys.

I turn to Wally and I ask him You ever hear me goin off about goosin easy?

He shakes his head no.

I turn back to the guys in fronta me, and I know what's comin outta Mash's mouth before he's hardly got it open.

He says to me It really felt like you were just trying to cover your bases for us specifically. Because we're, you know…we're tough guys. Wally's not. No disrespect Wally, you seem like a good guy.

Wally tells him None taken. Just stating a fact.

Yeah, a fuckin fact. Are these fuckin facts? How do I know these guys ain't playin me somewise? I can't remember a thing I ever said to em. So yeah, that means I mighta talked about goosin easy. But I also mighta said anythin *but* that.

So I ask em What was that other shit you were sayin? I don't talk the same?

Harris nods towards Hatch and tells me And you're more aggressive. Not just with him. With the bartender, with us…

Childs says The Samuzzo we worked with knew his own strength, but in a way that gave him peace. You weren't quite as…

Mash says Demonstrative.

Childs nods and says Yeah. You had the longest fuse of us all, by far.

Knew his own strength, he says. I get a recollection I

ain't lookin for. Flippin over that fuckin car. Replayin that crunch in my head and figurin it wasn't the fuckin mirror.

That don't make me feel any kinda fuckin happy. So I look at Wally and I says to him You seein any fuckin nuggets of truth in here?

He's takin a long forever to answer, which, that's a fuckin answer. Finally he says to me It's harder for me to say, because I see you pretty regularly. Long-term changes like that, I might not have noticed as much.

I tell him That ain't a fuckin answer.

But that ain't quite right. I just got *two* fuckin answers. I don't gotta hear what comes next.

Only I wanna so I don't dive over the fuckin fence. Insteada that I just sit on this tiny fuckin stool and listen to Wally sayin But, I guess, now that I'm thinking about it…there are definitely some behavioral differences. Noticeable, I guess I'd say.

I says to him Now that you think about it, huh.

He bugs his eyes out like he's sayin to me Hey whaddyagonnado.

I look around at the whole lot of em, even Hatch, even though he ain't brought a fuckin thing to this, good or ill. I says to em This is just fuckin typical.

But that's all I can fuckin think to say to em. So I says it again.

Harris looks at me and asks me When's the last time you looked at a photograph of yourself, Samuzzo? An older one, before you went to France?

Wally puts his head down like he agrees with whatever point Harris's makin but don't wanna stick around to see how do I take it.

I ask Harris I'm all kinds of eager to hear what the fuck you're drivin at.

He says to me You don't look so good.

Childs tells me You just look like you've…been through a lot. Like, above the neck.

So I says Oh, right, I ain't agin like fuckin Fairbanks so that's how come I'm all fucked up, is that it?

Mash says to me That's not it.

Harris says It's a lot more than that.

So I says to em all How about this.

Then I wanna say to em all sorts of shit, like how about I ain't a fuckin dope, I ain't stupid, and how about you quit tellin me I gotta do this or that, I gotta go get my head fuckin checked or I gotta get jelly squirted into my fuckin brain, and how about you quit pretendin I'm some kinda fuckin unusual suspect for losin bits and pieces as I'm steppin yearly from my youth, and how about we go outside I take you all in one go, even Hatch and even fuckin Wally, and how about we call in Godric and everybody who ever fuckin figured they could tell me I'm stupid, I'm a fuckin dope, I'm losin bits and pieces. I fuckin ain't. And if I am, then how about they can explain how'm I still whole enough to be pullin bits and pieces offa *them*, on accounta I'm a fuckin bruiser and a fuckin tough and I ain't the kinda guy gooses or zonks and I sure as shit ain't the weepin sort, so let's fuckin rumble, I'll take you all.

But then I get a fuckin pause. On accounta Daff's in

that group I just visualized rippin to bits and pieces. I didn't even fuckin think about it. Only I gotta say I didn't think it as in an intentionalwise thought, on accounta I *did* think it, unintentionalwise. I thought about it so fuckin hard I could feel arms leavin sockets.

I figured on fuckin up everybody I fuckin care about, and I didn't even fuckin figure on how fucked up it is that I had a figure on it.

...

That gives me fuckin pause.

So I take a fuckin pause.

Everybody takes a fuckin pause.

Then I says to em I'm gonna level with you fellas. I got no recollection of the shit you're sayin to me. I got no grip on who's the Samuzzo you guys said you worked with. I gotta reckon with I got a short fuse nowadays, but I can't find the headspace for what's it like to string out a long one. I'm...but see the thing is, I don't even figure it makes sense I'm sayin sorry. I ain't sure how'm I sorry about, what, I got bonked too many times and now I got loose meat in my attic? I mean, how's it I'm on the fuckin fire? It ain't like I walked down to the boardwalk and paid somebody to tune my fuckin face up. I'm just bein me, and I don't gotta fuckin

Then Wally says to me my name and somefuckinhow that reels me in. I'll tell ya, it's pretty fuckin astoundin what that fella can do, socialwise.

I'm tryin to get clear. Everybody in my life keeps tellin me they got love goin my way, they're the ones tellin me I ain't got sufficient floats for throwin a parade, you see what they're sayin. I tell em take a fuckin hike with that kinda talk. Then these guys I ain't seen in ten years, they ain't seen *me* in ten years, but they come in and say the same thing to me and it fuckin clicks. How's that? Maybe I'm pretty fuckin freaked on accounta it's gotta be real obvious for them to spot it so quick. Maybe…

Ah, fuck it. That's probably it.

On accounta if it ain't, I got no fuckin clue what's the deal with that.

The inside of my fuckin ribs start slitherin and squeezin like I got an anaconda livin in there. Then my eyes start itchin.

So I says Son of a bitch, but I don't excuse myself from the fuckin situation. I just sit there and water my cheeks. On accounta why the fuck not. I do all sortsa shit a tough ain't supposed to do. And I don't figure I can do anythin worse than quit trustin the folks got big hearts for me. So yeah, I sit in a fuckin proletariat bar called The Tusk and I water my cheeks a fuckin smidge.

And goddamnit if everybody else don't just sit with me til I'm done.

GO FIGURE

So I go to this new house belongs to a guy looks a lot like me (oh and anyway I ain't got any old photos but lookin at myself in the mirror, I figure I'm lookin pretty good for my years) named Frank Patricks and I tell Daff I had a fuckin realization what gave me a pause and she can't fuckin believe it. She says to me That's great, and I figure that's a funny reaction on accounta she's sayin it's great I was imaginin rippin her arms off and slappin her with em. So I says as much to her. She tells me she was thinkin more about the realization than the fakeization what made it.

So I tell her I feel real sorry about not listenin to ya, but I also gotta make clear I ain't goin to a fuckin doctor. The doctor shit Godric's been yakkin on about, he keeps sayin they got *new* tests some fella with a white coat's lookin to hammer out. I ain't fuckin with nothin ain't got a success rate better than a little ball clickin around a red and black fuckin wheel. I says to her I get it, I maybe got some issues I ain't quite realized about. But I still got a fuckin line ain't for crossin.

She says to me about how she agrees about that, which I wasn't expectin.

So I says to her Then what've you been pushin me for, you didn't want me doin Godric's doctor stuff?

She says to me Well, in the interest of full disclosure, Godric and I never expected or even wanted you to take an interest in medical treatment. The fact of the matter is, if you're suffering from

I set her straight about I ain't sufferin.

So she waves her hands and says Right. Poor word choice. But, well, there's a gentleman in Newark, his name is Dr. Martland. He's developing a theory around a condition called *dementia pugilistica*, and while he hasn't published yet, well, Godric got wind of it, the list of sympt-, um...

She takes a deep breath sounds sad. Crazy how air's got fuckin feelins too, huh? Anyway she keeps sayin However you want to describe them. It seems likely you have the condition Dr. Martland's describing, and if he's correct, then the...*issues* are likely irreversible.

Now she's gettin a soggy face. So I pull her in tight and tell her Well that don't make em special. Most things're irreversible. Particularly in my fuckin vocation.

She looks up at me and says I'm sorry, this isn't about me, I just...I'm just really happy you're finally re-cognizing this.

172

Go Figure

So I says to her I still ain't so crystal on what I'm meant to be doin, if reversin's in the trash.

She says to me There are other kinds of help. W-

I set her straight on this ain't about *help*. I don't need fuckin *help*. I'm just tryin to get the scope of what I got. I feel rotten for sayin that, only it just sorta came out. Feels kinda iminical to my fuckin ephipany, or however them words go.

Anyway I only said those last two sentences inside my noggin. Far as Daff knows my thinkin stopped at tryin to get the scope etfuckincetera. So she says Right again, only it sounds like she means to say Wrong but I ain't got time to set you right. What was the fuckin word for that? Anyway she keeps sayin Ok, well, there are other ways to get that scope. Specifically...there's this group Godric found.

And to that I says Oooooh *Jesus*. I'm gonna fuckin *talk* my brains back in?

She just keeps pressin her cheek into my tummy and starin up at me, eyes shinin like she gave em a real good polish this mornin.

I'm lookin back down til I says Most times I love you but sometimes I don't like you so much.

So she smiles at me and turns her eyes up louder.

I shoot some air outta my mouth maybe sounds sad. Then I ask her Alright, where they doin this thing?

Danbury fuckin Connecticut. Supposed to be quote neutral territory unquote for all the toughs in the tristate area. Makes sense on accounta who's gonna be

173

pullin jobs in Danbury fuckin Connecticut? Only muscle these chumps ever seen was in a bowl at a seafood shack. It's the kinda city's got one paper, and it runs headlines like *The Other Shoe Drops On Socks! If They're So Great, Why Do Mine Smell Like Old Fruit?* It's the kinda city called fuckin Danbury.

So I gotta drive all the way out there on accounta that's where do they have their meetins for Paci-FIST. I guess it's this fuckin group for bruisers caught the emotions and wanna give em to somebody else. Godric tells me he knows plenty of guys cycled in or out. I don't gotta ask him how come he never told me.

They're doin the meetin at the home of the guy who runs it. Guy called Chet Crowder. Just right in his fuckin livin room, he does em. I figure he figures nobody's gonna be startin any shit in a guy's livin room. Soon as I walk in, I can see how come he figures that. And it ain't just on accounta he says he's made it twenty years with zero issues, and who wants to be the fuckin ass breaks that streak?

No, it's also on accounta his livin room's a fuckin delight. Looks like somebody babyproofed the room what the Declaration of Independence got scribbled out in, only the baby was *really* fuckin stupid. Everythin looks old, only it don't on accounta it's all padded like a room in the nuthouse. Which maybe ain't the best look for a buncha wide-shouldered screwballs talkin about how'd their hearts melt their brains and now the big job's keepin the pink puddin from oozin out their headholes, but it sure is puttin me at my easy. How fuckin stupid would a guy feel, pickin a fight in here?

Well, turns out that's a question I gotta ask myself. On accounta I just spotted a face looks real fuckin familiar to me. Last time I saw it, I was givin it a fuckin massage. Guess I wasn't gettin the deep tissues, on accounta there he is, standin by a table's got a load of little sandwiches on it. He's got one of em halfway to his pie-hole when he spots me.

Tommy Fuckin Toothpick.

GO FIGURE

Tommy Toothpick ain't jivin around like he was on the night of the hook. The night he stabbed me in the fuckin shoulder. Oh no. He's real still now. Like right before shit went south. Mainly for him. Only not so much as I'd figured.

I can't even get my head around they let him in. He ain't small as Wally was in the Tusk, relativewise to everybody else, but his nickname still works, put it that way.

Chet comes up to me and asks me if I might be Mr. D'Amato. I know this big fuckin rectangle guy's Chet on accounta he's got a tag says as much stuck to his titty.

I figure it's a dumb question if I might be Mr. D'Amato on accounta Godric told him I was comin, and what's the chance of a guy looks just like me, well, that's one right there. What's the chance of a guy looks just like me? Not a lot. Then you add on that guy walkin in here the night I'm meant to show? Dumb question. But Chet's bein a good host, and I seen with Scar at the Tusk it don't help matters gettin wise with somebody's bein a good host, so I tell him Uh-huh.

Then he says to me Thank you for coming, I'm so glad you could make it. I'm Chet, though some of our Paci-FISTs are more comfortable using last names only. If so, you are more than welcome to call me Crowder.

Well this guy's eager, ain't he? I put out my hand and tell him Samuzzo D'Amato. I'm likewise on not carin which name you wanna call me, only don't go rootin around for a fuckin nickname.

Somehow Chet's got a nametag sticker and pen in the hand I just shook. Like I palmed em to him or somethin. Creeps me the fuck out. But he ain't fixin to dazzle by his wizardry. He just says to me These name tags are completely optional – some of our members prefer to stay unlabeled entirely – but it's just a nice way to help people keep track of names.

I shrug and take em. Write SAMUZZO on it and slap it on my titty. Chet nods and says Excellent, excellent. Well, welcome to the Paci-FIST family.

I figure Chet figures I did the tag to join the family. I don't figure he'd be half as happy knowin I did it on accounta I'm tryin to front hard at Tommy Toothpick. I mean, it's kinda too late to look hard after you're in a room for hard guys're really soft on the inside. But not hidin who am I, namewise, that's gotta be an ok way to start walkin that soft bit back.

Now Chet starts pointin me to the sharin circle and the snack table and this and that, but I ain't quite listenin. I'm just starin at Tommy Toothpick. He's still starin at me. Only he's started eatin the little sandwich so I guess he ain't scared enough to lose his hungries. He ain't like Pezet, less I catch him at an angle lets me split his tummy.

Tommy Toothpick finishes his sandwich faster than Chet wraps up his spiel. Then Tommy starts walkin my way. Lickin his fuckin fingers as he does.

I can't believe it. Is he really gonna start some shit here? After what I did to him last time? And with how fuckin cozy that readin nook over there looks?

He takes a few more steps and I can read his name tag. You wanna guess his name? You wanna take a shot?

It's fuckin Thomas.

So I start laughin. And then he's close enough Chet notions Tommy's gone and welcomed himself to our two-man family.

He says to Tommy Yes Thomas?

Tommy says to him Remember the story I told you? A few weeks back? The incident that made me feel emasculated and ineffective?

Chet nods and says I do.

So Tommy fuckin points to me and says This is the guy.

Chet snaps his head around at me with his lips in a little O, like after hearin Tommy's story he wrote me a theme song and now he wants to whistle it at me real quick.

I look at Tommy and say You in third grade? What is this tattletale shit?

That's when the whole fuckin room *stops*. Everybody freezes. They quit talkin. They quit walkin. Then they all start rushin towards me like they just found out the last one touches me's a rotten egg.

A guy over Tommy's shoulder says to me This can pass without fists, only the way he leans on *pass* and *fist* makes me figure he's torturin the word pacifist til it gives him somethin he can use.

Another guy right next to me says This is why we have the Ring of Resolution!

Chet, right on the other side of me, tells my other ear It's OK Samuzzo. This happens a lot more than you'd think. Ours is a community with a great deal of overlap, and it's inevitable that two men who have found themselves at cross-purposes before will cross paths once again.

I says to him Hang on, what's the Ring of Reso

Then he nods his noggin at the rest of the crew and he says But remember: this time you meet on neutral ground, and among family. We have the tools to terminate the cycle of recrimination.

I says to him Lemme guess, the Ring of Fuckin Resolution?

Chet says to me It's just the Ring of Resolution. But, uh, yes.

I look at Tommy and I open my mouth so I can say

to him Remember the time you stuck me in the fuckin shoulder? But then I look at the rest of the guys in the room. They got faces say it ain't just the charm keeps shit from startin in here.

So I throw my hands up and says to em Fuck it, get me in the ring.

Go Figure

THEY drag a load of chairs from all over the house into the livin room. Everybody sits. This is my first good look at who's Paci-FIST. Twelve of em, not includin me, which I figure makes thirteen. We all got wide builds, short hair, tight jackets, short ties…

I gotta say, I'm kinda fuckin stunned at how much do we all look like each other. Some's a bit shorter or taller, some's a bit darker or lighter, some's a bit stockier or sleeker…but that's just like we're all showin our fingerpaintins we made when we only got three colors to choose from. I figured I was really somethin outta the ordinary. I just didn't figure that depended on what ordinary was I in.

They tell me sit on one side. Tommy's on the other. We're whaddyacallit. Antipodal. Holy shit, where'd that one come from? I was just about to say I'm Shackleton and he's Santa. But it don't matter, on accounta I remembered about…whaddyacallit. Son of a shit.

Everybody gets quiet even though nobody told em to. Then Chet says to em Well, here we are again. New family members can sometime dredge up old grievances. But, you know my motto. If you don't like it…

And then all of em together says Put a Ring on it!

And then all together they says Or, rather, put it in a Ring!

Then they fuckin clap and I'm tryin to figure out did Godric and Daff send me to camp for guys can't go to the bathroom without a chaperon.

So Chet asks em How many of you remember Thomas' story?

They all but four raise their fuckin hands.

Chet says to Tommy Why don't you recap, for those who might have missed it the first time?

So I ask Any of you wanna hear what I got to say about it?

Chet says to me We absolutely will. But it's important for you to hear Thomas' side too, just as he is going to hear yours. Then he nods to Tommy and he says Thomas, like in a way actually means Go ahead.

Tommy Toothpick says Thanks. So, I was hired as part of a three-man hit squad to ambush Samuzzo.

And my jaw fuckin *drops*. I figured he was gonna spin it like I came at him from outta nowhere. Like he was crossin a bridge and I swung up from under and clubbed him on accounta he didn't answer my riddles. But no, he says right up top that he was gunnin for *me*. And none of the guys raised their hands before are makin faces like it's anythin they ain't heard already.

Tommy tells it like he didn't know the other guys before the job, no better'n he knew me, which was not in the fuckin least. He says he just gets briefed by the boss that he's gonna be like bait. They're gonna set it up seemin like Tommy's gonna goose me, on accounta I goose easy. It's my own fuckin fault too, on accounta apparently I just can't wait to tell every fuckin meathead I see about it. Anyway, that's their plan and it's goin exactly great til Tommy fucks it up by tippin me off with a glancewise look. And he even fuckin tells em he's the one fucked it up! He's just tellin em all the shit he did wrong, but it ain't the kinda tellin like the tellin I told when I told my scab buddies bout me goosin. Tommy ain't tellin on himself to cover. He's doin it to do the fuckin opposite.

He tells em about the fight, and it's all some quality fuckin reportage til the part where I put him to bed. Then he says he came to quick enough there hadn't been no interest from guys wear hats with tiny brims, so he went slinkin home. The end.

Then he leans forward so he's starin right at me, and he says Samuzzo, what I want to say to you is that I'm sorry that I tried to kill you. It was a job, a quick buck, you know? Purely business. Which doesn't make it right? But it's true. I really have no ill-will for you. So you trying to kill me? I get it. I *get* it. I don't blame you. And if my forgiveness is something you want, I've got it right here, in my heart. But if it isn't…I don't blame you for that either. All I can say to you is, I'm sorry.

Everybody claps for him. Some guys are wipin their eyes, or makin owl noises. Then they finish clappin and look at me. Chet asks me Well, Samuzzo. Is there anything in Thomas' account you wish to dispute?

So I says Uh… Which is fuckin unusual, on accounta um and uh and er ain't a part of my fuckin vocabulary. I mean, a lot of shit ain't a part of my fuckin vocabulary. But I don't do fillers is what I'm sayin. I say what I'm gonna say or I ain't sayin nothin. My speech is fuckin whaddyacallit. Economical. Ain't no words comin outta my mouth ain't gotta. Straight to the fuckin point, that's me. I'm…well. You see what'm I sayin.

Then I tells em No, no, I ain't got disputes. I…yeah.

Chet nods and asks me What do you think about what Thomas said to you at the end?

I look at Chet, then at Thom-no, *Tommy*, then at Chet again, then at Tommy again. And I says to em …

So Tommy says Please speak your mind, Samuzzo. I promise I will only be offended if I feel you're censoring yourself to spare my feelings.

Jesus Christ. I close my eyes real quick and shake my head around. When I open em I ain't in bed with Daff sawin logs next to me. I'm still in Danbury fuckin Connecticut. This is real fuckin life.

I look at the other bruisers in the Ring. Or I figure they *are* the Ring. It's like seein twelve Samuzzos from different fuckin dimensions. All of em're studyin me like they got a test comin up.

Chet says to me We're all friends here, Samuzzo. We're all family. Please, tell us what's on your mind.

So I says to em Ah...I mean...I'm kinda fuckin confused about why's Tommy gettin

Tommy says to me If it's alright with you Samuzzo, I prefer to be called Thomas?

I ain't really thinkin straight so I don't mean to say to him Yeah, but Thomas Toothpick don't sound right.

I don't mean to say that to him, but I do.

Everybody around the circle starts makin more barnyard noises.

The quote this can pass without fists unquote guy, who I can see now his titty says he's called Donnie, he says to me That wasn't a nickname, was it?

Another guy to my left who's one of them don't like the tags says We don't allow nicknames here. Which I figure is pretty fuckin rich comin from the guy don't want anybody knowin his real name. Must be he's got a name's real easy to nick-ify, like Stuart Bagina.

Chet says to me Samuzzo, weren't you yourself expressing to me, just minutes ago, your distaste for nicknames?

So I says to him Yeah, but I was talkin about for *my* name. But fine, whatever, I'll quit callin' him Tommy Toothpick out loud.

The barnyard's back.

Chet shakes his head and tells me That's not enough, Samuzzo. You can't just change what you do on the outside. You have to change what's inside. You have to stop viewing people as fundamentally different from you, or opposed to you, or something to be dehumanized as just a funny nickname.

So I says to him Jesus, what fortune cookie you get that outta?

The guy sittin next to Stuart Bagina's titty's called Gunther, so I gotta figure the rest of him is too. Gunther says to me I understand that impulse, Samuzzo. I want to share with you that I too have a history with glib, off-the-cuff remarks. But I've come to understand that they're just a defense mechanism, to keep myself distanced from my work. Which is absolutely allowed. We all have to make a living, and that distance can be essential to our doing our jobs well. But you have to know when it's safe to shut that defensive part of you off. When it's safe to open up.

The barnyard fuckin approves.

What the fuck is…what the fuck? That's all I got, is What the fuck?

No, ok, I got a thing.

So I says to em Ok, well. Then I says to Tommy, How about I wanna know who kicked you cash to hook me?

How's everybody know to make the same fuckin noise at the same fuckin time?!

Another guy named Flynn says to me Those are all concerns outside the Ring. You two can pursue those independently if you wish, but for now, our focus is with the emotions passing through the Ring, between the two of you.

So I says to Chet I gotta ask you, and I want a

straight answer. Is this a fuckin cult?

Chet tells me no but he smiles like it's fuckin yes. Then he asks me Would you like to tell Thomas your side of the story?

I tell him I just…I got fuckin nothin to add.

Everybody makes aaahhh noises like they're tryna sell me fuckin toothpaste. At least they're makin human noises this time though. That's some kinda fuckin progress.

Chet asks me What's your reaction to hearing an account with which you can find no fault, coming from the man you consider your enemy?

I says to him Honestly, I am just so fuckin confused right now.

Everybody says Ooohhh.

Then Chet says to me Now I would like to ask *you* a question, to which I would hope to receive a similarly straight answer. If I had asked you to tell the story first, do you believe you would have done so in such a way that Thomas could have found no fault with it?

I ain't got an answer, which, you know, I always figure for an answer.

Seems like Chet don't figure the same on accounta he asks me again in half as many words.

So I says to him No, I don't figure I woulda.

Then he asks me Do you think you *could* have?

I ask him The fuck does *that* mean?

And he says Exactly what it means.

I try really fuckin hard, but I can't make myself pass out. So I gotta think of a thing to say.

The thing is, I know I can just fuckin tell him I forgive him and they'll let it all go.

But I *don't* forgive him. So why'm I gonna say a thing what ain't true?

And why don't I fuckin forgive him?

Because he tried to fuckin kill me! And you don't forgive a guy tries to kill you!

Except he just did for me.

But mine was only on accounta his!

But his was only on accounta a job. Which I get. I do jobs all the time I ain't got no feelin one way or the other bout the guy I'm hittin. I just do it on accounta that's the job. So I gotta imagine he was feelin the same even when's he stabbin me in the fuckin shoulder.

I guess I'm just cross about this time I'm the guy on the wrong end of a job.

So, yeah, I ain't gonna pretend I ain't still kinda cross about it. But I fuckin understand a bruiser bruises on accounta bruisin's what he does. And if somebody's payin for somebody else comes and bruises me, I ain't gotta be all fuckin *about* it. But I can't figure a reason right at present why I can't *get* it.

I wanna figure a good way to say that to em. Then they all start clappin on accounta I've been sayin that out loud the whole time and didn't even fuckin notice.

Thomas stands up from his seat and starts walkin towards me. Ok. I get it. Like how Hatch and I were cool. We're gonna be cool now.

I ain't quite ready to be cool with him, but I'm fuckin hungry and I wanna get one of them little sandwiches. So I figure it ain't a lie if I just shake the guy's hand. I stand up and start walkin towards him.

Then Thomas wraps his arms around me and I'm bracin up to swing him over my fuckin shoulder when everybody says Awww.

Thomas is givin me a fuckin hug.

So...I just pat him three times on the back. Like how grown men hug, like they're worried about catchin a disease. But Thomas don't let go. He's stuck to me like a barnacle.

Well, what the hell.

I take a deep breath and settle my arms on his back. Everybody starts clappin and cheerin. Eleven big mean Mr. Potato Head bruisers sittin, now standin in a circle and gettin misty over two more Potato Heads huggin it out in the center. On accounta we ain't got no problems with each other, we just maybe got bosses got problems with the other guy's bosses. I ain't got a fuckin boss, but it's a metaphorical, so we can fuckin hug it out, I guess.

I ain't sayin I'm all fuckin *about* it. But I *get* it.

GO FIGURE

THEY done such a good job stitchin me up about the Ring stuff that I completely fuckin forgot why'd I come here til halfway through Gunther's story about he mighta accidentally run over somebody's foot. Don't seem like such a big deal to me but he seems real broke up about it. Maybe he ain't never been so trustful of fuckin automobiles, what do I know. So I keep fuckin mum. Then I forget again. Then the meetins over. Then I remember. I remember I came here to talk about I'm bummed I flipped a car and I can't figure out to solve nothin without punchin noses and I ain't got the memory I used to and I flipped a car. Which I guess is fuckin funny. And I guess it means I gotta come back. I ain't laughin about that.

Still. Seems like a swell groupa guys. Couple of em says we're goin out for some fuckin moonshine, who's comin. I don't say nothin but then they ask me How about you Samuzzo? So I says to em Sure, what the fuck.

Thomas Toothpick's in the group too. So now I'm gettin fuckin corn juice with the guy tried to kill me. Maybe I'll ask does the bartender got two straws, we can split a fuckin milkshake.

We all ride over in our own cars on accounta nobody's got one big enough for five bruisers. Too bad Cleveland ain't amongst the fuckin livin no more, we coulda used a car ain't got a roof. Lucky we ain't gotta worry about carpoolin on accounta bruisers don't get drunk. Either the bruiser runs outta cash first, or the bar runs outta booze.

Speakeasy's called Tops Down. I guess that's a fuckin play on Bottoms Up, if the play's a fuckin tragedy. I figure they see the Paci-FISTs all the time on accounta they don't look put out none when five guys come rollin into the backroom got the same volume as the rest of the fuckin clientele combined.

Whaddyaknow, we got five fuckin stools open at the curvy parta the bar down there. Used to be three open, then two kids maybe ain't regulars got a look at us and then it was five open. So Me, Thomas, Chet, Stuart Bagina and a guy called George I didn't clock much at the meet all take a seat in that order.

That don't quite work for me. So I says to Thomas Hey pal, I figure I'm right under some kinda vent or somethin. You mind we switch spots?

Thomas reaches up to pat me on the shoulder, then he fuckin thinks better of it. He says to me Not at all, on accounta he's some kinda brazen and all kindsa simple. So we switch spots.

Now startin from the other end, it's George, Stuart Bagina, Chet, Me, then Thomas. Then the fuckin wall.

You see where I'm goin with this? Just on accounta we got big hearts at each other don't mean my fuckin brain got wiped.

Bartender asks us can he see some I.D. I says to him You fuckin serious? You worried we ain't legal drinkin age? Ain't *nobody*'s fuckin legal drinkin age!

Chet plops his hand on my forearm and says That's why he wants to see them. He wants to know who's coming in here.

From my other shoulder Tommy says He doesn't want folks coming in giving fake names. Helps him anticipate and adjudicate turf wars.

He don't try touchin my fuckin forearm. Good call, Tommy.

So whatever, we hand over our personals. Barkeep hands everybody's back except mine. Then he just stares at me.

Takes me a second to figure it. Ah, right. I look at my tit. Look back at Bartender. Far as he's concerned, I'm a guy called Frank with the word Samuzzo on my titty.

I tell him We was playin the game where you write a famous fucker's name on your titty and ask people clues and then they give you clues and then you gotta guess who's your titty say you are.

Bartender turns to me and asks So who's Samuzzo?

I says to him You ain't supposed to tell me! You gotta give me fuckin clues! Then I rip the tag off my titty and I says to him Now I'm outta the fuckin game. Thanks a lot.

Bartender mumbles about he's sorry and hands me Frank's personals back. Stuart Bagina's lookin all cocky just on accounta he's scared of nametags.

We all get some drinks and laugh about shit like we're old boys got the first fuckin thing in common besides bein sad about bein toughs. You read the dimer about the guy's gotta solve a crime in forty-eight hours only he can't get off this horse what's he on or his son's gonna blow up? You hear about those Canadians cuttin whiskey with the water they boiled out of fuckin syrup? You ever notice dogs're real picky bout where to bathroom outside but inside they just get straight to business? Dumb shit like that.

I give it til the second round. Then I turn on Thomas. I lean harder on the bar, bringin my shoulders up. Kinda cuttin him off from the others, but not so obvious anybody stops and says somethin.

And I says to him, real quiet, Listen, I'm real glad we're pals now, you and I.

He nods and tries to listen around me. Guess he likes what're they sayin back there. But I ain't gonna get louder to talk over em. I ain't gotta.

I says So, as pals, why don't how about you tell me who calls you up and says we got a Samuzzo problem.

Thomas sits back in his chair like I just told him to clean his room. He says to me I thought we had resolved this matter in the ring.

I tell him We resolved *our* thing, sure. I buy that. But I still got a thing with somebody's name I ain't fuckin privy about.

He says Think of it this way, have you been attacked since our attempted ambush?

So I says …I dunno. Only he knows and I know what I dunno really means is *no*, just with an extra *I dun* stuck on the front.

Then he says This is a matter of professional confidentiality. You understand that, surely? You wouldn't just divulge a client's information because somebody asked you nicely?

So I asks him You want I don't ask you nicely?

He leans back and he says to me Was everything we went through in the Ring a lie, then?

I says to him No, but it sure as hell weren't no promise neither.

So he says I really don't want to talk about this right now. The whole idea of grabbing a drink after the meet is to unwind.

So I ask him How much did the guy pay you? I'll pay you that and half besides.

Thomas says to me I'm finished with this conversation, if you don't mind?

What I wanna do is punch through his ear and rip his spine out, help him unwind for keeps. Only that's what the old Samuzzo woulda done, the Samuzzo ain't been through the Ring. The new Samuzzo *wants* to do that, but instead of doin it he uses his words.

So I says to him What I wanna do it punch through your ear and rip your spine out, help ya unwind for keeps. Only that's what the old Samuzzo woulda done, the Samuzzo ain't been through the Ring.

Thomas don't look scared as I'da expected. But he don't look *not* scared. To that he says to me Well, that is a kind of progress.

I says to him This shit don't happen all at once.

He says Oh, I understand.

So I says Maybe it ain't happenin fast as some other things might happen.

And he says You're still threatening me?

So I says No, I'm just unwindin.

Then he makes whaddyacallems with his mouth. Blowin air out fast enough so it flaps his lips real fast. Raspberries. He says to me Ok, how about this. I like people being able to trust me. So I can't betray a client. But…this isn't a client I'm on especially good terms with. Let's just say if he wasn't happy that I failed to take you out, then that you failed to take *me* out wasn't much of a consolation.

I says You had to foot your own medical?

He nods and says So if I were to mention something kind of…no, if you were to ask *me* some questions, and I responded, as one buddy to another, but nothing I said could be misconstrued as me just *telling*

So I interrupt him and I says to him You wanna give me fuckin *clues*.

More raspberries. Then he says to me Yes.

I says to him You got information cloggin up your

fuckin noggin could save me all kindsa headache and clear some space for you to fill with new words describe your feelins, and you could just fuckin tell me on accounta when the guys' dead who's gonna know I got him through you, on accounta who's gonna fuckin know who killed him, on accounta I ain't plannin on leavin a forwardin address. You got that, and what you got for *me* is a fuckin *clue*.

He says Potentially more than one, if your questions are on point.

So I says to him I wanna rip the leg off your barstool and jam it through your eye before you even start tippin over.

He asks me do I got anythin to say ends in a question mark.

Now *I'm* doin fuckin raspberries.

Go Figure

GODRIC puts his head down on accounta he's tryin to thinka the politic way to ask it. He don't find it so he just looks up and asks me Why didn't you just follow him home and beat it out of him?

I gotta give him a little shit about that. I says to him On accounta what I learned in the Ring of fuckin Resolution is how come.

He just sorta smiles and shakes his head. He starts fiddlin with the framed pic of the dipshit kid the lady's comin to pick up soon. Folks across town didn't do such a hot job, on accounta Godric didn't shell out enough for such a hot job. So he's doin his little touchups, mostly tape and paint.

Then he asks me Alright Socrates, what information did you *inquire* out of your dear friend Thomas?

I open my fist in fronta my face and start tickin off fingers.

To my thumb, and yeah I start on the fuckin thumb because the thumb is a finger, yes it is, it's a fuckin finger, and some motherfuckers start with the pointer which is stupid on accounta then you go out to the pinky and then you gotta go *all the way back* to get the thumb like it's this lady's dipshit kid her husband pretended to have left at the gas station on accident.

So anyway to my thumb I says the first thing I learned and that's This guy ain't goin after *me*, he's goin after somebody's a buddy a mine. Only he don't know how to find my buddy to go after *him,* so he's gotta go after *me*. So he wanted Thomas to get somethin outta me he could use to get to my buddy. So I guess this guy *is* goin after me, but only on accounta he's gotta so's he can get to my buddy. You got anybody wants it in for ya I oughta know about?

Godric shakes his head and tells me Not unless somebody discovered who actually does their framework.

That's a joke so I says to my first finger They ain't come after me again so far on accounta they ain't idiots wanna stub their toe on the same chair twice. They figure they got another lead on my buddy they meant to be goin after when they were goin after me.

Then to my middle finger I says This guy's got a hell of a lotta money behind him, which is how come he can just throw some goons at me and not even take it personal when none of em send him a Christmas card. This guy figures it's cash burned, instead of people. So, this is me just havin an omen, I gotta figure whatever does the guy wanna find a buddy a mine for's more than likely's got somethin money about it too.

Godric don't say nothin for a second on accounta he's makin sure he lays the tape flat as can be over the corners of the frame ain't touchin right. After he's got it he asks me Is that just because you assume anybody with a lot of money is going to be primarily involved in schemes to get more?

I says to him Yeah.

He tut tut tuts me and tells me Don't discount the personal. These rich types are often more volatile than you or I, emotionally speaking.

I explain to Godric about how That's like a prejudice, ain't it?

He says Yes, I suppose it is as he's rubbin this little brush what a mouse might use for mascara over top the tape.

I ask him Godric, ain't *you* some kinda rich type?

He smiles and tells me I'm rich. That's not the same as a rich *type*.

I shake my head and look back at my fingers. One two three. I wake up the ring finger and I says to it the fourth thing I learned and that's This guy ain't goin after *me*, he's goin after somebody's a buddy a mine. Only he don't know how to find my buddy to go after *him,* so he's gotta go after *me*. So he wanted Thomas to get somethin outta me he could use to get to my buddy. So I guess this guy *is* goin after me, but only on accounta he's gotta so's he can get to my buddy. You got anybody wants it in for ya I oughta know about?

Godric looks at me and frowns. Then he says No, Samuzzo. I don't.

I wish I had a a fifth thing I learned for my fifth finger, only I didn't learn no fifth thing so I got no reason to dig up the pinky. So I put it the whole thing away and I ask Godric Whaddya think?

His tongue pops outta the side of his mouth, which I guess helps him paint better. He asks the dipshit kid in the frame I don't know, what do *you* think?

I says to him You *do* know, you're just bein fuckin whaddyacallit.

He says That I am. Do you have a theory as of yet?

I look down at my hand, still got the four fingers sayin hi and the fifth stayin in its room on accounta nobody *gets* it. Then I say to Godric Well, I only got two good buddies got a lotta money, a lotta privacy and maybe a lotta not-so-friends.

He asks me And who would that be? Like he don't know already.

I says to him Wally and you.

Godric stops paintin and leans back. His eyes are dartin all over.

I says to him I figure if I figure who's the bad guy actually comin for, I'm gonna be able to figure who's the bad guy and start goin for *him*. And maybe Wally and you, whoever's the one the bad guy's comin for, you don't know he's even comin for ya yet on accounta he ain't sure how's he gonna find you. But he's got somethin in the works, sounds like. So, I'm gettin close. And one way I can get closer is findin a way Wally or you links up to Paul Pezet, like as a for instance if maybe you were some kinda friends with Pezet such so ya get the droopies when I tell ya he got whacked and then I carved him on accident.

Godric starts to say somethin so I keep talkin and I say I gotta see who knows him in a way Paul mighta got knowins of my business and my goosin, *but* ain't got knowins of where you keep *your* abouts.

He says to me Or Wally's.

So I says Sure. But all I'm sayin is, I ain't got fingers enough for the guys'd wanna clobber Wally. That's what pen and paper's for. And I know if I asked him, he'd give me everybody's name and social and starsign and shoe size and he wouldn't fuckin stop til I asked him three times. He don't do secrets. And he don't know Pezet. So all I'm sayin is, *you* keep secrets. You're real good at it. I'm thinkin maybe you're not keepin somebody else's secret this time. Maybe you're keepin yours. I ain't sayin its anythin bad.

So he says You're just saying.

And I says Sure am.

Then he breathes real deep and says You're insinuating that I have a deeper connection to Paul Pezet that I have been hiding from you, because...

I says Maybe you're embarrassed about somethin, or scared, or you just ain't the sharin type. I dunno. I'm sayin you're a cagey motherfucker on the personals, and don't even pretend you ain't. You married? You got kids? I don't fuckin know. I don't ask on accounta that's your business you wanna tell me or not. But maybe this time you got some business *made* itself my business. So I'm in it now, and I ain't gonna sit around with my thumb up my ass… Then I lift up my thumb but the other four fingers are still up so I gotta put em down with the other hand …my *thumb* up my ass and watch a guy I got a big heart for gettin done in. I wanna help you like you're always carpin about *me* gettin help. And I went to the fuckin meet, didn't I?

He says And you turned it from therapy into interrogation.

So I remind him You asked me how come I didn't follow him home and pulp him!

Godric shrugs his shoulders and puts down the brush and shit and he says I really do appreciate your concern. And no, I can't say with one hundred percent certainty that nobody's coming after me. I have to assume somebody *always* is, from both sides of the law. But what I can say with a modest majority of certitude is that I have never had dealings with Paul Pezet, professionally. Perhaps a middleman who never identified himself as representing Pezet, that's something to which I also cannot speak. But, to the best of my knowledge, we were never more than acquaintances.

I nod and tells him You do got a real good memory.

And he says I like to think so.

I scrute him up and down. If he's lyin, he's the best in the biz. I ask him How'd you'n Paul meet, you never done business with him?

Godric looks real embarrassed, scrutin at his knees, then he mumbles Squash club.

GO FIGURE

I ask him What's that, a sex thing?

He says No. No, Samuzzo. It's a sport. It's just kind of…well, it's a bit…embarrassing. It's for, ahem, rich types.

I gotta admit, it tickles me somewise, seein a fella's got so much of the dignities squirmin like Godric's doin just now. So I says to him Alright. Never seen a fella get so tetchy on accounta a buddy's tryin to help him, but alright.

He says to me It really does mean a lot to me. Your concern. But I'm just a very private person, you understand. It's my nature.

I says Not somethin ya do, somethin ya are. That sorta thing.

Then he looks at me like I just told him whatever secrets he ain't tellin me nor anybody else. And he says Yes. Precisely that sort of thing.

The bell says tingle ingle ing on accounta somebody's comin in. The lady's back for her picture. I figure I ain't got anymore business here, so I head on out. I crawl into the frames to clear the little way for her to mosey.

She says Thanks.

I says No problem. Then she and Godric are jawin and I'm just thinkin about how'm I gonna jog Wally's fuckin memory about does he know Pezet or not.

I'm headin out the door when I hear Godric tellin her all about the frame. The work he did. Woodwork, he says. He's fulla shit, but the man's got a shovel and a can-do attitude.

Damn it if I don't find myself believin his bullshit just a little bit. Even knowin full well it's fuckin bullshit. Huh.

Tingle ingle ing sounds the same on the way out too.

WALLY ain't no fuckin help. I just call him up and I ask him You for certain sure you ain't got no links to Pezet?

And he says to me Sorry Charlie, but I'm positive. You've nailed that down as the strongest lead again?

So I bring him up to speed about Paci-FIST and Thomas and the shit what'd I learned. Some about myself and also about who was tryin to wax myself.

Wally tells me That is vexing. Hm. A friend of yours who's ticked off some wealthy somebody as a means to an end definitely sounds like I'm the end. But I haven't really had much rumpus or riff-raff lately. Nothing out of the ordinary, anyway.

I ask him What's ordinary?

He says I meant it as a joke. Just normal stuff like earaches and electric bills.

I ask him You pay electric bills?

So he says I meant that as a metaphor.

So I put it to him Maybe you wanna acquaint your sayin and your meanin for the rest of we're on the phone?

He makes a noise like he figures that for a swell idea.

Then I says to him Could be you, that's for damn sure…but I got a feelin about Godric. He ain't an open book like you. You're like a book's got the covers ripped off I figure, if anybody's a book.

He asks me how come I get to speak in metaphor.

I ain't got a good answer so I put that one to the fuckin side and I says to him I don't think Godric's hidin somethin on accounta it's bad. I figure he's just a real private fella.

Wally says Funny, considering how he's the biggest butterfly I've ever met. Socially, I mean.

I shake my head and says Business social's different from

Wallys says me Connection's going bad. Come again?

So I stop shakin my head and I says Business social's different from social social.

He says True, true. So what's next?

I says to him I just gotta go see what's Pezet gotta say for himself.

He don't say nothin for a second.

So I sigh real loud and say I ain't havin a rememberin problem. I know Pezet's dead.

Wally says You were speaking metaphorically.

I say Yeah.

He says Hm in a tone I ain't so cheery on.

Somebody's gotta fuckin explain to me why every fuckin light in Paul Pezet's glass fuckin house on now. At least the yard's fuckin dark this time, so, yippee or some shit.

Course, I have a think on it for a second and it makes all sortsa sense. Pezet was involved in all sortsa shit loves the shade. Cops might be figurin, do some of those shady shits wanna come toss the house, maybe relieve it of some paperwork got names and dates, and shit? Cops might also be figurin do they wanna shell out for ten grunts guardin this place, or do they wanna send two guys, run the lights and let the estate foot the fuckin bill?

I'da rathered the ten grunts, bein level.

So now Pezet's house looks like one of those things lives at the bottom of the ocean, can't figure is it a fish or is it a grand openin. A splat of light and color ruinin a perfectly good night. He's got a lovely fuckin house, don't get me wrong. Pezet does, I'm done talkin on the fish. Pezet's got a lovely house. I know on accounta I can see every fuckin inch of it.

Nobody inside at least. And no body. Just a chair looks like it took communion a few too many times.

Gotta figure we got some bodies outside, though.

So I figure I got two maybes. Maybe one is I creep around til I find a cop or two, I put em to sleep, then I go in. Only I got no clue how many cops do I gotta be lookin out for. For all I know I could lap the fuckin place twice and there's another cop lappin it from the other side.

Second maybe is…I go cut the power? I don't know how to cut fuckin power. I ain't the kinda guy cuts power. That even a real thing, cuttin the power? Don't seem like the sorta thing one fella can manage.

So first maybe's the only maybe's gonna work as a probable. Means I just walk around and waste a lotta time and maybe still get fucked.

But if first maybe's just *waste time and maybe get fucked*, why how bout I don't just make a third maybe where I maybe get fucked but at least I find out sooner?

I like that maybe best. That's my best maybe.

So I take my fuckin time strollin across that yard now that it's fuckin dark, right up to the cardboard's fillin the wall I fell through on the first round. I take a runnin start and jump at the cardboard on accounta I'm a nostalgic kinda guy.

It's harder than regular cardboard so I don't really blast through like how'd I figure I would. My top half makes it through, but then my belt gets wedged. I'm just kinda stuck danglin a few feet off the ground. Anybody'd been inside there, it'da look like Pezet'd gone and hunted the biggest fuckin game short of somethin's got a trunk.

A bit a shimmyin and I fall onto the floor of the livin room. Ah, old times. Only I ain't got time for the sentimentals on accounta I ain't never been so lit up in my life.

GO FIGURE

I figure the cops they most definitely got out there, they ain't watchin the house too close. So I got maybe a few seconds before somebody looks up and wonders about what a guy couldn't sneak into an airplane hangar's doin crawlin around the livin room.

Now I'm runnin up these stairs can't figure out which fuckin direction they wanna climb and I gotta figure my seconds are up. Somebody's gotta be comin for me now. Drawin a gun I bet. They dumb enough to try shootin in this house? No clue. They probably couldn't figure anybody's dumb enough to walk in with it all lit up.

The hallway up here ain't even a fuckin hallway. It's just a balcony with more glass walls on one side and a drop to the ground floor on the other.

Even glass on the inside! There's nowhere in this fuckin house you ain't seein from any otherwhere! Either Pezet was a monk or kids lookin to get learned on human fuckin anatomy hike up here for homework.

I hear somebody outside shout Hey!

Shit.

I duck in the first room and it ain't an office.

Back out into the hallway. I look down and see three cops bumblin their way outta the dark, headin towards the door, clunkin and runnin into each other like a new stringa anal beads figures it's gonna grow up to be a necklace.

I ain't thinkin straight. Why'm I duckin into the rooms? I can see right the fuck into em.

Looks like an office down at the end. Fourth door.

So that's some time saved.

I run in there while the cops are unlockin the front door and leapin through.

Good news is I got eyes on the cops from the office. Bad news is likewise, just opposite.

I got no fuckin clue what'm I lookin for. I really figured I'd have all the time in the world for perusin at my fuckin leisure. So I rip a drawer outta the desk in fronta me. It's one of those deep ones. Eight inches, give or take. I'm gonna take.

First Cop yells up at me Stop what you're doing!

I tell him Ok, then I grab a juicy lookin folder sittin on the desk and stuff it in the drawer. It don't really fit but it'll carry.

Third Cop tells me Stop *everything* that you're doing!

I tell him What about my fuckin autoerotic funct-ions?

The cops all slow down for a second. I'm usin that second to stuff every paper I can find into the fuckin cranny I got left in the drawer.

Second Cop says He means autonomic!

Then they all get back to runnin up the stairs.

Ain't nothin left for me to cram into that cubbyhole. So I put it on the desk and grab a gold trophy says it's for runnin real fast, like I give a shit. Shaped like a little fella I gotta figure ain't modeled on Pezet.

I put my hands up and says to em You got me boys, I'm turnin myself in. I step out into the hall that ain't a hall at all.

They finish strugglin up the stairs and clump together at the other end of the ain't-a-hall. Nobody draws nothin. No guns. No tazers. No chance.

Third Cop tells me We sent our partner back to town. Reinforcements are as good as on their way.

I tell em Ain't you gotta have enforcements before you can re- em?

First Cop points to the trophy in my hand and asks What's that?

I says to em It's a hip hooray for hoofin it.

Second Cop says to me Aah please don't throw it at the

So I throw it at the glass we're standin on, hard as I can. This shit's gotta be all kindsa reinforced, so I hope the cops ain't the thoughtful types. I got a good arm and the glittery little dipshit flies true. It taps the cat-walk with its itty fuckin forehead. A huge crack shoots up the whole thing. I dive back into the office. The cops take a shortcut one story down to the foyer, where they'll be waitin foy-yuh backup! HA! Remember like I said that one time? Foy-yeir? For their. Eh.

Anyway, they ain't takin a shortcut on accounta the catwalk shatters. On accounta it *don't*. It cracks, yeah, but it don't shatter. They just figured it would, and they leap over the railing all at the same time, like it's fuckin protocol, like that's some kinda better they slam onto the ground on *their* terms.

On accounta yeah, they fuckin slam. Guess they missed the how-to-land-easy class.

I was figurin I'd have to use the drawer to bash a hole in the windowwall and just jump down a story. But on accounta they're all rollin around down there and moanin, and the catwalk ain't broke, all I gotta do is stroll on out the front door.

So I grab my drawer full of shit and stroll nice and easy into the ain't-a-hall and it explodes into a million pieces. A lotta glass shows me howta take the Cop's shortcut after all.

The glass gets to ground first. Then I fall on toppa that. Then the drawer falls on toppa me.

Now we're four guys rollin around and moanin in a dead guy's foyer.

I try to pick the drawer up offa my chest real careful. Don't look like nothin spilled out in the tumble. I packed it real tight, I guess. I put it down to the side and roll the same way. Lots of crackin sounds as I'm pushin myself up. Can't tell what's glass from what's bone.

I wanna say somethin to the cops gonna save me some face, only I can't figure a single fuckin thing'd do. So I just tell em all At least mine was a fuckin accident and I pick up my drawer and limp on out the front door.

Go Figure

Daff tweezes another piece of glass outta my back so I says to her Ouch.

She don't say nothin about that. First couple times she said sorry, but then I said ouch more times'n she wanted to say sorry. Instead I just hear the glass tell me Ding as Daff drops it into a bowl full of more glass.

The bowl's full of more glass on accounta it's the rest she pulled outta my back. Just wanna make it known we ain't got bowls full of glass floatin round the house. We do got some bowls *made* of glass, but we ain't puttin the glass into a bowl made of Ouch.

Ding.

I'm all hunched over a chair but I still got enough breathin room to thumb through the shit I stuffed into the drawer. That juicy folder I got's got *real* fuckin juicy, on accounta turns out I bled on it a whole lot. Or else Pezet left it on the desk all bloody and I missed that fuckin detail. Either or, I got nothin what can I do with that unless Godric can find me some fuckin dweeb knows how to get blood off a fuckin page. But on the level, I'm thinkin I maybe might keep Godric outta the loop on this bit. Not that I figure he ain't worth trustin. Just, you know. You can never be too Ouch.

Ding.

So right now I'm readin the pages been stuffed into this other envelope. Lots of finance shit. Charts and numbers, charts *of* numbers. The kinda shit I'd be takin to Godric any other day. Daff don't do numbers so she can't help. Maybe I can see does Janis got anythin goin Ouch.

Ring.

Ding.

Ring.

I ask Daff Ah shit, can you grab me the candlestick?

Suddenly it's right next to my head on accounta Daff's got it in her hand on accounta she's always on toppa stuff and I got no clue what I'd do without her. I tell her as much and her face turns into a tomato.

I grab the phone and say Yeah? It says Ring. I take the talkin horn off its shelf what says Click then I say Yeah?

The phone says to me That's how we answer the phone now?

I says Hiya Agnes.

She asks me Are you allowed to read the paper through the zoo glass, you fucking zoo animal?

I says Ouch.

Go Figure

Ding.

She asks me What, I getcha too good with the zoo excoriation?

I tell her No, Daff's pullin glass outta my back.

So she says I'm gonna guess that has something to do with why I'm reading about you in the funny pages right now.

Daff pulls out another piece of glass. I don't say nothin. She leans forward and asks me You good?

I says to her Let's why don't I grab a towel and we go see if we ain't got a periodical on our porch.

Ok, so it ain't awful like Agnes had me thinkin. What they got's a sketch of what'd the three cops figure I looked like. I guess it kinda's got a resemblance. Enough for Agnes to spot. Not enough so's I'm worried about somebody's never seen me before makin me on the street. Hell, you take that sketch to a Paci-FIST meetin and it could be anybody.

Still, Daff ain't so happy about it, on accounta I guess I left em some fingertip prints when'd I pick up the statue of the little golden fella loves to run. They drew them prints on a page and sent em off to fuckin Langley or whatever, so they ain't got confirmation, but some of the local dicks're figurin the fingertip prints look like ones they already got sittin round the fuckin office. So the article ends with they're sayin maybe Michael Berns's the one came and took some shit from Pezet's place, and why not have a gander at this resemblance of his mug, assumin this guy's Michael Berns after all. Which, you know, just on accounta they're right don't make this anythin other than subpar fuckin reportage. What if they're talkin two different fellas here, you're gonna derail lookin for Berns by putting the wrong face on it? I tell ya, they don't make the fuckin gumshoes like how'd they used to.

But anyway, seein as they *ain't* figurin wrong, Daff figures I oughta start frettin. They're gettin a fuller picture, sure. It ain't like I don't get why're Daff's nerves janglin. But Michael Berns ain't amongst the fuckin livin no more, and that picture don't look enough like Frank Patricks or Douglas Barker or especially not Samuzzo D'Amato to be givin *me* the jangles.

I pick the phone back up to my face on accounta I ain't never hung it up and I ask it How'd you spot it was me?

Agnes says to her phone The forehead, mostly. The shape of the jaw too. Mostly the part about the chowderfaced piece of shit breaking a glass floor and then falling through it himself.

So I ask her That's what they're sayin on continued page 6, huh?

She grunts like she's sayin Just about.

So I says to her Say you ain't never seen me before. You see this picture, then next day you see me on the street. You figure you're gonna line em up?

She says I'm not the person to ask. Maybe tomorrow I don't remember today at all. Comes and goes, my memory.

To that I says Hm. Then I ask her How do you

know you can't remember somethin? Like, you remember you can't remember?

I figure I can hear her face crackin into a smile while she says to me Mostly, it's because somebody tells me we talked about something I can't remember talking about, or they've already heard a story I'm in the middle of telling. Assuming I can trust them further than I can fucking throw them, that is. So, like it matters to you, that's why I'm a bit less of a glitter-faced bitch than I used to be. I can't afford to keep company with anybody who can't keep my confidence.

I remember the guy she shooed from the yard sale and I says You gotta cut loose the Alans, huh?

She says That's exactly right.

I stare at the paper. At my fuckin likeness I hope ain't so like. And I'm just lookin at it, thinkin on how people comes down to two types. You got your Alans, and you got your Agneses. I got a lotta Agneses in my life, and I'd say that makes me some kinda fuckin lucky...but I maybe got some might be Alans after all.

So I ask her How'd'ya tell an Agnes from an Alan if you can't be sure you ain't forgettin somethin'd put one into the other?

She don't miss a beat, sayin You just have to do your best, dear.

We talk for a bit longer, then we hang up. I pick up the files what'd I cadge from Pezet's place and I start combin through em again from the beginnin. Only this time, I'm doin my best. Can't remember if I was before. But that don't matter, on accounta at least know I am *now.*

Daff finishes pickin glass outta my back, then she goes to write a song about it. I ask her does she wanna leave the door open on accounta I wanna hear what's she comin up with, if she wants to. She wants to.

I ain't got the words to explain a song I'm hearin much past it's a piano and it's makin my ears happy. Brand new piano, I oughta mention. Ain't no way she was gettin the one from Berns's place outta dodge. Anyway it's piano's ticklin my ears, and it's helpin me focus on the paperwork, I figure. Daff helps me do my best in all sortsa ways, even when she's just doin her thing, ya know? I figure that's why we make such a cute fuckin couple.

This time I look at charts and numbers, and I ain't just thinkin Boy do I wanna take these to Godric and then puttin em to the side. No, I'm really lookin at em, *squintin* at em even. They ain't exactly swirlin into somethin makes sense though, so I think Boy do I wanna take these to Godric and then I put em to the side.

What else we got in here? Some telegrams, which I gotta figure's got somethin incriminatin on somebody on accounta why else you wanna keep fuckin telegrams in this day and age? I look through all the names on em, all the businesses. Ain't a single one what I recognize. And I can't make sense of which bit's the incriminatin one, if any of em are. Reads like one half a dull fuckin back'n yak on who's got which investments where or whatever. Maybe somebody's doin the whaddyacallits? Goofin on the...? Well, it don't fuckin matter on accounta I got no way of knowin. So I think Boy do I wanna take these to Godric and then I put em to the side.

I think that same fuckin thing for everythin I pull out. One folder's got somethin looks like blueprints for a tiny house, another's just a packet looks like Pezet's pitchin somebody or else somebody's pitchin Pezet about investin in a better kinda anchor chain specially for boats, another's got somethin looks like a getaway package with passports and foreign money and shit, and speakin of shit, here's a piece of shit sketch of somethin's either figurin to be a dog or else it's a wheelbarrow. Like, I ain't an art guy, but Jesus, somebody's gotta take a fuckin class or three.

Seems like hours go by. I'm thumbin through this drawer, hardly even believin how much shit I managed to stuff in. Daff's in the other room writin music, playin a bit then goin back and playin it better then goin back and now it's worse and then now it's even better. The whole time, feels like my face in the funny pages's squintin at me, tryna read *me*. Only it ain't *my* face. Or anyway, it's like my face if whoever drew this fuckin wheelbarrow named Rover drew my face. Don't matter is it my spittin image or what, it's still starin at me. It's eyes still got fuckin teeth.

Now maybe it's on accounta I got Michael Berns over *there* and Daff over *here*, and me in between. Maybe its somethin else entire. I ain't so sure. But there's some kinda gear catches in my brain makes me go back to that getaway package. Somethin makes me pour it out on the table and scrute it some more. Somethin makes me go for the passport. Start flippin through pages. Lookin at em, squintin at em harder'n I ever squinted at anythin in my life.

Maybe it's on accounta Berns and Daff, maybe it's just some fuckin hunch I got, maybe I don't fuckin know. All I do know is, whatever's that somethin made me look at the passport is the somethin found me another fuckin lead.

That page of the passport's got Pezet's face and name and all that shit, down on the bottom corner, there's a real little smudge.

Kinda thing somebody ain't worried about somebody's never seen it before spottin it.

Kinda thing looks like OM.

If you're lookin for it.

Go Figure

I show Odette Pezet's passport and her eyes go kinda big. She takes it and flips through it and looks it all over and says to me Wow, yeah, that's mine alright. But, God, I did that one *ages* ago. I read that name in the paper and thought it sounded familiar, but I never made the connection. I just assumed it was because he was an entrepreneur.

I says to her It was ages ago, huh?

She says Yeah.

I ask her How old're you, again?

She rolls her eyes and says Yeah, ok. But age is relative. Then she hands it back to me and looks real serious all of a sudden. Older, for sure. She tells me I can imagine you're here for information. But I've got a certain reputation to uphold, you know?

So I says You're gonna tell me you can't tell me all that much on accounta you got discretions, am I right?

She nods.

225

I says to her People keep sayin that to me.

She suggests it's on accounta I got friends got a lotta honor.

I suggests to her No, that definitely ain't it.

She smiles a little, then unsmiles. She tells me Here's everything I'm willing to tell you. So please don't ask me any follow-up questions, because that's just going to be awkward for both of us. Ok?

I says Ok.

She sighs and says Ok. Paul Pezet isn't his real name, I remember that. He came to me, gosh, maybe four years ago?

I says Ages.

She waves that away and says He moved here from out west somewhere. Hears about me, I didn't ask how. Doesn't really matter to me. What mattered was, he came looking for a new identity strong enough to conduct business with. He'd burned more than a few bridges under his birth name, but had no intention of removing his straw from the myriad milkshakes into which he'd stuck it. So I gave him Paul Pezet. And that's all I can tell you.

I says On accounta your scruples and discretions.

She says That's right.

I says You can't tell me what was his real name.

She says Right.

I says Even though he's dead and ain't gonna mind.

So she says It's the principle, see. If I'm happy to burn somebody's identity after they're dead, that's going to tell prospective clients that if they get rubbed out,

I won't think twice about jeopardizing their family or any other dependents they'd been sheltering under the new name.

So I ask her How many dependents has Pezet got?

She tells me I don't know, but that's not the point.

I recall to her The point is the principle.

She says Yeah.

I also recall And the precedent.

She says Uh-huh.

So I stare at her a really long time. Squintin like she's her own fake papers.

I like Odette. She's real smart and real nice and real good at her job. I'm feelin pretty fuckin pissed at her right now, on accounta she's makin simple shit hard for me and callin it professional discretions like everybody else in my fuckin life. But I also get that I'm bumpin up against the same discretions're gonna be coverin me should somebody ain't my pal come knockin on her door. I'm just pretty fuckin pissed on accounta I happen to be gettin put out by the scruples just now. So even if I *do* wanna punch her into a sharin mood, I know that ain't an option. Also on accounta I learned some fuckin lessons in the Ring and a guy's learned lessons don't punch his buddies, speakin generally.

So I says to her You like me bein a customer?

She tells me Sure I do. You're one of my best. She says that with a tone like she's givin me a bit of a shine for seein her so often lately.

I ignore that and says to her Well, I don't get to the bottom of this Pezet shit, I might not be purchasin your quality fuckin wares anymore. And maybe I'll haveta tell folks, you don't wanna be dealin with Odette Muntry, she's some kinda bad news.

She looks real hurt by that. I wanna tell her I'm sorry on accounta I don't like makin her look real hurt, but I can't do that yet.

She says to me That's a shitty thing to say, Samuzzo.

So I tell her I'm sorry on accounta I don't like makin you look hurt. But I got a problem's got a solution sittin in your fuckin head, collectin head dust. And on accounta I ain't gonna punch it outta ya, I gotta lean on ya through the fuckin free market.

She don't look convinced so I keep talkin, sayin Listen, these are circumstances been extentuated. I ain't lookin to make this a habit. I can't make a fuckin figure on what do you figure me as, specially right now, but for you I got a big heart. You're a pal to me. I'm just askin you, one pal to I gotta hope another, for a favor.

Now she's startin to get a gleam in her eye. She asks me A favor? Would you say, then, that you'd owe me a favor in return?

Oof. I ain't a fan of owin favors on accounta the person feels owed always comes back with somethin ain't in the same league as the thing they done for you to get the favor. I got lucky Janis only asked I helped her mom out, though I figure Janis figures helpin her mom out's a lot worse than it is. But I got a feelin I ask Odette to say a name to me for a favor, she's gonna come back askin me can I rig who gets to squeeze out the next Dalai Lama.

But that's gonna be then, whereas now's now. So I tell her Yeah. You tell me Pezet's real name, I'm gonna keep fuckin mum about it, *and* I'm gonna owe you a favor.

She ain't done though, she asks me And you'll be recommending me to any close confidants who express an interest in personal rebranding?

I says Yeah yeah. You got me over a fuckin barrel. Why don't we let's hear the name already.

She tells me Greg Horowitz.

And for that, I gotta be in her fuckin debt? I'll tell ya, I ain't sure did I ever meet a scruple I really got on with.

WALLY'S the kinda pal who somebody talks shit about him and all you can really say is Yeah, but he's a pal. He's a good guy, don't get me wrong. He's just the kinda guy's good in spite of his bad, ya know?

So like here's a for instance. Wally calls me up for a how's-it-goin and I says to him Real glad ya called, I got somethin I wanna run by you.

He says to me Ok, shoot.

I says to him Not on the phone.

Now I don't figure anybody's standin over his shoulder pushin their fuckin cheek up to his, but I wanna be extra careful on accounta I said to Odette about here's my word and I'll do ya the free fuckin favor that I ain't gonna go blabbin nothin she told me if I ain't gotta. Ain't sure I can say I'm honorin that if I ain't lookin a fella in the eyes. And even puttin all the Odette shit to one outtatheway, I wanna be lookin at Wally's face for when do I say Greg Horowitz at him.

So he says to me Oh, ok.

And I says How about I swing by yours?

He says I'm actually, uh, busy just now.

I says Well can it wait?

He says Not really.

I says The hell are you up to over there?

He says Over where?

I says Your place.

He says I'm not at my place.

Then I says Where are ya?

He tells me Um…also not on the phone.

So I says Then why the hell'd ya call me for?

He says to me I thought it'd be safe to talk!

I have a big old sigh and I says to him Ok, well, how about we figure a place for meetin ain't either of ours, and what's ok to say on the phone?

And he says I mean…now that we've indicated to anybody who might be listening that we're both engaged in things we'd rather not discuss on the phone, it seems ill-advised to tell them exactly where we're going to be next, right?

To that I says …Wally.

So he says Alright, alright. How about…how about we meet at the place we met when I told you I maybe had mentioned your propensity to startle to my legal representation?

I gotta think about that for a second. Then I ask him

Which one was that?

He says to me I...I can't say without just telling them where it is.

I says to him I don't figure there's gotta be a *them* there.

He says Then why did you not wanna talk on the phone?

I says I'm just bein cautious on accounta I gotta keep this thing I gotta ask you on the mumside for a friend of mine.

So he says I get that, I'm just trying to keep the thing *I'm* doing quiet, for my own sake.

I tell him There ain't no *them* listenin. I was only doin the due diligencies.

He says Well then say your thing.

I says to him Why?

He tells me If there's no *them* listening, *definitely* no *them* listening, then you should be happy to say your thing.

I says The word *definitely* never came outta my mouth.

He says Then we can't be sure whether or not there's a *them* listening.

I says I mean like a hundred percent sure? I ain't never been a hundred percent sure of fuckin nothin in my life.

He says So to err on the side of caution, we should maybe assume that there *is* a *them* listening.

I says Wally.

He says I just have to be careful about these things,

you know?

I says Wally.

He says Yeah?

I says Maybe I call you back at yours in an hour, you can be not doin the thing you ain't gonna tell me about on the phone?

He says Well now *them*'re just gonna know to start listening again in an hour.

I says Then how's this, I'll never fuckin call you again. Now *them*'s gonna know they ain't gotta listen ever again.

He says I think *them*'re smarter than that, Sammy.

So I hang up and go to his fuckin house.

He don't open the door, so I let myself in. I call for him up the stairs and he says to me I'll be down in a minute. He says this to me when the sun's still up. Ain't til 4 in the fuckin A.M he comes downstairs. Skippin two steps at a time like he found his virginity and can't wait to lose it again. He sees my face, and lemme tell ya I'm makin a fuckin *face* at him, his skip barely dips.

I ask him What're you so fuckin skippy on?

He tells me You heard about Armstrong joining the Fletcher Henderson?

I says to him One more time?

He says Louie Armstrong. The Fletcher Henderson Orchestra. You've heard of them.

I shake my head like no I ain't heard of em.

He says You've heard this song, right? Then he starts makin root-a-toot-toot noises with his mouth.

234

And then I says I ain't never heard a song even the singer can't remember the words.

He shrugs and tells me Well, Armstrong joined the Fletcher Henderson Orchestra. They're over at the Roseland. Very hot ticket. Some of the hottest tickets in town. And when I say the Roseland, I should add, I mean the *big* room at the Roseland. Not one of the little ones. They're too big to play the little ones. Fame-wise. They're normal sized people.

I tell him So what, ya asked a girl to go the fuckin Opry with ya and she had a think about it prior to she said No?

To that he says Ha ha, no. I'm happy because as mentioned, those tickets are some of the hottest tickets in town this year. And I own eighty five percent of them, to be resold at the astronomical markup of my choosing.

I says Jesus, Wally. How the hell'd you manage that?

I quit listenin on accounta I remember about I don't give a shit. I just tune back in for the end bit where Wally starts clappin and he says I own eighty-five percent of the hottest tickets in town. The rate I'm jacking the price up, if I sell even *twenty* percent of my tickets, I break even. The rest is pure profit!

I says Ain't Fletch and friends gonna be pretty fuckin stumped their sold out show's only thirty-five percent full?

Wally shakes his head and says Less.

I says No, you said you got eighty five, and eighty

He says I see what you did, but the twenty percent I

just mentioned was of the eighty-five, not one hundred. So that'd probably be, like, a little under six percent of the full hundred.

I says How's that?

He says Well I'm just doing approximations in my head to make it easier, but if you

I says to him That ain't why'm I lookin to twist your ear, though.

He looks kinda disappointed he ain't gonna get to do math at me. He says Alright. Well.

I says Listen, that's real swell about the Flick Strongman tickets. I ain't lookin to rain on your fuckin parade. It's only just I'm bein some kinda scattered on accounta I got my own parade I'm runnin, and it's gettin some rain on it and I'm tryna figure where from. But I ain't lookin to fuckin detract from your parade, or rain on it, or what the fuck.

He gets all smiley like it ain't 4 in the fuckin A.M. and he says to me No sweat, my friend. Why don't you come on up, we'll have us a nightcap and get down to business?

I don't figure it's a nightcap at this fuckin hour, but mornincap don't got quite the same ring. So I just says to him Sounds like a plan, pal.

WALLY'S pad's not what ya might expect. I mean, I dunno what're you expectin. But it probably ain't what's he got.

What's he got's a real tasteful fuckin cottage-lookin thing with a kinda nice view in an alright parta town. He keeps the place clean, but south of spotless. Real middle of the road furnishments. He lets his Saint Bernard he calls Rooster walk all over em, but he's got a towel's some kinda useful for dabbin up slobber he lays down. It's just a nice, unmemorable place is what I'm sayin. Which maybe ain't what you'd expect for a guy's got all kindsa quirks and the money to indulge em. Or maybe that's just fuckin precisely what you was expectin on accounta I already told you he don't spend the money. I don't fuckin know what were you expectin, but shame on you for prejudgin a man's livin quarters.

Anyway Wally's pad is borin as shit, so I pour us two drinks look like the pee of a guy's had more'n two drinks. I take em over to Wally's couch, only Rooster's takin up the whole thing. So I hand Wally his and we just kinda stand there between the carpet part of his livin room and hardwood part.

He says Cheers and shows me his drink. I says to him Cheers and my drink gives his drink a little kiss. Then we drink our drinks, just standin there while Rooster's droolin at us on the couch.

Way I figured this'd go, we'd shoot the shit for a while, then I'd jump right in. Only the best segue into shit-shootin is you flop back into a comfy chair and you says Aaaahhh, then you start shootin shit. It's like a transition. Aaaahhh. Now we're relaxin.

Only we ain't got that transition on accounta it ain't kosher sittin on a dog, even one looks like a comfy chair, so there ain't no line between we're walkin in and we're settled. It's fucked up.

So I says to him You remember Paul Pezet?

He asks me Is this what you didn't want to say on the phone?

I says Yeah.

He says Yeah.

I says Huh?

He says I was answering your question.

I says Does your dog wanna get off the fuckin couch?

He says Probably not. He really likes the couch.

I says So do I.

Wally sips his drink and says It's really comfy.

I says Almost seems like a waste, we're standin here and the dog's got the couch.

He says We can sit over there. Then he points to some borin fuckin chairs at his stupid fuckin table.

I says Nah.

He says Why not?

I says It ain't about sittin. It's about who's in charge.

Wally gets this smile on his face and he says So you're literally standing on principle, aren't you? Eh? Get it?

That's enough of that shit. I cut to the chase at him and I says So you remember Paul Pezet. I ain't gotta remind you who's Paul Pezet.

He says to me No.

So I says Ok, well turns out Paul Pezet ain't Paul Pezet. Turns out Paul Pezet's Greg Horowitz. That's his real name, I'm sayin.

Wally's forehead frowns.

I says to him That name ringin a bell for ya? Greg Horowitz?

Wally's havin a good think about that til he says You know…it is. I remember the name, but I can't remember where from. Um… Then he holds his drink at me and says Hold this. I do and he scampers, fuckin *scampers* down the hall.

I tell the counter the hold these drinks and I walk over to the couch. I sit on the edge of it's got Rooster's head. I look at the hound. Hound looks at me. We both look at each other while Wally's crashin around the other room.

We only quit makin eyes at each other when Wally comes crashin back into this room. He's got a paper in his hands what he hands in to my hands. I give it a fuckin looksee. Greg's name just about jumps off the page and doinks me in the eyes. So I look at the top of the page. Then I keep lookin up at Wally and I says The pyramid gag. On accounta that's what's this a list of.

He says Yeah.

The sheet what he gave me's only got H names on it. Hop-Hos names. There's gotta be a hundred names on this piece of paper, written real fuckin small. I can't even make up a fuckin number for how many people did Wally rope into his scheme ain't yet got called the Ponzi. But I ain't gotta make up the numbers for how much're these hundred-odd suckers out for.

Greg Horowitz, he's down a cool quarter million.

I says to Wally You musta had a lotta fuckin marks.

He says This was 1919 though. Ages ago. He says it like he's sayin sorry, like he didn't hear what the fuck I just said.

I says to him Age is relative.

Wally folds his arms and says That's my bad, man. I really thought I wasn't connected to this guy. I had no idea he'd changed his name.

I tell Wally Ah, cut that off. Ain't like I knew neither. I'm just fuckin remarkabled by your memory. How the hell'd you remember one name outta the list from quote ages ago unquote?

He says I didn't. Not specifically, anyway. I just keep

240

very good records.

I stare at the sheet for a minute. Ain't ever somethin I pegged Wally for, keepin very good records. Only I figure now, ya wanna keep all your gags straight, ya probably gotta have some kinda fuckin system.

So I says to him So you got an alphabetized list of everybody you ever scammed or what? Figurin that for half a joke.

He shrugs and says to me Easiest way to keep track of everybody who might have a grudge against me.

I get another one of my omens now. A big one. I says to him Can I glance at your fuckin dewey decimals?

He says My room's kind of a mess right now. But, hang on. Then he runs back outta the room. I look at Rooster again. He's done with me. More interested in the fuckin wall.

Wally comes back in with an armful of fuckin looseleaf. His 1919 pyramid punks. I start lookin lookin lookin, only I ain't findin what'm I lookin for. I'm frownin fit to set fire on his fuckin papers when Wally pats me on the shoulder and asks me 1920 or 1921?

I says to him 1920, and Wally goes and gets me the 1920 names.

This time I ain't gotta go lookin lookin lookin. Just two lookins, and I see the name.

Son of a bitch.

I'm a little bit annoyed, on accounta I coulda put this all to bed a while back if I'd thought to ask Wally did he remember *this* name's out for half a fuckin million. But whatever. We're here now.

Wally sees me smilin, he asks me what am I smilin about.

I says to him I got the who, the what and the why.

He asks me How?

I says I'm frettin more on the where.

GO FIGURE

I could give Godric a ring on accounta now I know he ain't somebody I ain't gotta not trust no more. Only...I wanna have this shit all wrapped up when I give him a ring. He ain't gonna believe I done all this figurin on my own, and I don't wanna give him a chance to figure somethin I ain't figured and then he gets to figure he figured more than he did.

So instead I call up Operator and I ask em When's a guy named Denver Eustis gonna be anywhere, or where's he live or what? That don't get me far so I ask Daff for help. Her help is I oughta ask Janis for help. I tell her This is the thing with askin for help, it only makes you need more help. Daff tells me there's a difference between needin it and welcomin it, only she don't elaborate.

So I call Janis up and for some howcome she's the one pickin up, instead of Reception. So I says to her I'm tryin to figure out when's Denver Eustis gonna be anywhere, or where's he live or what. And she says to me I'm sorry, who is this? And I says to her It's Samuzzo. And she says to me Oh. Um, hang on.

Then I'm on hold for a while. Then she comes back and says Forgive me Mr. D'Amato, but may I ask why you're calling me?

I explain to her I'm tryin to figure out when's Denver Eustis gonna be anywhere, or where's he live or what.

She says Yes. I heard you. I'm more referring to the fact that we had completed our quid pro quo, and with that our business was concluded. Is this business you're conducting on Mr. Zwillbin's behalf?

I says to her Yeah. On accounta that ain't totally a lie.

She asks me So if I call Mr. Zwillbin, he will know precisely the purpose for which you are calling me?

So I says No, it's a surprise. So don't call him on accounta then you'd ruin the fuckin surprise.

She sounds like she's in a tornado for a second, then she says Mr. D'Amato, I'm very appreciative that you're…you've been very decent to my mother. More decent than I believe she deserves.

I says Oh, she's a cuddly old fruit bat. What'd she do to you, huh? Forget to take you to the fair?

Janis' voice gets real quiet now, so I gotta imagine her turnin her head away like we're in a fuckin Shakespeare while shes sayin It's…beyond the scope of this conversation, and let's leave it there. Her voice gets back to regular volume when she says to me What I'm getting at is, another exchange of favors has suddenly occurred to me, thanks to your unexpected call. So I'll pretend I believe you're doing this for Wally, and

I interrupt her and says I am though.

She says I'm going to choose to believe that.

I says No I mean, I really am.

She says And so you are.

So I says Your voice's still rollin around.

She says That's sarcasam, Mr. D'Amato.

I says to her Why ain't you listenin to me?

She says I am.

I says No, but you ain't, you figure I'm being a wisenheimer.

She says Aren't you?

I says No!

She says Oh. Well, ok, but, um, people who special-ize in the extralegal such as yourself typically disguise intentions, levy threats, or avail themselves of plausible deniability through irony.

So I says to her …

And she says Yes, well. Ok. What I was laying the groundwork for was another quid pro quo. I will help you out with finding Denver Eustis, which will in point of fact benefit Mr. Zwillbin in some way. And in return, I would like you to terminate communication with my mother.

So I says to her …?

She says As I may have mentioned, I believe you have accorded her more decency than is her just port-ion. I would like to see that decency brought to an end.

I says Jesus Janis. That's your own ma! She's a swell enough lady, you get past all the insults.

I can hear Janis's mouth gapin open, words garglin around her throat. What she finally comes out with is Does her needling feel good-natured to you? Chummy?

I says Sure.

She says Perhaps you should consider that, in just the way I mistook your sincerity for irony, you are making a similar mistake with my mother. I would also ask you to consider the fact that you have not the least idea what lies behind those…superficial cracks of her.

I shudder and says to her Never heard a daughter talkin about her ma's superficial cracks weren't licensed to practice.

Janis asks me A joke?

I tell her Yeah.

She says Just checking.

I ain't feelin at my easy with this, turnin my back on Agnes just like nothin. She mighta fucked up Janis somewise I can't even figure, but there's plenty of folks you ask em is Samuzzo D'Amato a good guy, they'll say Hell no, on accounta I knocked em around some. I figure me for a good guy though. You just gotta ask the right folks.

Or get to know me, right? What the fuck?

So I says Ok. Only I tell myself I'm sayin Ok to Janis sayin Just checking, and not to her sayin I gotta quit chattin with Agnes.

Janis says to me Just so we're clear, you're agreeing to cease all communication with my mother, in return for my locating Mr. Eustis for you?

Ah, shit. I says to her Yeah.

Then I hear a little wet noise at the end of the line.

A smile's another kinda superficial crack, when ya think about it. So I guess it ain't just fingertappin runs in the family.

Go Figure

I'm figurin she's gonna get me Eustis' lobbyin schedule, so it'd just say shit like CAPITOL – 0600, HEARING – 0730, BATHROOM – 0900, then I'd have to creep myfuckinself into a government buildin and it'd be a big fuckin headache and I'd probably end up burnin Frank Patricks along with the other one for good measure. Whaddyacallim. Douglas Barker.

Instead, I don't know how come I ain't thoughta this priorwise when Godric's givin me Denver's lobbyin schedule, or come to think on it how come Godric didn't come to think on it: Janis gets me Denver's home address. Lives in Virginia. Right outside D.C. No shit, right?

So Frank Patricks buys a car and drives on out, only this time he checks double checks fuckin *triple* checks

249

he ain't goin west. He gets where he wants to go in a day, ain't even gotta stop to take a leak not once.

Denver Eustis' house looks like its got blueprints were drawn by a second grader. Blue sides, orange roof, square windows and a big white door with a nice yard and a garage thrown in. Betcha anythin his real estate hookup's got a beehive for a haircut.

Gotta say, ain't what'd I picture for a big-time lobbyist. Only maybe he ain't so big time, he's out rattlin branches for Big Grocery. Gotta figure that's why's he still smartin, ten years on, about how'd he get stiffed, about how'd he get fuckin pyramided. Only he ain't mad at me. Smart money's on he don't even remember me.

Well, we'll find out real soon, huh?

Now when we're talkin a stake-out, even on a good day, there ain't no good days. I ain't no good at blendin in. Ain't like I can scoot my seat back and lay down. And anyway, if I'm sittin in a car, the car's tiltin my way. You can see it from outside. First time Wally saw me in a car, he couldn't talk for the fuckin giggles. Some cars, I take a left turn too hard and I'm shellin out for a new side mirror.

So I can't just park across the street and watch his house. It's a fuckin grassy-lawn neighborhood. I'm gonna stick out like a thumb on a fish. This place ain't never seen nobody my size weren't being projected on a sheet over top a guy playin piano. First I'm thinkin I'm gonna just keep circlin the block, only then I see I ain't seein cars. Creepy guy parked is intimidatin, but maybe you just cross the street and leave him be. Creepy guy cruisin around a neighborhood's a sex pervert, maybe. Now the cops're gettin lotta calls from folks want em to meet me.

But I gotta keep eyes on the house. I gotta know when's he leavin, when's he comin back. I could hit him there, yeah, only I ain't lookin to fuck with his family. That's heat I ain't courtin, and besides, I ain't gonna wager they got the slightest fuckin clue this guy's on my case. Assumin he is. I'm pretty near fuckin sure. Only I wanna hear him hear me sayin it to him, then he says Yes, or Yep, or Yeah. Just somethin's affirmative so's I can says Your goose is cooked, then I'm pullin his teeth outta my knuckles. Only that line don't make *so* much sense since he might nota known about that goosin rumor at all. Ah, what's he gonna do, keep livin on accounta he don't like the sign-off? Fuck him.

Assumin.

Which as it happens is what the fuck I'm gonna be round this place. On accounta *un*assumin ain't an option. Only I ain't lookin to be *so* assumin folks start rememberin my face, maybe recall they seen a Picasso version in the daily rag. Body, I can't fuckin help that. Face, why'm I gonna go givin em a good look? So anyway, it ain't like I can just stomp around the fuckin neighborhood, orbitin this one house, until Pezet goes somewhere I can follow him and ask him a few questions I might already got the answers to.

No sweat. I got a next-best to the door-to-door.

I drive into D.C., followin the rails. Every stop, I get

out, go into the train station and have a look-see do they got a bulletin board or what. First station they got one's full of shit. Pamphlet askin You want some X-ray specs. X's too fuckin goofy a letter, and anyway, canvassin ain't for cuttin-edge technologies, don't believe what the guys wanna sell you a fuckin vacuum say. Rest of em are just coupons, pull tab pages for do you wanna buy my dresser, that shit. Second station, more of the same. Third station too. Four stations on, sun's goin down and I'm startin to get mighty fuckin frustrated.

Oh, lo and befuckinhold! The very thing what was I lookin for. Poster's got a real good drawin of a dog on it. Tiny little cute one, too. Couldn'ta asked for one better. On top of the drawin says LOST DOG. On bottom says too fuckin much. Basically it's Hey I can't find my dog, it's called Crunch and it's real fuckin friendly, kinda scared of people til it gets to know em, loves food, wary of communists, etfuckincetera, bring it back and I'll bung ya twenty bucks. Which like, Jesus, you budget twenty bucks for your best buddy? Maybe Crunch ain't so great after all. Assumin Crunch's still in the present tense.

But whatever, Crunch'll do for me. So I unpin the poster and go to a store got pen and paper and I buy a buncha both. They got a table too, which I ain't got in my car, so I make myself fuckin comfy and get crackin on copyin the poster a hundred times. I ain't gonna be able to copy the drawin of the dog too pretty, but what the hell, my artisticals ain't done with a brush.

The lady behind the counter comes around and sees

what'm I doin with my purchase. She says to me I'm so sorry to hear about Crunch. I hope you find him!

My pen says Scr, Scr on the fuckin page.

I says to her Cost of livin around here's pretty high, huh?

Scr, Scr.

She says to me Um…do you not live around here?

Scr, Scr.

I says I'm just bein rhetorical.

Scr, Scr.

She says Ah! So I shouldn't answer.

Scr, Scr.

I says That ain't what I mean.

Scr, Scr.

She says But…that is what *rhetorical* means.

Scr, Scr.

I says Ah, hell. What's the word what'm I lookin for?

Scr, Scr.

She says I'm not totally sure.

Scr, Scr.

I says Well anyway, I'm just sayin. Twenty bucks ain't gonna carry you across many finish lines round here, right?

Scr, Scr.

She shrugs and says Well, that depends. That could be groceries for, I don't know, a week or two.

Scr, Scr.

I laugh on accounta I gotta appreciate the coincidence about the groceries.

Scr, Scr.

Then she says to me Twenty isn't nothing, that's for sure. If it's all you can spare…

Scr, Scr.

I says to her No way's that all can I spare. You give me a sheet and some plastic cement, I'll take twenty *thousand* fuckin banknotes, build a boat out of em and shove it down the Potomac without even wavin goodbye. I got more money'n I know how to burn. Twenty's nothin.

Scr, Scr.

She just stares at my pen like it's whisperin somethin to her.

Scr, Scr.

I ain't used to people don't say nothin after I do the tough guy thing at em, so I lean on it and I says to her Crunch was a shit dog. Crunch was a piece of shit. Crunch is what I hope his skull says while a garbage truck's rollin over it.

Scr, Scr.

She's listenin real hard to what's my pen tellin her.

Scr, Scr.

I figure I might leaned a bit too hard.

Scr, Scr.

I figure I got another funny somethin to say, only I snap outta it and realize I ain't sure why'm I doin this. It started off like it was gonna be a funny somethin, like a funny somethin toughs do. Intimidatin the locals. Buildin your legend. Kinda thing we all grab a beverage and have a fuckin reminiscence on. Classic bruiser shit. I figured I was doin one of them things when I started bullshittin this lady. Only now I ain't enjoyin it so much. Why'd I figure this'd be fun?

Scr, Scr.

By fuckin golly if I don't have a thought I ain't never figured on thinkin before. I think, What would the fellas down at Paci-FIST say about what'm I up to, hm?

Scr, Scr.

I says to her Ah, I'm sorry. I'm just kiddin ya. I got a rotten sense of humor. Sometimes I'm some kinda fuckin stinker, I ain't afraid to say so. Bein realwise, I ain't got all that much money. But I do got a lotta love for Crotch.

Scr, Scr.

She says Crunch.

Scr, Scr.

I says Those ain't two words I like hearin so close together, ya know?

Scr, Scr.

She don't say nothin.

Scr, Scr.

I says Sorry. Sometimes it ain't easy to tell serious from irony. Even when's it comin outta your own mouth.

Scr, Scr.

I says Ya know?

Scr, Scr.

I pay more attention to what'm I drawin and turns out I been done with the poster for a while now. I'm just rerunnin the circle makes Crunch's head, over'n over'n over.

GO FIGURE

I take my fuckin duplicates and cruise back out to Eustis' part of town, only by then it's got dark so I'm back to lookin like a sex pervert. So I cruise right back the way where'd I come from, only this time lookin for a place to lay my weary fuckin head. I find a one-story dump's got a pool *and* breakfast. What a steal.

Frank Patricks pays cash and gets the key to room four. That's how you know the joint's classy, when you got the single digit digs. Frank Patricks says Thanks to the desk jockey, then Samuzzo D'Amato heads off to room four. Hey, not bad – they got a paper waitin for Frank on the fuckin threshold. So he, and I'm talkin bout me now just to be clear, me...*I* plop down in a piece of wood's been cracked into right angles so's it could hang out with real chairs and I snap open the pages to see what's funny. Ain't much funny. Democrats're gonna run a fella called John Davis, which sounds to me bout as real as Frank Patricks. Some new piece of paper says *ain't nobody mad at the Turks no more* got all signed up by the Brits. Same old same old. So I fold up the paper and pull out that piece of paper Godric doodled on way back when. Umbrellas coverin up letters. Crazy to me, I got this whole big umbrella chain of *this* union and *that* interest linkin me up with Eustis, and ain't none of it matters. The way I figure it at least. Yeah, I got this all figured out, and all that matters is Pezet, er, Horowitz, he's got a friend in Eustis. Both of em, they're after Wally on accounta he got em in his fuckin pyramid and they musta figured it out somehow. I'm only in this as a by-the-way.

The way I figure.

Not the way Godric figured.

Most times, I'd be all sortsa on board for followin Godric's gut prior to my own. But…I dunno…

So I get to a phone's plonked on the wall right outside the door to my room and I give Daff a ring, on accounta I gotta talk to somebody I got the trust-worthies for. We have a lovely fuckin yak ain't none of your fuckin business, then at the end she says to me I gotta call Agnes on accounta she's been ringin the safehouse round the clock. I ask her How'd Agnes get the fuckin digits for the safeplace?

Daff says I don't know, but she *definitely* has them. Then Daff gives me some digits for Agnes ain't the same as Agnes' last digits. That's fuckin weird. So I give Agnes a ring ain't got no Resolution about it, and she answers and she just makes a noise like a fuckin sea creature.

I says Huh?

Agnes says Huh? Huh? I called you up to hear Huh, did I?

I says to her You didn't call me, I called *you*, and I ain't even supposed to!

Which is true. Ah, shit. I forgot. I have a think for a second on what'm I gonna say. Janis kinda made me promise I wouldn't say nothin to her ma no more, and I ain't the kinda person breaks promises like they're wishbones. But Agnes's never done me crosswise.

So I says to her Janis told me I ain't supposed to talk to ya, Agnes.

She don't say nothin for a while. Then her voice gets real quiet and she says That ungrateful little shit. Then even further away another voice says somethin. Then Agnes' voice, still faraway only not as faraway as the further away voice, says Lemme ask. Then Agnes' voice crawls all the way back into the phone and she asks me Why's that, then?

I ask her Who's there with ya? Where are ya?

She says Sorry, was that my question echoing around your empty fucking skull?

I laugh on accounta I figure she's joshin, only then I remember what'd Janis say to me. So I quit laughin and I ask Agnes What's up?

She says to me You're on the news, that's what's up.

So I says You already told me that. I guess you forgot. And we say *in* for the paper. I ain't *on* the paper,

I'm *in* the

And she interrupts me and says Wow, I must have silly putty for brains if I've already lost a call I placed to you since you got to Virginia.

I says to her First of all, I placed this fuckin call to *you*. And secondwise, how'd you figure I'm in Virginia?

She says *Now* who's forgetting shit? You got a radio wherever you're at?

I says Ooooh. *On* the news. The radio news.

Lucky for me I recall there's a dinky fuckin plinker in the corner of my room. Maybe this ain't the fleabag I figured it for. Huh!

I let the phone hang and run in my room and click the radio and fiddle with the knob.

There's another rat-a-tat bastard sayin words I know right away ain't his. It's a fuckin quote. He's quotin the lady watched me make copies of those fuckin posters. When I was talkin shit, tryin to get all tough and funny like a bruiser's meant to, she was thinkin back to a sketch she saw in the paper. I didn't figure that sketch'd be showin up this far from Jersey, but I guess I fuckin figured wrong. Then I go and I say somethin about a truck runnin over a dog, she puts it together. This here's Michael Berns, guy the funny pages says killed cops and Paul Pezet and how much time ya got.

So I says to the radio Godfuckindamnit! But I do kinda appreciate my good timin on turnin the thing on just when're they talkin about me.

The phone what's hangin on its cord out my door yells Don't talk to me like that! in Agnes' voice.

GO FIGURE

I go out and pick up the talkin horn and I says to her I wasn't talkin to you, you old bear trap!

She says Well then who's there with ya?

I hang up on accounta I'm sick of the fuckin echos.

Ok. I gotta think. Now they're gonna be lookin for Michael Berns in Virginia. That's gonna make tailin Eustis even harder. Maybe I just lay low, and ah shit, apparently whoever runs this joint's real big on current fuckin events. Newspaper at the door, radio in the room.

Probably don't much matter what'd I tell him my name was.

So what do I do? Sit tight and pray like I figure it might do somethin?

Course not. I brought nothin with me here, so I can leave with nothin. All I gotta get's the lost dog posters outta my room, and I'm walkin away from it like before. Which, *FUCK*, the car's registered to Frank Patricks.

I turn around and see a cop car pullin in. Ain't runnin its gumdrops. Which means it's here on accounta coincidence...*or*, it's tryin to creep.

Sure as shit, the old fella jockeyin desk loves his current fuckin events, and he's got a quick finger on the dial.

I dial Daff's number and make her disappointed in me again.

She says Hello?

I says I hope you ain't makin music.

She says What? Only it ain't so much a question as that.

I says Frank Patricks mighta met an untimely demise.

She says Wh…F…might have?

I look over my shoulder a little bit. Old fella's heaved himself out from behind the desk. He's talkin to the cops. Nobody's pointin my way, but only on accounta they ain't gotta.

Shit.

I says to Daff Yeah, Franky bit the big one.

She says What did you do this time? Did you hurt anyone?

I says to her No, I didn't flip no fuckin cars or nothin. I mean, I got folks I *wanna* flip a car on, only I ain't done it yet. But I fucked up with the verbals this time. I was tryin to be a fuckin big tough bruiser. I blew it, Daff. I'm real sorry.

She starts sayin Fucking shit, only she don't get further than Fucking sh prior to the phone decides it don't wanna hear no more of that kinda talk.

Just rotten, that's how I feel. Mostly on accounta I let Daff down again.

But then I go back to my room to grab the fuckin dog posters and now I got a new reason to feel rotten. This one's on accounta I'm in a motel room with only one window's facin the same fuckin direction as the door, and that's a door's got cops on the other side.

I maybe shoulda left the posters, huh?

I have a little peek out the window.

Oh, good. Here's another cop car.

GO FIGURE

WORST thing I can do is stand here wonderin what'm I gonna do. Every second I'm scratchin my chin, that's another second the cops got to yell numbers at each other. Numbers that're code for shit like More guys pronto or more cars pronto or airplane pronto, just different stuff they want done real fast. Hey, you know they got an airplane? Not these ones, the cops I mean, but the New York blueshirts? They got an airplane! The fuck're they gonna do with an airplane? Wild. But that don't matter much for this present fuckin predicament.

Anyway, they're yellin numbers and less I wanna get sliced up by bullets sized like carrots what they shoot outta the plane, I better be faster'n the numbers.

Actually, now that I'm havin a think on it, worst thing I can do's open the door and surrender. But even then, that ain't as worst as runnin a bath and drownin myself. There's all kindsa stuff worse than me standin here wonderin what'm I gonna do.

Lotsa stuff's better though.

Ok, so what do we got?

Outside we got four cops maybe twenty yards away. Three of em are outside their cars. One of em, passenger on the one just pulled in, he's sittin there with his arms folded like Dad brought him to meet the special lady's gonna be his New Ma. The old desk jockey fella fuckin narced on me's out there with em. I see some lookieloos pokin outta their rooms. And then we got me. I brought nothin in with me. I got nothin can shoot or stab or spray. I just got me. So far, I ain't never found that wantin. So far.

That's figurin I got em within huggin distance though. I pop out that door and start tryin to close the distance we *do* got, they'll pull out their peashooters on accounta they can't hang on for the carrotshooters in the plane, and plug me before I got both feet on concrete. Peas or carrots, either way it's veggies for old Samuzzo.

Other option's wait til they get close before I pop out, but I got no guarantees that's happenin prior to the funny helmet brigade shows up and knocks on my door with somethin's longer than it is wide.

So I gotta make up a third maybe'll close the distance without wastin time.

Ok.

I rip the comforter off the bed and wrap it around

my head. Just tryin not to think of how much biology I got crawlin around my seat of fuckin consciousness right now. I ain't so sure this quilt ain't one giant fuckin single-celled germ.

Before I open the door I crouch down low as I can without scrapin my knuckle on the ground. I keep my head down, give myself fuckin lice by pullin the cumforter up over my hair, then I scream as high pitched as I can.

I ain't got the voice of an angel, but considerin most people'd figure my voice is how them heads on Easter Island'd talk, mainly the tones, probably not so much the words, but I'm sayin at least my high scream don't sound quite like that. Sounds like the He's *safe* might come outta the big umpire Jesus they're buildin in Rio.

Then I swing the door open and scramble out, keepin myself low as I can, body-wise. Voice-wise, I'm goin high as my pipe's'll humor me.

I have a little peek towards the cops. They're all lookin at me alright. Fourth guy's outta the car, even. Ready to meet a real special lady, yes sir.

Still high as I can, I shout at em He's in there! He's in there! I almost reach back and point, only they might start raisin eyebrows about the little lady's got arms like orangutans. Not arms like an orangutan's arms. Arms *like orangutans*.

Still shriekin at em, I am. I shriek He's unarmed! He's in there!

I look up and all four cops are runnin my way. Three of em's headin for the room. One of em's comin to see how's the big little lady holdin up.

The three run past me first. Then the one reaches me.

I throw off the blanket.

He makes a face like he just remembered the stove's on at home.

Then I reach him.

By the time I'm throwin him at his buddies, he's snorin through a bloody nose.

Go Figure

Now don't you go fuckin thinkin I killed nobody back in the parkin lot. I checked. Every one of em, once I'm done, I go around and put my pointerprints on their necks. All of em are doin the fuckin Charleston, pulsewise. I learned my onions with flippin the car. I was a good fuckin boy last night.

Come mornin, I'm back hangin Lost Dog posters round Eustis' part of town. Or maybe it ain't me. Maybe it's Frank Patricks. Actually nope, he's dead like I hope none of them four cops from the motel are. I really checked. I put my pointerprints on their necks and everythin. Though at this point, ya know, who gives a shit. I burned *myself*, on accounta I was tryin to be a cool guy or somethin. They already know I got a body count.

Only that ain't the kinda thing the boys from Paci-FIST'd wanna hear, now is it? That ain't the way I oughta be thinkin. Ain't done, for a fella to be goin around offin folks like there ain't no such thing as ethics, then call himself a good guy. That ain't a good guy. I'm a good guy. Therefuckinfore, that ain't me. So I gotta hope they ain't dead. I don't figure they are. Like I said, I checked.

I can't believe I'm even still thinkin about that stupid fuckin sharin circle as I'm hangin posters.

Only am I hangin em? Or is Douglas Barker hangin em? Is he still kickin? Did I do anythin tells folks he's some serious kinda pals with our dearly departed Franky boy? That fuckin murderer?

But anyway, wasn't it Frank Patricks and Michael Berns killed all those guys? It ain't like it was me done it. It ain't like it was Samuzzo D'Amato. Samuzzo's killed some guys, make no mistake. But he ain't killed no cops before. Well, he ain't killed *lotsa* cops. Not without gettin paid to play, anywise. That ain't the kinda thing Samuzzo'd do. But somebody did it. So who?

Am I just doin a whaddyacallit? Puttin distance between me and the thing? Whaddyacallit? Ah, hell.

Somethin behind me says Hey mister. Sounds creaky, like a rockin chair's sick of gettin sat on.

I finish staplin the poster to the tree, then I turn. Only not all the way. I knicked a pair of spectacles outta the pockets of one of those cops got real sleepy *but not dead* last night, so I don't look *totally* like the picture those cops from Pezet's house drew, and the new picture I'm sure the cops from the motel are drawin, on accounta they're for sure still alive goddamnit. But I'm close enough to the motel, folks're gonna be hearin bout me, keepin an eye out. I'm just really bankin on the lonely guy hangin a Lost Dog poster disarmin people's suspicions. I got no better ideas on how'm I gonna keep an eye on Eustis. And I gotta talk to him. I gotta. I gotta tell him I got it figured, he tells me I'm right, I tell him his goose is cooked, and then it's fuckin over. Him, I got no problem puttin his lights all the way out. He's got it comin, on accounta he's comin for my pal, and he had a stab at comin through me.

So yeah, I gotta be hangin the posters. *Somebody* does. Same somebody's wearin dopey glasses what got the glass popped out, half-turnin to talk to this squeaky little kid.

She looks up at let's just say me and asks me You lost your dog?

I wanna say to her No, I'm startin a band called Lost Dog, you play drums or what? Only then I remember where bein a wisenheimer got me last time. So I says to her Yeah. He was a good fuckin boy.

The girl says to me I think he still is. I think he's just confused and ran away.

I says Is that right? On accounta I got no clue how do ya talk to kids.

She says Yeah. I think he loves you, but he's just confused.

I says And ran away.

269

She says Yeah!

I says If he's confused, how come he didn't just stay put til he ain't confused no more? How're you gonna go runnin all over creation just on accounta you're confused?

She says Dogs don't think like us.

I says I don't figure most folks think like each other anyway, so that ain't no excuse.

She just nods about that. Too much fuckin wisdom in that nod. It's ghouly-like. Now I'm thinkin maybe she's some kinda therapist's got her birthdays all fucked up like the guy in the fuckin Fitzgerald story about the guy's born old then gets more and more a baby til he turns into a button. That one's got the word quote case unquote in the title, but it ain't about a fuckin detective. Just a warnin to ya.

I ask her You wanna help me find my dog?

She says Yeah! Only her eyes are still lookin like she knows prayers ain't real but she's playin along for her little brother.

I hand her a bunch of posters and I says to her Stick these up somewhere, will ya?

She asks me Where should I stick them?

I says Somewhere. Somewhere ain't here. I got here covered.

On accounta *here*'s got a clear bead on the Eustis place. I don't tell her that though.

She says I don't have any nails or anything. I, well, my dad has nails for fixing his bookshelf, but they're small so they bend sometimes and then he says bad words.

I says Oh, no shit?

She just says No and then keeps on talkin like she's heard it all before. What she keeps talkin about is she's sayin What should I stick them with?

I says I don't fuckin care. Bubble gum. Chew it up and stick it on. You got that at home?

She says to me Yeah. Then she goes home.

Which is right down the street.

I'm lookin right at it.

Can you guess which fuckin house it is?

I'll give ya a hint, rhymes with Blenver fuckin Blustis.

Can you believe that's Denver fuckin Eustis' kid?

I can. I gotta.

Fuck this. Fuck me not just goin inside. I'm sick of this shit. I'm sick of everythin's gotta be hard and confusin when it's really easy. I'm sick of Godric's drawin me diagrams don't mean shit when a straight line'd do it better. I'm sick of I'm drivin all over creation snappin up posters for some dead piece of shit dog I don't care about so's I can look at a guy's house, and all I got to show for it is wasted time, plus the money it's gonna cost to turn into yet *another* new son of a bitch, all these problems I wouldn't have fuckin had if I'd just gone bargin in to begin with. I'm sick of I gotta feel bad about throwin around some cops wanted to take me to a small room ain't got newspapers or radios in it, on accounta I got a little voice in my head called Crowder wonderin is this how we solve problems or what. I'm sick of bein confused about what's goin on and why's it goin on and who's makin it go on and do I gotta feel bad about it's goin on or what. Or fuckin what.

What I'm sayin is, I ain't just sick of this shit or that shit. I'm sick of *shit*.

And besides, not sittin around waitin for more shit is what got me outta the motel, right? So why ain't it gonna work now?

I head over to Denver Eustis' house. Try the knob on the door around the side to see is it locked.

It ain't. The handle turns. So I turn it.

I tromp through a mud room and then another door and now I'm in a kitchen. There's that little girl standin at a counter, talkin to a lady I gotta figure's her mom.

I says to the girl I thought you were gettin fuckin bubblegum?

Mom says to me What the f…get out!

I says Ah, sorry. I didn't figure we ain't cursin. You a Eustis?

She circles around a free-floatin counter like nothin I ever seen before and hugs her daughter from behind. She asks me Who are you?

I says to her Relax lady, I ain't lookin to hurt nobody.

The little kid tells Mom He's looking for his dog.

Gotta figure ain't no point leadin em on no more so I says to her Actually some poor fuc…some poor guy or gal a few miles east is lookin for their dog. That was a whaddyacallit.

Mom says A lie?

I says A pretense. I gotta talk to your husband, assumin your husband's name is Denver Eustis.

Mom asks me What do you want to say to him?

I says I gotta ask him somethin. Best kept between us two, him and me.

Mom says to me Well, he's not home right now. But if you try coming back later tonight, maybe around seven, he

I interrupt her and I says Just on accounta I look like a fuckin space-age appliance don't mean I'm dumb as one. Frickin, I mean. Frickin space-age appliance. Anyway, I figure I come back here round seven, you show me a chauffer wants to take me straight to a place got iron in the windows. So when's *Denver* gettin back?

She looks at her feet and she says I don't know.

I look at how many bowls does she got sittin on the counter and I says That's a lotta food-type paraphinalia for two ladies couldn't tip a scale against a, I don't know, somethin small. A lizard. A small lizard.

Mom says If you must know, we're expecting guests.

I says to her Oh, lemme guess, the national guard? They comin at seven too?

She just frowns at me.

So I ask her Whaddya call yourself?

She says That's none of your concern. Whereas I know *exactly* what you call yourself. Frank. Or is it Michael?

I sigh and says Yeah yeah, good job. Most folks just look at the picture.

She says I started paying more attention when I read you were in the area.

I says Word travels fast in the fuckin space-age, huh? *Frickin!*

She asks me Do you really expect me to believe you only want to *talk* to my husband?

I says No, but seein is fuckin believin. So why not let's have a fuckin game, a *frickin* game of flip the card or burp loud or whatever the kids are playin these days. Then I look at the little girl and I says What're ya playin these days, anyway?

The girl just looks at Mom. So I ask the little girl Whaddya call *your*self, huh?

She says Misty.

I says Misty Eustis, what a…*frickin* tongue twister that is. Jesus. How's the sea shell racket treatin ya?

Misty don't get the joke. So I move on and point to Mom and say Last chance. Tell me whaddya call your-self or I'm gonna pick a name for ya. Might be a word Misty here ain't never heard before.

Mom says Grace. And so Mom turns into Grace, just like that.

I says Terrific. Anybody else in the house I oughta meet? I'm only askin on accounta I ain't so good with surprises.

Grace curls up her lip. Misty jumps in and tells me My little brother's upstairs. He's five months old though.

I says Huh. How old're you?

She holds up all her fingers save her thumbs, which like I said are fuckin fingers. Anyway she's got eight eye-pokers showin and she tells me This many.

I nod, only I don't get it. Havin a kid's beyond me. Havin a kid, seein how much of a fuckin nightmare is it over eight long fuckin years, and then havin *another*? I wanna ask em how the hell'd that happen, only it's my business like Misty's in seashells.

Instead I says to em Alright Misty and Grace. Let's why don't ya give me a little tour of the place. Make sure there ain't nobody here slipped your mind. And just so's I can put my mind at its easy about the other kid's still smaller'n a loaf of bread.

The kid's tiny and sleepin in his crib, and the rest of the house's empty like a song on the radio. Ain't no extra beds or framed pictures of dipshit kids might set me wonderin maybe they ain't tellin me somethin.

My mind's at its easy, so I have em show me where do they kick back. It's a real nice livin room type deal, kind with a fireplace and carpet looks like they got the means for choosin what color's gonna go best with the furnishments. I tells em Sit and they sit. I pick a spot's got the wall at my back. I tells em Let's play a game, pass the time. They got nothin. Looks like Grace's bein scared of me's rubbed off on Misty. That's a damn shame. I tells em again I ain't here to set finger on either one of ya. I just wanna ask Denver a question and be on my way.

Yeah, I ain't mentionin how if it turns out I'm right about what'm I theorizin, I'm gonna have to say to Denver Your goose is cooked even though that ain't gonna make all that much sense to him, and after I says to him Your goose is cooked I'm gonna kill him in some kinda way or another. For the fuckin inconveniences he's been dealin me, if nothin else.

They ain't sayin nothin so I throw my arms up and say You ain't bein gracious hosts now. I'm tellin you you ain't got no worries, so let's play a frickin game! Misty starts cryin and I feel bad so I ask her What games do you like playin, huh?

She tells me Um, I don't know.

I says to her You don't know? What kinda kid don't know do they play games or what?

Grace says We have cards. We could play that.

I gotta figure Grace's suddenly volunteerin shit on accounta her sleeve's got more'n her arm up there. Only I figure I start gettin suspicious, I just pull her arms off and whatever's up the sleeve's gonna come slidin right out. So I says to her What a swell frickin suggestable, Grace.

DENVER Eustis comes home about three hours after that, and I'm actually kinda annoyed about it. It was just Misty and me playin at first, only I wasn't sayin Go Fish half as many times as she did. So Grace starts gettin all invested, just little by little. First she's still got her arms folded, only she's whisperin stuff to Misty like Don't keep asking for that, he'll keep telling you to go fish. Then she kneels down and knee-walks over to Misty so's she can peep her daughter's deck more easywise. Then til now, we're playin it proper. I win a game, then Misty wins a game mostly on accounta I *let* her win it, then I win one again.

Then Denver's back.

He walks in the door and says Honey?

Grace don't even look up from Misty's cards, just calls to him We're in here!

He walks to in here, eyes fixed on me the whole time. He asks Um, who's this?

His who's-this puts a little crack in whatever fuckin fairy tale logic got Grace kneelin at the game. So I jump in and says You ain't recognizin me?

Denver's eyes go real small, then real big. He says Holy shit. You're the guy in the paper!

I says to him I ain't just that, far as you oughta be concerned.

Grace and Misty look at each other like they just seen ants crawl outta each other's noses. Then they both look at me like they just noticed I'm one giant ant's got a human nose.

Denver's lookin at me like I'm a giant nose with ant legs. He says Is that a threat?

I shake my head. I says to him I'm just layin it out.

He says That doesn't really lay anything out for me.

I says to him Listen, we can talk turkey in fronta your family, but seein as you're a lobby guy, you gotta figure any business a guy looks like me wants to talk maybe ain't the kind a family oughta hear. So I'm suggestin we lock em in a closet, just so's I can be at my easy, then we go talk somewhere else.

Denver's lookin at me like, like, some new fuckin variation of ants and noses I ain't got the time to figure right now.

So I remind him Or we could just hash it all out right here on your carpet looks like a big teddy bear sicked it up.

Denver quits lookin at me and looks at his family.

Go Figure

They look at him.

He asks em How's Alex?

Grace says Fine. And so are we. But we're not going in a gee-dee closet. If you're involved in something that brings a lunk like this to my house, I think I'm entitled to know about it.

Denver starts to say somethin, only I cut him off by sayin I figure it's settled then. Take a seat.

He don't sit quick as his family did. So I says it to him again. Slower. Lower.

I says Take a seat.

This time he does it *real* quick.

I look him in the eye and I says to him Your goose is cooked.

Ah, FUCK! I said it too early! He ain't got the least clue why'm I sayin his goose is cooked!

So no shit he just sorta looks at me somethin somethin ant nose. And I just remembered, that's a thing people say anyway. That's why'd I come up with maybe I'll say it prior to I kill the guy told everybody I goose. But anyway, turns out that was me, so none of this fuckin works.

Nobody says nothin for a while, then I just tell him. I tell him Maybe you don't recognize me on accounta

He interrupts me to tell me I just said I *do* recognize you. From the newspaper.

I says I mean not from that. And don't fuckin interrupt me.

Misty gasps.

I says to her Sorry. But the fuck, that ain't the first

time you heard me curse.

She says It's the first time in front of my dad!

I say Who fuckin cares? Then I says to her Ah, sorry. That ain't the Paci-FIST sorta thing to say. Then I says to Denver, I says Guy gettin money from you tried to hook me a while back. You know. Set me an ambuscade. Buddy of mine figured it was on accounta this crazy connection we got, on accounta I scabbed a thing your grocery union was doin. I figured, some of these guys got real long memories, like this buddy of mine got. So when it turns out none of the other guys scabbed with me are gettin visits from the kinda guys don't smile at the waiter, I figure, heck, maybe Denver Eustis ain't got nothin to do with it. Just a whaddyacallit. Coincidence. Real funny stuff. I ain't a stranger to em. You follow?

He don't say yes, but he don't say no. So I keep goin.

I says Then I get another bright idea. I do some research on it. I'm talkin searchin through cabinets, writin down numbers and pointin at em. Pulitzer winnin stuff.

Misty says to me Pulitzer, only she says it like *pyoo-litzer*.

I don't take my eyes from her daddy, but I do wag a finger ain't appreciative of the correction. Then I says to Denver And that's how'd I figure actually it *was* you paid a guy to whack me. Only I'm still pointin at Misty when I says it, so the moment ain't got fuckin gravitas like I planned it.

He says I have no idea who you are beyond the guy

from the newspaper. I know you've killed a lot of people. But when I woke up today, I hadn't the slightest idea you existed.

I says On accounta you figured maybe I didn't anymore. And it weren't me you was gunnin for. I was just how were you gonna find the guy what's been keepin you up at night. Figure the guys you sent to hook me had some extracurriculars about makin people hurt til they say somethin useful. You remember 1920?

He says Um…anything specific, or just the year as a whole?

I says Your company, what's it called again. America's Country Workin Whatsit?

He mumbles Working for the Country America Institute on accounta he knows it's fuckin dumb.

So I says Yeah, that's the one. You remember 1920, maybe you get some money from them and you make a fuckin investment? Guy tells you hey, this is easy money, big returns, that sorta line? So you give half a mil, five zero zero, zero zero zero, hopin you're gonna get easy returns big money? That sorta line?

He says Of course I remember that. We're not so rich we can sink that much into an investment without thinking about it.

I says Great. You remember Paul Pezet? You mighta known him when he's called Greg Horowitz?

Denver gets all hangdog like I just told him Greg's dead. Only I didn't do that. So yeah, he remembers Greg, and he musta heard about how'd he spend his summer vacation.

I says Well then I gotta figure you can recollect Greg invested similarwise with the same guy in 1919. Fuckin

He interrupts me and says Huh?

I says 1919. One right before 1920. Greg sinks a quarter mil into this pyramid same as the one you threw cash at the year after.

Somethin tells me Denver don't precisely know what I'm talkin about. Mostly the somethin's his face. The rest of the somethin's him sayin I mean...I knew Greg was diversifying his portfolio, but we never discussed specific investments. We never really discussed much of anything, specifically. He was a friend from school. We kept touch pretty sporadically.

Grace says Sporadic. That's a good word for him.

Denver nods and says He's...he *was* a free spirit. No doubt about that.

Grace harrumphs.

Denver says to her I'm not defending the guy. I'm just saying, you can't deny this, I'm just saying he marched to the beat of his own drum.

Grace says You're right. I can't deny that. Only she says it sidewise.

I ask Denver So you didn't know you both got ripped off by the same guy?

His face drops like a penny off the top of a skyscraper. He says Excuse me?

I says You guys gave to the same scam pyramid and never figured?

He just shakes his head a bit and says I had no idea that was a scam. We got paid back, and then some. We

Go Figure

got money out of it. What was the scam? Someone tried to scam me out of half a million? Who?!

I says How the hell'd you…you got money?

He says Yeah!

None of this makes fuckin sense to me, til I figure on how Wally told me this pyramid thing works. You just keep gettin new investors, then you use their money for payin the old ones. Works like a dream til you stop gettin new investors. Denver and Pezet, they ain't new investors. They're old investors. So they got paid. So then there ain't no reason they'd be comin after Wally.

So maybe I ain't got this as figured as I figured.

I says So it probably ain't like you and Greg work this out one day, and then you decide you're gonna find the guy built the pyramid and kill him only you can't find him, and then one day shit goes bad for Greg so he moves to New York and starts workin his under-the-bridge hookups til he finds a buddy of mine who's the guy who a guy's talkin about when he says he knows a guy, only in this case the guy, my buddy, *he* knows a guy's a girl and she helps Greg turn into Paul, only somehow she lets on she knows about the guy made the pyramid, so PaulGreg calls you up, writes you a letter, what the fuck, anyway Greg Pauls you up and says You're never gonna believe it but I found the pyramid guy, only you can't find him direct so you gotta find a guy's in thick with the pyramid guy, and that guy you find's me, so that's why're you payin guys to come whack me on accounta you want they can ask me not

285

so nicely where's Wally?

All three Eustis' are lookin me like I just talked Latin at em. Then Denver asks me Wait, what?

Grace just shakes her head and traces her fingers around the air and asks me Who was the girl the guy knows?

Denver says to me I have no idea what you think is going on here, but nothing you just described tracks to…uh, reality, as far as I know.

Misty says You've got a lot of buddies, mister.

Then Denver asks Is Wally the pyramid guy?

So I says to him Ah, shit.

First thing I do is I start imaginin. I figure I can make it look like one of them murder-suicides, like Dad snapped and wiped em all out and then himself. I gotta figure the cops'll be addin this one to MichaelFrank's tab in the end, but I can at least make em work for it.

That ain't right though. It ain't done. That ain't done by a fella been through the Ring.

But then what'm I gonna do? I just told em Wally's name. True, ain't like I told em his fuckin surname too, and I figure there's gotta be a buncha Wally's in the city.

Hell, lemme tell ya, I got half a mind to smoke the Eustises anyways just on accounta I got the embarrassments. I really figured I had it all figured. What'd I figure? Fuckin shit. How'd I figure it?

I got some real specific help. Real specific. Help.

Hm.

Help.

I look around on accounta somebody's sayin Help

real quiet.

I says Who's askin for help?

Denver blinks at me and he says You are. You're mumbling it under your breath.

I shrug and I says to him Ah. Fuck.

Then I stand up and I says it again only louder.

They're lookin at me like I'm a turnip rolled off a truck and said Hey how's it goin I got some strong opinions on wealth distrubtion, so I sit back down and I explain to em I'm at fuckin cross purposes. I really oughtta give you folks a tour of the fuckin basement, only that ain't done.

I fold my arms and look at my balls and then I says to em, bein my balls, Shit. Then I look back at the Eustis family and I says to em I just…it's fuckin hard. I got no clue what am I supposed to be doin no more. I'm just a fuckin…I'm a fuckin bruiser, yeah, but I think I gotta have a wrestle with maybe I ain't the brightest shiner anybody ever got, you know what I mean. I…I got accustomized to you call me up and tell me where do I gotta stand, who do I gotta punch, I do it, I get paid. I ain't cut for figurin. I ain't the kind of guy sees somethin don't make sense and says to himself Lemme figure what's the sense this ain't makin. So what the fuck am I doin, you know? Why'm I tryna be somethin I ain't? That's the problem here. I oughta just fuckin asked for help, like Daff said. I got a fuckin skillset, and but so then I figured I was gonna go and ply a fuckin trade I ain't fit to ply.

So Denver says to me Listen, I have money. Just let

my family go, don't hurt us, and I'll

So I cut him off and I says to him I ain't gonna fuckin kill ya. I was throwin that out on accounta I'm sayin I ain't gonna do it. I ain't that kinda bruiser, no more'n I'm the kind's fit to figure a fuckin whodunit. I was also figurin maybe I take the kid upstairs, go somewhere safe, leave him and give you a call. I'm sayin, quit yellin, I'm *sayin* that on accounta I ain't gonna do it.

Grace is still yellin and she yells at me Then what do you want?

I says to her Honest?

She gets a rotten face and says Yes.

I point to Misty and the parents get all itchy. But I says to em I just wanna play another round of cards. Then I'll fuck off and you can call the cops or whatever.

Denver and Grace look at each other like I'm sniffin glue right in front of em. They turn back and Denver says to me You just told us you were thinking of killing us, and now you want to play cards with my daughter.

I says to em No, you got shit in your ears? I just told you I *ain't* thinkin of killin ya. But yeah I wanna play cards. With the three of ya's. It ain't been a cheery buncha weeks for me, and I ain't done nothin recreational since time outta fuckin mind. Ya been swell hosts and I ain't lookin to fuckin capitalize on your hospitality even if it ain't somethin you woulda offered, I didn't come in lookin like a scribble in the funny pages.

I sniff and I wipe my eye only I ain't worried about doin a boo-hoo on accounta I ain't the yesterday kinda bruiser don't do shit like that. Then I says to em You ain't lookin to deal another hand, you tell me to take my wares fuckin elsewhere, I'm gone. It'd just...it'd mean somethin to me if ya let me stay for another hand.

The Eustises all look at each other. Misty's the first to talk. She says to me What about a different game?

Her parents look some kinda shocked. I figure they weren't figurin that'd be the next thing anybody's sayin to me.

I ask Misty What different game you got in mind?

She says Bunco?

I laugh on accounta that's a game they play at the fuckin speakeasy. I ask her You know Bunco?

She says Yeah I know Bunco.

Then I frown on accounta Bunco's a game's got dice. I ain't so fond on dice rollin. You know that, I fuckin said so. Ages ago.

Only what kinda fuckin guest ain't gonna play what does the host wanna play?

So I says to her I'd fuckin love a rounda Bunco. Frickin, is what I meant to say.

RIGHT about now I wanna be screamin down the highway, pedal to the fuckin metal. I got a fuckin figure about that *real specific help* what I figure's the right figure, and I got a hunch on how'm I gonna check-see. Only it probably ain't such a great idea I'm drivin a car's got Frank Patricks' name on it, so I gotta find another. Only I got no clue how do I boost one, so I gotta get one legit.

So I says to Denver You mind I use your ring-a-ding? He says no on accounta we got some kinda fuckin pally after a few rounds of Bunco. Turns out I ain't such a rotten guy after all. Go figure.

So I give Daff a call and she picks up and says What now?! Another getaway?

I says I don't figure it'd be too hard, half the stuff probably ain't even unpacked, right? Don't hang up!

She hangs up so I give her another call and she picks up first time this time, ringwise. She asks me What the fuck do you want right this second?!

I ask her Do you know is the guy ain't Frank Patricks still alive?

She says Douglas Barker?

I says Yeah him.

She says Are you asking me if the name's been blown?

I says Yeah that.

She says I don't fucking know. How would I know that?

I says Yeah I dunno.

She don't say nothin for a while, til she says Samuzzo. There's no easy way for me to say this, so I'm going to just rip the band-aid right off. You've been getting sloppy lately.

I says to her I'm real sorry, I know I got a fuckin

She cuts me off and she says Let me finish. I don't know if you've just lost your touch or it's something more, but this recklessness…it's endangering you, and it's endangering me. For both of our sakes, I think it's best we…just temporarily, I think I should go stay with friends or family for a while. Until you've figured this out.

I says to her Wait! Daff! I figure I got it figured!

She makes a cluck cluck noise and says You know that brawl in the motel parking lot?

I says to her *You* know that brawl in the motel parkin lot?

Go Figure

She says Of course. It was on the radio. Two of the cops died, Samuzzo.

I says to her No! What? That ain't…that ain't happenable! I checked em! It was a whoopslike, I'm bein so fuckin straight with ya you could hang a picture with me! And it'd be a nice picture, of a flower or some shit!

She says I believe you that it was an accident. But… that's my point.

I says to her Look, I'm callin you from the Eustis home'n fuckin hearth! I just played cards with the family, I ain't so much as tousled the kid's fuckin hair!

She says I believe you. But I can't keep changing homes every

I cut her off on accounta I'm gettin near weepy and I says to her I'm sorry! I figure you got the probable fuckin cause for bein upset, but I'm doin better! I'm gonna quit tryna be a thing I ain't, I been figurin past couple days, you know, what would the boys at Paci-FIST figure on what'm I doin! I'm workin! Please don't fuckin vamoose!

I hear she's gettin weepy too and she says At a certain point, I'm worried I'm just enabling you. This isn't me leaving, Sammy. I just, for my own safety, I think I need to give you a wide berth until things cool down. I'll give Godric a number where you can reach me, and you can

I interrupt her and I says Give it to Wally. I says that on accounta I ain't gonna fight her no more, she's got her heart set and it's a strong heart ain't easy to budge.

She says Why not Godric?

I says to her I just got a figure I gotta elasticize.

She gets real quiet. Then she says I hope you know what you're doing.

I tell her I'm tryna get my life right so's I can get you back in it.

She makes a boo hoo noise and says I love you, Sammy. I really do.

I says to her I got the likewise in reverse.

We says see ya to each other and hang up. I'm wipin my eyeballs and I turn around and the Eustis family's standin behind me.

I says to em Jesus, you ain't never hearda personal space?

Grace points out that's rich comin from me on accounta I just sorta waltzed onto their private property, and I says to her about that's a fair point.

Denver asks me Who was that?

I says to him That was my lady. She's a fu…a frickin saint for dealin with me, lemme tell ya.

Denver'n Grace nod a bit too eagerwise.

So I sigh on accounta that's fair too. So, alright, I guess, what'm I doin now? I gotta go to a car rental joint and see can Douglas Barker rent a car without a cop car falls on his head? How's that different from a ball goin click click click round a wheel? It's just more shit, and I'm done with shit. I just gotta think up some clever way ain't shit to get a car ain't shit.

So I says to Denver Any chance on you givin me a ride to the big apple?

Misty says to me I spy with my little eye something green.

I point out the window and I says to her Is it that tree over there?

She points out the back window on the car and she says No, it was that one back there.

I says But anyway, it was a frickin greenage, huh?

She says Duh. I told you I spied something green.

I fold my arms and I says to her I ain't sure I agree with the frickin premise of this amusement. So I lean forward and I asks Mom and Dad in the front seat We almost there yet or what? On accounta I got impatient waitin for em gettin ready. They figure, let's turn givin Samuzzo a ride to the city into a fuckin family farkle. So they gotta pack up a weeks worth of shit. Meanwhile I'm sittin there hopin I ain't misjudged this whole thing somethin fuckin serious wherein here I am stickin my thumb up my ass while they're callin the cops in the other fuckin room. Turns out I ain't, and neither'd they on accounta they wanna give me a ride to the city. What a decent buncha fuckers. Can't hardly believe I meditated on do I wanna pulp their skulls or what.

Grace turns around and she says to me It's gonna be a while.

I says harrumph to that and I lean back. I look out the window and I says to Misty I'm peepin somethin's

Then she interrupts me and she says Are you trying to play I spy?

I says Why else'm I tellin you what do I see out the window?

She says You have to say I spy with my little eye something, and then you say a color.

I ask her Says who? You caught my frickin what do I mean.

Misty says That's just how you play the game.

So I says harrumph to that too. Then I says Fine. Ok. I spy with my eye, somethin

She says You have to say *little* eye.

I tell her My eye ain't frickin little.

Denver says over his shoulder Did you know the eye doesn't grow? It's full-sized when you're born.

Grace says No it's not.

Denver says Yes, it is. I read it in the paper.

Grace says That's not true.

Denver asks her How do you know?

Grace gives her teeth some sun and she says Because I gave birth to, and raised, two children. Then she throws a thumb at Alex who's sittin in Misty's lap and she says Do you think Alex and Misty's eyes are the same size?

Denver says I can't look right now, I'm driving.

I ask em You folks mind can we stop off somewhere's got a phone? We ain't gettin to the city for somewise, I gotta make a call.

Denver just sorta grumbles, only it sounds like a grumble means yes.

So I says to Misty I spy with my little eye somethin blue.

She sighs and asks me if it's the sky.

So I says to her Why don't we let's play a different

game.

We gotta figure it ain't so safe for me to be usin the phone at the diner on my lonesome on accounta I got a face for radio, you know what I mean. So the whole Eustis family comes in with me, doin their best to make it clear I'm one of em, I'm on their fuckin side and they're on mine. Denver's layin it on a bit thick, you ask me, slappin my back and the like. Feels like maybe he's tryna take somethin out on me, way he's hittin me, only he's gonna need some fuckin pointy tools he wants to do any damage.

Anyway, lucky for me my fingers're smarter'n my brain. They ring up Janis. This is the last of my due fuckin diligence, checkin my figure. But I figure I already know what's she gonna tell me.

Reception picks up and I says Remember me? Then the phone rings again and Janis comes on and she says Get what you were looking for?

I says I mean, kinda. I got a new theory I gotta try out. But I gotta ask you one tiny little favor. Real tiny.

She sighs and says Why did you tell my mother I had asked you not to speak with her?

I says Well shit, I didn't know I ain't supposed to tell her I ain't supposed to be talkin to her! All kindsa tight spots you two're puttin me in! Ain't you never seen me? I ain't fit for tight!

She says Mr. D'Amato, your physical size is unrelated to your discretion!

I give a looksee around the diner and I says to her You'd be frickin surprised.

She asks me Frickin?

I says to her I'll tell ya another time.

She says As long as you're telling *me*, and not my *mother*.

I ask her Why does it matter what does your Ma think of ya all of a sudden?

She says It's not about that, and excuse *me,* but I really don't have time to brief you on my filial history just now.

I says Oh yeah?

She says Yeah.

I says Kinda funny, every time I call up your office, there you are. That ficus runnin the desk never says to me Janis is in court today.

She says What is it you want, Mr. D'Amato?

I tell her I'm just wonderin can you look up them papers you gave me about all Paul Pezet's connections. Remember those?

She says Yes I remember those.

I ask her You still got em?

She says I gave them to you.

I ask her You're gonna pretend you ain't made copies?

Now she's the one harrumphin.

I hear papers rufflin over there, so that's alright. So I figure I'll fill the empty fuckin space and I says You know your Ma's got a buddy now? I heard em on the phone.

She says I'm sure she's making all sorts of *buddies*.

I says Huh?

I hear papers going rrf rrf rrf and then she says Ok. I'm looking at the information I provided you. What is it you want me to be looking for?

I says to her See is there a guy named Denver Eustis on there.

Rrf rrf rrf then she says No.

I ask her How the heck'd you check it so fast? The alphabet, I just recalled. Nevermind about that question. How sure are ya?

She asks Should I mind about that one?

I says Har frickin har.

She says I'm positive. Closest match to Denver I'm seeing is a Bible study group in Colorado that made a joint donation.

I says This ain't the frickin city of Denver, trust me. Easy mix-up though, anybody coulda made it.

She tells me Ok then. Denver Eustis isn't on here. So what

I cut her off and I says Thanks a million Janis, you're a fuckin pal.

Then I hang up and I turn to Misty and I say Listen here, foul language ain't got no place in civilized societies, only sometimes you got a pal you got so much heart for ya gotta get a bit blue to tell em, you know?

Grace shakes her head and she says to her daughter No. Swearing is *never* acceptable.

Misty laughs and says to me I spy with my little eye something blue!

I ain't proud to say so, but it takes me a second to figure out what the fuck's she sayin.

Go Figure

I tell the Eustises just drop me off at a motel in Brooklyn, and they do. They tell me they hope I find what'm I lookin for. I tell em You oughta get to Manhattan, they got some swell frickin museums. They say Sure, only I figure it's the sorta sure means maybe not so sure. Whatever though, are they gonna see some old canvas or not ain't my frickin, my *fuckin* problem. I wave em goodbye and I says to myself Fuck fuck fuck, on accounta I gotta make up for lost time. Also and anyway, on accounta I'm nervous about who'm I gonna see and what'm I gonna say tomorrow.

So anyway it's tomorrow, and I'm walkin in to I've Been Framed! Godric's got a customer when I make the bell say tingle ingle ing. So I says to the customer This guy don't do the framin himself. He goes across town to another guy does it for half what you pay here.

The customer looks at Godric, and Godric's lookin at me all cheesed-like, so the customer can see just from lookin at Godric lookin at me that what I just said's true. So he says somethin about how this is outrageous and he's gonna tell his friends. Godric ain't so happy about that.

The door says tingle ingle ing and then Godric looks at me and says What the hell, Sammy?

I walk real icebergwise to the door and lock it slow as I can. Only the door's got one of them latches on the floor so you really only got one speed for lockin. I wanna turn around a sign from OPEN to CLOSED extra slow, on accounta that's the real unnervin part. Only he ain't got one of those so I just gotta turn around and walk back to Godric like I'm pushin through syrup.

The window says Knock knock knock. I turn around and the customer's out there bangin on the glass askin about What the hell? What kind of fly by night operation is this?

I says to him We're closed.

The customer says I forgot my portrait in there. I stormed right out and I forgot my portrait.

Godric's sittin there holdin the customer's fuckin portait out to me. It's of the fuckin customer. He's sittin in a cushy chair makin a face like he just shit himself and don't half mind the smell.

I says Ugh and I walk over to Godric, grab the picture from him, walk over to the door, unlock it, open it, hand the picture to the customer, close the door, lock it, then walk back over to Godric. And the mood's all fuckin ruined so I just punch Godric in the nose and he falls off his little stool. His green visor thing stays on though. Must have some fuckin Velcro on it or somethin.

Sounds like the landin hurt him more than the punch. Makes sense for a fella his age, I figure. He splutters and gawps a bit like a fish just figured out the hard way there ain't no fish rapture happenin, it was just pelicans. Then he tries to scoot back a ways, maybe to get all of me in view at once, only he backs into a frame and it slumps down on him. Now he's wearin it like a scarf been fashioned by a fuckin blockhead.

I says to him That's the first framin you ever done yourself, huh?

He asks me What in the fuck did I do to deserve that?!

I take a few steps forward and crouch down so's I'm loomin right over him. I says Me sayin about the framin, that's one of them twicewise entendres, right? Only it ain't in a sexed way like most of em. Just a thing means two things. Whaddya call that, eh old timer?

Takes a few seconds for him to say anythin. I figure he's usin them seconds tryin to figure how much I figured.

So I guess that means I actually fuckin figured it right! Finally! I gotta tell ya, it's real hard on the old self-esteem when ya get it all kinds of wrong like I been doin. What a weight off, gettin it some kinda right! I wanna smile, only that'd ruin the mood even more. So I keep frownin. But somewhere inside of me, Douglas

Barker's got a grin so big you could play horseshoes with it.

Finally Godric says to me What is that supposed to mean?

I put my hand on his dusty fuckin foot and I says to him You keep playin dumb and I'm gonna unscrew this til it pops off. I got no fuckin patience for you playin dumb. On accounta you figure me for bein as dumb as you play. You're playin me, when you do that. You *been* playin me.

Now I'm playin *him*, on accounta I ain't got no intention of unscrewin his foot. I ain't the kinda guy does that to a pal. I been through the Ring, right? Hell, I pulled my punch when I popped him on the nose. He oughta know that, on accounta he ain't got a brain full of nasals. Only it ain't like I'm sayin, jeez, the rough stuff ain't good for nothin. It's still got some fuckin usefuls. Specially when a fella ain't so sure how much of the rough stuff you're gonna be trottin out.

Speakin of trottin, Godric's starin at his foot real hard. I figure he wants to keep it on accounta he says Sorry.

I nod but I keep my hand right where I got it. I ask him Why the fuck did you play me? I thought we were fuckin pals. You knew I had a big heart for ya. You knew there's all kindsa trust comes with that. So what do you do? Somebody tries to hook me through you, I come to you and say I need some h…a hand with this, what do you do? You say Jeez Sammy, it was all this guy Paul Pezet. So I go get some papers about his buddies, and I bring em to you on accounta I fuckin *trust* you're gonna help me f…gimme a hand. What do you do? You tell me there's a guy on em called Denver Eustis. And you got this whole fuckin map on how Pezet gets to Denver gets back to me and some shit I did ten years ago. Then it turns out the other guys from ten years ago are all happy as fuckin clams, no hooks in sight. *Then* it turns out Denver's got no clue Wally's pyramid was fuckin flimflam, which I figure is the only other reason he'd have any fuckin interest in sendin some ungentlemanly types my way. So if the other scabs ain't in it, and Denver ain't in it, now I gotta wonder, is fuckin Pezet in it? Or did you just work out this whole fuckin goose chase for me to go on, ha, ha, goose chase, did you work out somethin to keep me lookin everywhere but here? You hire guys to go out and wax Pezet just to make sure your yarn kept on spinnin? My figure is maybe you lied to the guys you hired to wax *me*, Thomas Toothpick and them, so when Tommy comes back wonderin hey, who's this guy ain't lookin to come through now that I got myself fuckin banged up on the gig, he figures your name for Paul Pezet? Just so when I go and talk to him, he tells me what do I wanna hear? What do *you* want I hear? Did you hire those fuckin guys to wipe me out on accounta you and Daff figure I'm losin my marbles? You think I'm just some fuckin liability, some dumbass too fuckin dumb to take care of himself anymore? So you figure it's time to send me to a fuckin funny farm upstate? Is that why'd you want me fuckin dead? Did I just say a single fuckin thing you wanna look me in the eyes and tell me ain't true?!

I guess I been gettin a little worked up as I'm sayin all this, on accounta I'm leanin on his foot a bit. It's crackin too far to the inside. Godric's sayin Hee hee hee, only it ain't a laugh. So I ease up. Not all the way.

When he quits pantin like a dog, he just shakes his head and the rest of him along with it. He says I'm so sorry Sammy. I'm so, so sorry. But you have to listen to me, I need you to hear me. This was all a misunderstanding.

Now I let the smile out and a little laugh besides. I says to him I am all fuckin ears.

Godric puts a hand in his mouth, roots around for a bit, and pulls out a tooth. He looks at it like it just won Most Improved Player. Then he puts it in his pocket. For the fuckin fairy, I figure. I wanna tell him sorry about the dental work, on accounta I ain't meant to knock bits of him off. Only that'd kinda cut my whole fuckin spiel off at the knees, so I don't say nothin.

Anyway then he says You're right about almost all of that. I've been misleading you. But I did not, did *not* at any point suborn your murder, or do anything that I believed would harm you.

I says No, you just sent me on a ha ha, a ha ha ha *goose* chase what made me burn through a bunch of papers and help the cops build up my fuckin portfolio.

He says That is not my… Then he stops in fronta the next word, which I figure was gonna be *fault*. Good call on his part. Instead he throws it into reverse and backs up from the ledge. He says I am truly, truly sorry for that.

I says Maybe you forgot already, on accounta I know your memory ain't as fuckin spectacular as I figured, but at present I'm all fuckin ears. You tell me who wanted me hooked or you're gonna be…no fuckin feet, and that's just a start. I'm sayin as like a twist on all fuckin ears. No fuckin…eh forget it. Anyway, you wanna see how many ailments I can give ya to whine about?

He closes his eyes, takes a deep breath, and tells me Agnes.

I says to him Ha ha. Then I says Ha ha ha. Then I'm laughin fit to burst. I got tears comin out of my fuckin eyes. We get to the end and Godric's this shitty a liar? What woulda happened if he ever got collared and the boys in blue shined a bright light at him? He gonna cop to shootin Lincoln and Garfield *and* McKinley?

Agnes. That don't work on *any* level.

Okay, so here's a whoops: I got some muscle memory takin over right about now. It's like the fingers ringin the phone numbers my brain ain't got on file, ya gotta keep that in mind. It ain't *me* liftin up Godric's leg and crankin the foot hard til it's facin the wrong way around. It's just my fuckin muscles.

I says to him Sorry, only I don't figure he hears me.

GODRIC tells me Aaaaaaaah, and then again when I put his leg back down. The foot just flops like there ain't nothin in the shoe.

I says to him Ah fuck, I'm real sorry. I was just, I mean, ah, it ain't like I was comin in here sayin to myself, I'm gonna

He cuts me off and he says Stop! Wait! Let me explain!

I says Stop apologizin? I'm just sayin, I'm real sorry about

He still ain't hearin me on accounta he's too busy sayin I swear to Christ, it was Agnes! I'm not saying she was *specifically* trying to have you killed, because she wasn't! She didn't know!

So I lean back so's I'm sittin on my heels and I put my arms fuckin akimbo and I says Just generally, huh?

Then he spits blood at my face and says Fuck you, Sammy!

I frown and I says to him I already told you I'm some kinda broken up about unscrewin your foot. You ain't gotta be so fuckin sour on it. This rate, I'm worried we ain't gonna be able to keep bein buddies when's all this through.

Boy, I never figured Godric for such a shit listener. He's back to yodelin and he's sayin Just fucking listen to me! It's fucking simple! Agnes' husband died. The house, that big house of hers, was in his name. For some reason, he gave it to Janis, but wrote into the will that Agnes still gets to live there. And for some *other* reason, Janis decided to sell it while Agnes was still living there. Family stuff. They hate each other, if you haven't noticed. I don't know why. I wasn't digging for dirt. That's not who I am, you know that.

I just wave my hand in a circle like let's hurry it up already, I ain't lookin to get more blood spat in my fuckin face.

He spits some more blood only this time on the floor, then he whimpers a little and he says to me So Janis sells it without even getting it appraised, through an agency called Bullsomething.

I says Bullington.

He looks at me like I'm a sandwich just told him You forgot the mustard. Then he says Yes. Bullington. Janis puts it up and it sells almost instantaneously. Bear in mind, nobody came to look at it. It just *sold*. And since Agnes is a little bit on the way out, as far as cognition goes, Janis spent a lot of time trying to convince her that either she was being foreclosed on, or Agnes herself had sold the property. But in her lucid moments, Agnes recognized the deception and started hunting for someone who could help her throw a spanner into the works. She found me.

Now I can see the whole fuckin thing. The whole stupid fuckin thing. So I says to him And lemme guess, she tells you she's got money and she wants a guy can hunt down whoever runs Bullington and lean on em, find out who bought the house. She figures, knowin her own brood, it's gotta be Janis. And it is.

Godric nods and says But not just Janis. And that's why the people I contacted on Agnes' behalf ended up ambushing you. Without my knowledge, I might add.

I'm noddin now. I says to him Wally. It's one of his gags, right?

Godric's still noddin like he's scared what's gonna happen if he stops shakin the snowglobe. He says This is what I didn't realize, what I only put together after you'd had your trouble. Bullington is one of Wally's dummy companies. He's a slumlord, amongst his many ventures. Buy cheap, paint, flip. And as soon as Janis got the house from her dad, she went from abettor to accomplice.

I says She had Wally's company snatch away the old lady's house, on accounta, what, she's still pissed about bein sent to bed early?

Godric says I have no idea. But I do know what the goal was, now that she's accomplished it. She did all of this to put Agnes into a home.

I says Why's she takin her out of a home and puttin her back into a different home? Why ain't she just gonna keep her in the same home?

He just rolls his eyes and says to me A *home*, Sammy. An assisted living facility.

Oh swell, we're still on Sammy terms! If he was callin me Samuzzo, I'd be worried he was mad for keeps. So I says She put Agnes into a fuckin old timers' home? Only thinkin about it now, that line about how Agnes is probably makin a lotta friends makes more sense now.

He nods and says Yes.

I have a good long think on this. Everythin I've been havin good long thinks on lately, it's been bullshit what'd Godric tell me to go step in. I scrunch my nose and I ask him So if Pezet ain't got nothin to do with this, you just pulled his name out of a fuckin hat, how'd he get so dead?

Godric hangs his head. Another tooth falls out. He slurps up some blood and says I did that.

I says You frosty little son of a bitch! I'll tell ya, you ain't never gettin on no moral high horse with me ever again! Fuckin *shit!*

So he starts shakin his head again like he can't believe he ever stopped and says You think I'm proud of it? I...pretended to be Paul. Everything was going wrong, the man you call Tommy was demanding payment, naming you by name as the target of a failed hit...I panicked, and I thought of a name, and it was Paul's. Then what they did to him, and...once I realized my role in this farce, I...well, I didn't want to admit it. That I'd accidentally facilitated an attack on my friend, my fucking *friend*, Sammy! I didn't want to admit it to you, and I *couldn't* admit it to myself. So I created this...elaborate story. I just plucked some names out of my memory, mixed and matched them until I found some that worked together. And I...this sounds nasty but, I expected you to be so overwhelmed by the complexity of the connection that you would just tell me to handle it.

I says Uh...Um...Ah... Then I shut my mouth on accounta I hate those fuckin not-so-words. Finally I get my shit together and I says So all this shit you put me through, and I'm even puttin aside the hook on accounta that was just a funny fuckin coincidence, but the rest of this shit that cost me my lady and two identities

He says Daff? Did she

Only I'm still talkin so I says This shit brought all kindsa shit down on me heatwise, got some cops and other schmucks killed, made me sit in a fuckin Ring and learn a fuckin lesson, all of this comes from you didn't wanna admit you fucked up and just say Sorry, my bad? Instead you figured it'd be easier to just make up some big fuckin conspiracy involves controversial groceries and got some dope had enough problems in his life killed in a *real* bad way, and gutted on toppa all that? You figured it'd be easier to do all that on accounta you figured I'm so fuckin dumb I'd hear about it and just say Well shit Godric, I can't make heads nor tails of this, why don't you take care of it for me? When the fuck have I ever said anythin like that to you?!

Godric's got nothin.

So I says to him I wanna hear you tell me what's all this shit about.

He asks me Huh?

I tell him I wanna hear you say to me, that all this shit's on accounta you didn't wanna say sorry, and you figured I was fuckin dumb.

He's still got nothin. So I get up and I wanna walk on his knees. They're old, ain't up to supportin my weight. I can already hear what sound would they make. Crack snap crunch. Only that ain't done, is it? Maybe my muscles coulda done it like they done his foot, and I'd say, hell, that was my muscles, not me. Only my muscles ain't done it, so now it's my brain's gotta decide do I wanna walk on his knees or what.

I sigh and I crouch down again and I says to him Look at us, huh?

Godric looks around at everythin but us, and he says to me What?

I laugh a little and I says We're just two fuckin schmucks, huh? Two big fuck-ups. I see where're ya comin from, I gotta say. I'm walkin in your shoes. Like Crowder says, I gotta see can I state the presentwise case so's you ain't gonna raise a flag on it and say no, it didn't go down like that.

He smiles a little on accounta he figures I'm through givin him grief. Obvious he can't see I'm sittin on a fuckin volcano of angry, then. But the top of a volcano's a Ring, ain't it? That's my Ring at present. A Ring of fuckin fire.

So I put my hands on either side of the foot ain't been unscrewed yet, and I lean forward a bit and smile and I says to him Let's why don't we just make sure we got the situation clear and straight, huh?

He tells me I'm sorry! I'm so sorry!

I says That ain't it. Try again.

He says I fucked up, Sammy! Please just don't hurt me again! Jesus Christ!

I smile wider and lean a bit more forward and I says to him One more shot, then your hip's gonna start actin up.

I don't figure there's nothin wrong with just threats, right?

He makes boo hoo sounds and he says I was afraid to admit it! I was afraid to admit I fucked up! I was afraid to apologize! I was embarrassed!

I nod and I lean back and I ask him And what else?

He says Goddamnit, fucking Christ! I thought you were fucking dumb! Are you happy? Did I say what you fucking wanted to hear? Because that's all it is, you fucking ass! It's what *you* want to hear, not

I interrupt him and I say There, that's fuckin swell. So I ain't the only one learnin lessons, how's that? Then I put my hand out and I says to him I hope we can still be fuckin chums. I figure we're square, far as clownin on each other.

Godric looks at my hand like it's made of fuckin cactus.

I say Take my hand, I'll get ya to a fuckin hospital.

Godric frowns and slaps his hand into mine and he says You probably shouldn't be seen in a hospital right now.

I smile and I says to him Holy fuckin hell, you tellin me I *ain't* oughta be seein a doctor now?!

He says to me This is a wildly different context!

That's a good point so insteada answerin about that I says to him What, do I wanna hear about your fuckin ailments from a guy's got even more syllables for em than you? Course I ain't comin in.

Godric puts his arm around my shoulder and asks me How are we getting there?

I says to him I'm gonna put ya in a cab.

So he says Wow Sammy, you're a real gentleman.

I says Ya gotta know I didn't figure on unscrewin your foot. It was my muscles.

He says to me I *did* intend to spit blood into your face.

I says to him I can't blame ya, old timer. That was some kinda justified.

He says to me You're a fucking asshole.

I says I know. I'm workin on it. Maybe you wanna work on bein less of a fuckin weasel sometimes?

He says I plan to.

So I says to him Look at us, workin on ourselves.

RECEPTION stands up when he sees me come in. Glad to see he's found some fuckin manners since the last time when'd I have to look at him.

He says to me Ms. Kidderminster is out at the moment. She's in court.

I says Which is it? She's out or she's in?

He says Um…they're the same, effectively.

I says Well then I'm just gonna pop in and I'll pop out while I'm at it. Effectively.

The kid starts babblin and I just walk on past. Straight to Janis' office, which I figure is some kinda fuckin court on accounta there she is.

I close the door and walk over to her desk. Around to her side. I sit on the edge. Then I says to her I got two great questions need two great answers. Ain't no right or wrong answers. Just what's real. So don't try tellin me what do you think's gonna make me go away. I'll leave when I say to myself Gee, it's time to fuckin go. So here's my two questions I got: what'd you know, and when'd you know it?

She's leanin back, hopin her chair's gonna swallow her up. Thus far, it ain't givin her much save the lumbar support. She's got nothin to say.

So I frown and I says to her Why you gotta make this hard? It's so fuckin easy. Here, I'll start. I know *you* know you're the one snatched Agnes' house what was already yours out from under her, on accounta you *gotta* know that.

The way she's tensin up, I figure she knows a lot more'n she's gonna cop to. She ain't playin the Sorry but I simply don't understand what you're talking about game. I gotta respect that. Only for a little though.

She asks me Did Mr. Manfly…who told you?

I says You got it in one. Godric did. But if it makes ya feel better, it was only post I rearranged his skeletals a bit.

I don't mention that was on an accidental, on accounta I wanna get her figurin maybe I bought Godric a one-way to the Barrens.

She gets even smaller in her seat and says Where is he now?

I wasn't figurin on lyin outright, only maybe a lie's gonna keep my muscles from gettin into a position they're gonna be flexin on their own. So I says I figure that's down to what's your creed. Where does a guy go's got his head turned inside out?

Now she gets real big, just about launchin out of her seat at me. She says Mr. D'Amato, you didn't!

I tell her I did, and what's more I figure I learned from some mistakes I ain't lookin to make the second time. Then I put my hands on her shoulders and push her back down into the chair like it's time out for her. She don't look too happy her fuckin refuge got turned into a prison so quick.

Her face figures a way for gettin even less happy when I stick *my* face, which ain't happy only in a different direction from the way her's ain't happy, right into it. Her face.

Then I says to her Like I was sayin. It's real easy. Never gonna get easier. Just the two questions. What'd you know, when'd you know it?

She looks at the door like Reception's gonna come chargin in. Or maybe she's tryin to psych me out, get me to spin around and then she can brain me with a marble bust or potted plant or somethin. Or, who fuckin knows, maybe Reception *is* gonna come chargin in.

So I put one hand extra heavy on her shoulder and lean, turnin around all the while.

Reception's behind me, creepin like he's bashful about interruptin.

He says to me Leave her alone like it's a point proves itself I just ain't thought up yet.

I says I'd be leavin her alone if she'd left me alone. Now nobody gets to get left alone. Includin you, kid. You sit in the corner there and I'll be right with ya.

Janis yells at him to Call the police!

Reception looks at her like that's a point *he* ain't thought up yet, only that one ya gotta prove for. And he looks at her like he ain't done that provin yet. So I grab some scissors out of a little jar on the table and I wave em at him. I says to him Sit in the fuckin corner, less you think you can run faster'n I can throw these.

Reception goes and sits in the corner. You believe that shit? What, I stayed up nights practicin on how's the best way to throw a pair of scissors? What a fuckin chump.

So Janis says to me How the hell did I not leave you alone? *You* repeatedly contacted *me* for favors!

Ah, man. I guess she *is* gonna do the playin dumb thing. Why's everybody gotta go straight to that? When's anybody ever gonna go straight to bein straight, just say Oh shit, my bad. Sorry about that shit I done?

Is that so fuckin hard?

I says to her You're goin an doin it again.

She says *Doing what?!*

I says Takin somethin's so fuckin easy and makin it so fuckin otherwise. Then I lean in even further and I growls at her So lemme easify this. I'm gonna ask you my two questions one last time, expectin you to color in the lines I drawn thus fuckin far. You tell me you ain't got the least clue what'm I talkin about, I'm gonna turn your head inside out. You tell me somethin answers my questions, we'll keep talkin, just two pals.

Her teeth are chatterin but I think she says to me If you kill me you won't get *any* answers, unsatisfactory or otherwise!

I shrug and I says I'll go say hi to some fuckin medium, maybe ask em to ask you where does a gal go's got her head turned inside out. The rest won't matter no more.

She says Then why does it matter so much to you now?!

I says We already got two questions in line for answerin. We ain't addin another. Next words outta your mouth's an answer or it's not. I'm ready for either.

My nose is touchin her nose at this point. Her face's so close I can't actually really see nothin, on accounta my eyes can't cross enough to focus. So she's just blurry. I try to keep lookin mean even though my head's kinda hurtin from tryin to eye-cross.

I really hope she don't try for callin my bluff. I ain't lookin to turn her head inside out, and if she tells me to go ahead and do it…I don't know what'm I gonna do.

Two seconds after I tell myself She's got five more seconds for the second time, she says to me I knew a lot of it, I think. I had no idea my mother had contracted someone to hunt *me* down, because you have to remember, had the people she employed succeeded they would have found Mr. Zwillbin *and* myself. You were an unfortunate link in the chain that would have ultimately led to my doorstep.

I says to her Focus, Janis. Talk in a straight line.

She takes a deep breath and says Right. Ok. I didn't know that my mother had taken the money for the sale of the house, which I *did* let her have, she…ok. Ok.

Yes, I was trying to salve my conscience by giving my mother the money from the house sale. I didn't know that she used that money to hire a thug to hunt down the house's buyer, who *she* didn't know was *me*. Even after you were attacked, I didn't see the connection. I assumed your incident was unrelated to mine. The Pezet inquiries, the favors you asked of me, I don't think I would have made a connection between those and my unfortunate family affair even had I known to look for one. That's because, well, I'm sure you beat it out of Mr. Manfly before you…but there wasn't one.

I says I know. Keep talkin.

She squirms in her seat and keeps talkin, sayin I *never* would have made the connection, to be honest. Mr. Manfly made it for me. He called me up, and keep in mind I'd only ever heard the name Godric Manfly mentioned here or there, I'd never met him and still haven't…and never will…but he called me up and explained it to me. How my mother had hired a gun through him, and how the gun was pursuing me, and how your ambush was, as I mentioned, merely a link in the chain.

I ask her When was this?

Her nose curls up. She says I can't remember exactly. But it was before the call on which I asked you to stop communicating with my mother.

I says You wanted me to quit talkin with her on accounta she mighta let *somethin* loose mighta put me on your trail?

Ain't much I can see from this close, but I can see

her eyes are gettin wet. She says It's not my fucking trail! I didn't *do* anything to you! This is a family affair that you were roped in to, *very* tragically, like I just explained! I'm sorry this happened to you. Seriously. I will do whatever I can to make it right. But you have to understand, I am jus…I'm a victim too! My mom hired somebody to *kill* me!

I says Only she didn't know.

She says Not at first. But after? Who knows?

I nod and I says to her You knew enough to steer me the wrong way, though. You kept me chasin Pezet, kept me followin leads to nowhere.

Maybe she really figures she ain't got a happy endin comin, or maybe she just screws up some courage from way down deep. But either way she shoves me back a bit and says Because I fucking knew this would happen. I knew you'd be unable to distinguish the passive part I played in this from the more active role of Mr. Manfly.

I says On accounta I'm fuckin dumb, right?

She says Your words.

I laugh even though I don't feel in a laughin kinda way and I says Seems like everybody I figured was a pal's been playin me on accounta they figure they can, on accounta they figure I'm fuckin dumb.

She says From what Mr. Zwillbin tells me, you weren't always fucking dumb. You used to be just an average kind of dumb.

I says to her That's a hurtful thing to say.

She lifts up her chin and I gotta say, I got a hell of a lotta respect for her all of a sudden.

323

So I says to her I got a hell of a lotta respect for your fuckin moxie. Look, I ain't killed Godric. I unscrewed his foot, but that was my muscles, and anyway they only done it on accident.

She blinks at me and says So...wait...Mr. Manfly isn't...dead?

I says to her You think I'm gonna wax my fuckin pal? The kinda guy you figure me for, huh? But listen, you got vim'n fuckin vigor. I respect that.

She just blinks a lot.

I says to her Sorry I scared the bejesus outta ya. Then I stand up and leave, only I don't tender no fuckin apologies to Reception on the way out on accounta fuck that guy. I got no clue why, but fuck that guy.

GO FIGURE

WALLY don't wanna meet me
anywhere ain't a public place. I tell
him why don't he come on over, visit me at Douglas
Barker's. He says Aw, I wouldn't wanna put you out.

Maybe he got wise to I roughed up Godric, or
maybe Janis gave him a heads up I got some axes I'm
grindin. I figured one of em woulda said Hey, Samuzzo
ain't gonna knuckle you quite like he says, which would-
a been unfortunate on accounta there goes my fuckin
leverage. But then why ain't Wally lookin for quality
time? Maybe he got wise on his own fuckin whaddyacallit. Somehow, I gotta figure, he got some kinda wise.

I got no clue *how* wise til Agnes gives me another
ring. I got a fuckin omen it's her, so when I answer I
says Hello, how are you today?

She says to me Is this is a fucking pharmacist's office? Since when do you answer the phone like that?

325

I sigh and I says What bad news ya got for me?

She asks me What's *that* supposed to mean?

I says You don't call me less when you got somethin bad to lay on me. They got a sketch of my dick in the paper this time?

She says How do I know? I don't have a fucking microscope glass.

I walked right at that one, fair play to her.

So I says Ok, fine. What're ya callin me for today?

She says I have bad news for you.

I throw my arms up, only she don't know that. Then I says Well lay it on me.

She says It's you.

I ask her Huh?

She says You're bad news.

Did she hear about how I spooked her daughter or somethin? I don't figure that'd bother her much. So what, she just takin a summary view?

I says You wanna break that down?

She says You're in the news, and the news is bad. And I know I've called you up with this before, but…I mean, this time you're *in* the news. Your face.

I tell her They got my face already. Ain't done em no good.

She says to me Not the sketch. Your face. They're hawking extra editions in the city with a picture of you in em. One of the orderl…my friends brought one in. I said to myself, I wonder if he knows he's got birdshit on his reading material?

I says Lemme guess, then you seen it was just a picture of me.

She just laughs.

I ask her Where'd they get a fuckin picture of me?

She says A kid named Eric.

Reception. I ain't sure how do I know, but he just looks like a fuckin Eric. Somehow, somewhen, he got my daguerreotype.

I says to her Motherfuck. Eric.

She says Yeah. Eric. Got a clear shot too, makes for a real good look at your stupid fucking bulldog face as you

I tell her Don't call me stupid.

She says I'm not calling *you* stupid, you fucking idiot, I'm calling your *face* stupid!

I says Well don't do that either!

She says You done crying? I'm trying to give you valuable fucking information.

I says I ain't fuckin cryin.

She says Then why're you sniveling like that? You wanna come on over, I'll burp you and let you sick on your bib?

I says Yeah, sure, I'll come on down. What batty-old-broad's home you get stuffed into again?

She gasps and says That's the kind of sentence a man doesn't live to regret.

I says Whaddyawannado, hire somebody to kill me again?

She says Excuse me?

I says You hired a guy to see about who runs Bullington Realty. Remember that? Or'd it already slip outta your fuckin mashed potato brains already?

She says I recall that and a lot more besides, asshole!

I says Great, you ever hear on who it was owns the biz? I'll tell ya, it was your fuckin daughter. And the guy you hired tried to catch her through her money buddy, and he tries gettin to the fuckin business buddy through me. So what you did was take some money, give it to a guy, and then he's comin after me. Well, not anymore.

Finally, she's got nothin to fuckin say.

I still do though, so I says But you ain't gotta worry. The folks you hired ain't returnin your calls for a reason. Maybe now you wanna pay me instead, so I don't go chokin my way back up the chain. So I'll come collect from ya. Tell me which graveyard are ya rottin away in? Or do I gotta find out from somebody else, maybe work up some fuckin bile in the findin?

She says You're a stupid motherfucker.

I says to her Well I figured out this fuckin mess what'd you make, so I still ain't half as dumb as you.

She tells me Go check the extra edition, shithead. They have your face. They've got all your made up little names. They're putting together a map of every crime they can nail you for. Fingerprints, birdbrain, ever heard of em? And, oh, they're about to need a lot more red yarn, because as soon as I hang up here, I'm calling the fuzz and telling them the man they're looking for is actually named Samuzzo D'Amato.

My mouth's hangin open for a second. Then I snap it shut and I says to her Don't you fuckin dare.

She just laughs at me and says Or what? You said it

yourself, I've got one foot in the grave, and most days I can't even remember that. My daughter hates me. My home is gone. I'm miles and miles away from you, so it's not like you can rip up my fingernails or whatever meathead shit you do. What can you threaten me with, huh? Where's your power? Or do you want to try to persuade me? Have you ever done that without balling up your idiot fists in front of somebody's nose? Ever tried? Of course not. Because you're too fucking stupid to know how. You're only as good as the pain you can inflict. That's all you've got. And now here you are, talking to a woman beyond caring about pain. How does that feel, Samuzzo D'Amato? Maybe if my memory holds out, I'll remember to come visit you in prison and find out. More likely I'll fucking forget. Then you can see how it feels, to be stuck somewhere, alone, knowing that the only person who might have visited is indifuckingsposed.

I says to her I can't believe I ever figured the world was all Agneses and Alans, when it turns out the Agneses're just a buncha fuckin Alans anyway!

Then she says Oh! Don't call me an Alan, you fucking Alan!

I says to her *You're* an Alan! I'm more fuckin Agnes than you *ever* been!

She says to me No, you know what you are, is you're fucking ugly! I'm sure you're hearing all about how fucking stupid you are all the time, I'm just worried people don't have time to cover how much your face looks like googly eyes on a butthole. Shithead.

I says to her I used to wonder why does Janis hate you so fuckin much. That's another mystery fuckin solved.

She says Oh! and hangs up.

…

There's a lotta stuff I ain't sure did she mean what she said, or was she just sayin it on accounta I caught her out on dealin with unsavory types.

I ain't ugly, am I?

Also, she ain't snitchin on me to the cops, is she?

Now I'm all kindsa fuckin troubled. Even more when I think on Wally wantin to meet in a public place. He musta seen my fuckin handsome visage on the extra edition too. So why's he wanna meet me in fuckin public?

Does he…does he maybe want me caught and boxed? Maybe…maybe Godric and Janis ain't returnin his calls for some reason, maybe he figures I flattened em. Maybe I don't know. I can't figure. But Wally wantin to meet me in a public space, that breaks my fuckin heart a little. Puts me in the sorta mind I'd normally be callin up Daff for soothin. Only I figure she ain't gonna wanna talk just yet.

So I stare at the phone for a while and I'm imaginin Agnes' voice flyin through it to the cops. They're gonna have every fuckin name I ever got, even my real one. Well, they ain't got Douglas Barker, right? So I guess I'm safe at his place. Long as I go back now, and don't leave the fuckin house.

Too bad I ain't got no fuckin hobbies.

SO…what the fuck? Now what? The people been doin me down lately're all pals. I can't wax my fuckin pals. There ain't nobody for me to punch til their head rolls off. This is a weird fuckin situation for a bruiser.

Ok, ok. First things first. Where'm I at, what do I got.

I walked most of my way back to Barker's place. I done that on accounta I wasn't lookin for no cab drivers to match a face to a place, only I didn't figure about maybe somebody looked out their window and saw me walkin. Let's why don't we figure Agnes ain't blowin smoke when she says she's gonna snitch. I gotta assume all my fuckin assets're toxic, or whatever folks say. The floor is lava in any place's got Samuzzo's name on it. That kinda thing. Also I meant to say *my* name. And all the other names're me but ain't *me*. And maybe I gotta assume Barker's included in that anywise, on accounta maybe somebody saw my face while'm I walkin home. Long shot, but I ain't had the sunniest fuckin luck lately.

So I walk outta Douglas Barker's house not five minutes after I got back.

But what's fuckin furthermore, I can't really hoof it on accounta for the same reasons I figure I got burned walkin over here. Yeah, I know, not my smartest fuckin move. I cut the kinda figure draws the eye, and if it's my body's drawin all the eyes, I'm figurin it's the face what's gonna paint em a fuckin picture. So it ain't like I can just slum it on the public transits.

So how'm I supposed to fuckin go anywhere? And where am I lookin to go anywise?

I stuff my hands in my pockets, keep my head down and start poundin pavement. Barker's place bein outta the city seemed like a bright fuckin idea at first, only what made it bright's makin it seem pretty fuckin dim right at present. Ain't nobody on the sidewalk, barely any cars drivin by. Which means there ain't no bustle I can even fancy gettin lost in. I'm just clompin along bout as subtle as a full-grown moose.

Fuck this. I turn towards the house next door and figure I'll introduce myself to the neighbors. I won the Eustises over with my fuckin charismaticality, didn't I? I bet they got a deck of cards here, a pair of fuckin dice. It'll be another game night til I figure out what'm I gonna do. Let my pals cool down, Godric and Janis, then see what should I do about, uh, anything.

I let myself in and whaddyaknow, there ain't nobody

home! I help myself to some fuckin fruit they got in a bowl and wait for the homeowners to show up.

The cops come first.

They're flashin and wailin up Douglas Barker's driveway next door, funny helmet brigade and all. They surround the place and start wavin this way and that way like they all miss each other already.

I hear one guy yellin through a funnel at the house Samuzzo D'Amato! Come out with your hands up!

Ah, shit. So Agnes was good as her bad fuckin words.

Then Funnel starts runnin through all my other names. He says We know who you are! Samuzzo D'Amato, Michael Berns, Frank Patricks, Douglas Barker, Richard Freeman, Stephen Isaacs, Tony Berman! We have fingerprints linking you to all of these names!

Man, it's like a trip down memory fuckin lane. I forgot about a bunch of those! Odette's got a way with findin forgettable names, I gotta give her that.

I take another peek out the window. The cops are shuttin down the street. Parkin cars nose to nose and wavin hands for more. Only...they're shuttin it down wide enough I'm stuck in the shutdown.

Maybe I shoulda hunkered down in the house wasn't *right* next door to Barker's.

I start walkin towards the front door when it starts makin clunk clunk noises.

Keys!

I leapfrog into the kitchen so's I got a wall between me and the folks walkin in.

A fuckin family unit talkin to somebody. A cop or detective or *somebody* sounds like they put on a voice they got from some radioplay when they're quote debriefing the civilians unquote.

They all stop talkin at once on accounta I maybe ain't as hidden behind the wall as I figured.

I hear the kinda sound ya don't tend to forget, and that's the sound of the button on a standard issue cop holster bein unbuttoned, and a standard issue cop gun bein slipped out.

So it ain't a detective. Which means firearms trainin.

Cop says to the family unit Go find my commander. Tell him Trask is next door with a 10-10, reqesting 10-13.

I sure ain't happy about it, but I leapfrog back out from behind the wall and make for the window on the side of the house away from Douglas Barker's old claptrap.

The family unit all shout real loud on accounta they ain't figured on the extra edition showin up in their kitchen. The cop shouts too, then his gun shouts louder'n anybody.

Ain't til I'm just about at the window I realize it ain't wide enough for my fuckin shoulders. So I kick off and turn sidewise, left shoulder facin down, right up the other way. I gotta think so hard about turnin, I forgot to put my arms up. You'd think it'd be another job for my fuckin muscle memories, the amount of fuckin glass I'm breakin through lately. But whaddyaknow, my muscles and my brain both forgot.

Go Figure

So my face hits the glass first. Only that ain't enough to punch through. My neck crinkles up so my chin's on my fuckin chest. Then the rest of the chest follows up and gets through the window. I shatter through in the fuckin fetal position.

Turns out, remember how the backyard of the Barker safehouse slopes down a story so the basement's got a door leads to lawn? I didn't really clock it, but I remembered after I fall out the window, and keep on fallin after I figured I shoulda stopped fallin already.

Then I figure, shit, that's right. I guess all the yards on this block got the downslope.

Then I stop fallin.

It hurts but I ain't got time. I look up and I see the cop pop his head out the window. Then his gun. Then some bullets.

He's aeratin the lawn on accounta maybe he was sick for firearm trainin. I roll my feet under me and get movin before his buddies with the stronger constitutions show up.

There's a row of trees separatin this backyard from the one behind it. Just a row of trees shoulder to shoulder, ain't like it's woods or nothin. But it's *some* kinda cover, so I run through right when the buddies show up and start blastin away at the trees. The bullets hittin bark make it sound like the trees are applaudin me. So it ain't like I got *no* support no more.

I scramble up the hillyard of the house on the other side of the trees, on accounta I guess the whole block's built on a fuckin gully. Must be hell when it rains hard.

I'll tell ya, it's hell when ya gotta scramble up it even dry. By the time I get to the top, I see a cop car screamin down the street to my left. Another from the right. Damnit if they don't scramble those things faster'n I can scramble. In defense of me though, I ain't got the wheels.

So it's either I run across the street and into the next backyard, and keep on doin that til I can't run no more, which if I'm bein honest, won't take so long on accounta I ain't exactly built for relays.

Or, I can hunker down, only this time do it so's they're scared to come in.

The cars're closin in, like a fuckin math problem where you got one train comin east at one speed, and the other comin west at another. When're they gonna meet?

I ain't lookin to find out. You know how do I feel about maths.

So I run across the street and into another backyard. Only instead of crossin to the far side of the block, I double back and try the back door of this house ain't got a downslope, thank fuckin god.

The door's unlocked. Which is fuckin bonkers to me. Ain't they heard they got an extra edition in the neighborhood?

I oughta let em know.

Go Figure

I lock the door behind me and go chargin through the house. I don't hear nobody shout-in Hey or What or Uh Oh. So I find the door goes to the basement and jump down there. It's finished, carpet and table and couch and all that. So it ain't like there's a lotta places somebody could hide. I check what coupla spots there are. Nobody's hidin. I run back upstairs, fig-urin at this point the cops gotta figure I didn't bust through to the far side of the block, and now they're gonna be lookin at the houses. Findin a door leads to the garage takes me a second, but I finally do. Find it. Ain't no cars in the garage.

Ain't nobody's fuckin home. Which, you know, that's pretty fuckin annoyin. I was bankin on hostages.

Well, life gives ya limes, you can still squeeze em, piss in the cup to get some yellow and sell it like lem-onade, long as you're outta dodge before anybody tastes it.

So I rush back up stairs and look out the window. Cops're fillin *this* street now. More by the second.

I slide open the window and I says to em You jokers stay back or I'm gonna kill em!

A guy in a trenchcoat what looks like he's either in charge or else he wants to be stops, but everybody else is still scrabblin around. The hell's he doin with a trench in this kinda weather?

Trench shouts at me Samuzzo D'Amato! Come out with your hands up!

I says to him The fuck did I just say? Why'm I gonna say you guys gotta stay back and then come to *you?*

He shouts to me Who's in th... Then a cop pulls a funnel outta his car and hands it to Trench. Trench says into the funnel Who's in there with you?

Looks like I'm in a sittin room, the kinda room nobody uses save when company comes callin. I look for somethin with a name on it, mail or a diploma or a trophy or *anythin*. But there ain't nothin. And I can't just make up a name, on accounta I don't figure it'll take em long to figure whose house is this for real.

So I says to em The dad!

Trench holds the funnel in fronta his mouth for a second. Then he puts it down and says somethin to one of the cops next to him. The cop runs off to a place I can't see where's he goin.

Then Trench puts the funnel back in fronta his mouth and he says Just the dad?

Now I'm frettin the family here ain't got kids. Maybe Trench sent that other cop off so's he could chat up the neighbors. This probably ain't gonna go down as one of my sharper moments.

Trench asks me Can I speak with him, just to make sure he's alright?

I says No!

He asks me Why not?

I says He's sleepin and says he don't wanna be roused!

Trench puts the funnel down and says somethin to somebody else. Then he says to the funnel Alright, let's just take a deep breath. I'm going to ask my boys to all take a step back.

I says And girls, on accounta I see a lady cop.

Trench kinda rolls his eyes. Maybe he figures he's too far for me to see, only I can. He says to me That's right, boys *and* girls. I'm going to have them all take a big step back, so we can keep things nice and relaxed. There's somebody on their way who might be easier to talk to than me, so can you promise to just take it easy until they arrive, and we'll do the same?

I says to em Sounds fuckin swell.

Trench asks me Is there anything I can get you in the meantime?

I says You want I'm gonna ask you for an airplane and a million dollars? He rolls his eyes again, so I let him know I can see you rollin your eyes, asshole!

Now his eyes go real big. Then a cop comes up and says somethin to him and he says to me If you need anything, just holler! And then he goes away where I can't see where's he goin.

I shut the window and start drawin the curtains and barricadin the doors. Once I get that done, all I got available to me is wonderin when's it gonna be they catch on there ain't nobody else here.

TAKES a couple hours for Negotiator to show up. She's got a trenchcoat on too. The fuck is up with these people?

She walks halfway up the walk to the front door, not usin a funnel or nothin. She says to the front door How are you doing in the there, Mr. D'Amato? May I call you that, or is there another name you would prefer?

I creep up to a window and crack it open. I says to her Sammy's alright. We're fuckin pals, ain't we?

Negotiator half-smiles and says I'm not going to presume. We're meeting under rather unusual circumstances. But Sammy is how you would prefer I address you?

I says Sure, what the fuck.

She nods and says Well Sammy, how are you? How is Mr. Hornby doing?

Ah *fuck*. Why wasn't I lookin around for shit with a

name on it, instead of watchin them scrabblin around out there? Is the guy what lives here called Hornby? Or is this some kinda fuckin test, like if I say yes to the wrong name they all come roarin in? Only if they was gonna call shit on me, they'da done it already, right?

I says to her If that's what he's called, he's doin fine. Still sleepin.

She asks me Is he sleeping because you hit him, or because he's just sleepy?

I says It's a fine line, ain't it?

She nods like she's been thinkin the same thing and what a relief to hear it from another somebody. Then she says That's fine, Sammy. Just fine. I've got someone here who wishes to speak with you.

I says I figure everybody out there quote wishes to speak with me unquote.

Negotiator smiles and turns and waves at the cars behind her.

Daff walks up the walk.

I figure I'm supposed to be all broke up about this, only I knew she musta heard by now. I'm just bummed they roped her in, on accounta that must peg her as some kinda accomplice.

So I says to Negotiator You wanna give us some space?

She says to me I hope you understand, but I can't let her get too close, or go too far from me. Procedure, I'm sorry. But I can step back, at least a little bit. Would you like that?

I says Of course I fuckin would, what'd I just say?

Negotiator gives me a thumbs up and steps back a ways. Daff takes a few steps forward and then stops.

I can see journalists got little white tabs in their fedoras crawlin around the bushes now, tryin to get in earshot. Negotiator spots em too, gestures to the cops. The cops start shoutin at em.

Daff says Sammy, Sammy, Sammy.

I says to her I been real good. Gettin better. I swear to ya.

Daff just tuts at her shoes and says I know. I talked to Godric. He told me everything.

I says Listen, he

She cuts me off and says He's not mad. He was, but he's not anymore. I know you're trying. I'm just sorry this is how…things are happening.

I says Me too. I didn't want you gettin roped in. I'm real sorry.

She says to me I roped myself in.

I says Huh?

She says to me You need help right now. I'm not talking about, listen, don't make that face, I can see it from here. I'm not talking about psychological help or anything like that. I'm talking about legal. You're getting arrested today. There's no helping that. Because the only other alternative is you let yourself get gunned down, which I'm officially forbidding you from doing. So now it's just a question of, how can we beat this, keep you from getting the chair?

I says to her *We?*

Daff smiles. She says If you're willing to accept the

help. I want to help. But you need to want to accept it.

I says How the fuck're we gonna do that? They got me for killin cops. I don't figure Oops for much of a fuckin defense.

Daff says Janis is working on options. And, more to the point...Wally is.

I says to her Wally? I figure he wanted me fuckin done in, cop wise.

She looks back over her shoulders at all the cop cars got their gumpdrops spinnin, all the guys got their guns out and radios chirpin. Then she says to me Wally wanted you to get arrested because he's pretty confident he can pull on enough strings, in tandem with Janis, to close this nightmare out as cleanly as is conceivable.

I ask her Why the fuck didn't he say so?

She says to me What would he have said?

Fair point.

Boy, go fuckin figure, huh! Sure pays for a guy like me to have a guy does shady business with the whole fuckin food chain as a best buddy, huh?

Then she takes a deep breath and gulps real loud. She sniffles and says It's a gambit, for sure. It might not work. But...there aren't any other options. This is the best case. But for it to work...you have to come out. Step outside and turn yourself in.

I can't help it, I have a quick figure on maybe this is another fuckin gag, another somebody I got a big heart for tryna play me on accounta they figure I'm fuckin dumb. I don't figure that's the right figure...but I can't fuckin shake it. So I says to her Maybe I can figure somethin else ain't so

She says There's nobody in there with you. Everybody knows that. They're just trying to get you to come out so they don't have to go in. I'm their Hail Mary, though. If I can't get you out, they're going in. At which point, things are going to get a *lot* worse for you. You're a cop killer, Samuzzo. There's no getting around that. Cops don't like cop killers.

I says to her I ain't a copkiller.

She just frowns.

I says I ain't! I only killed cops on accident.

It ain't right, sayin what she's doin is *just* frownin.

So I says to her Alright, you answer me one question and I'll come out. I'm comin out however you answer, so you ain't gotta lie or crossdress the truth. You just tell me, once Godric figured out how's this all his fault, did he call you? I'm askin on accounta he called Janis who he ain't never had dealins with. And since you already told me he's called ya on other occasions tryin to get me committed at a fuckin loonybin or whatever you two were fuckin conspirin about, I just gotta wonder... did he call you? Did he tell about how'd all this happen and how's he tryin to steer me clear of him?

She asks me Why would he tell me any of this?

I says On accounta you two both wanted me to get lobotomized and locked in a fuckin broom closet.

She blinks wet and says No. No, he didn't call me. Me wanting to help you, to see you *want* to get help, wasn't part of some fucking conspiracy. It's because I love you and I was worried about you. Now are you gonna come out and let your friends help you, or…I don't even have a second thing, because not taking the help would be fucking stupid. And I know you're not fucking stupid.

Good thing I'm some sorta adrenalized, knowin I'm about to poke my head outta the door. Otherwise I mighta got to fuckin weepin again.

I have a big old sigh and I says to her Wanna see if I can get out there and give you a fuckin smooch before they pull us off each other?

She smiles and says Might be the last one for a while. You better make it count.

I figure I do.

GO FIGURE

SOMETIMES Wally comes to visit, only he don't talk so much. He figures the guy standin by the door's listenin in on the visitations so's he can write em down later, even though they ain't supposedta. I gotta figure he's figurin right, on accounta a lotta stuff happens at Yellow Onion ain't supposedta. I ain't sure why does he come to visit, on accounta the prison's all the way down in Virginia on accounta I gotta serve a buncha years in a buncha different places on accounta I ain't sure why. Maybe they wanna see do they run outta places first or do I kick the bucket. Unless my pals get my dumb ass outta here.

Whatever it is, it means Wally's gotta drive down to Virginia so's he can sit on the other side of some glass and just look at me and not talk so much.

I ask him How's it goin and he says to me It's alright.

I ask him You have any good conversations lately, meanin some of his judge buddies or whoever might owe him a favor. That's right about when he clams up. On the outside I couldn't never get him to shut the fuck up about what's goin on, only now I guess he's got a gag order far as his gags go. Don't wanna incriminate himself. Whatever, I get it. I just wish he'd loop me in on somethin. Gimme somethin to hang onto. I got no clue when am I gonna get out, how's it goin, what the fuck.

I tell him It's so fuckin borin here, pal.

He shrugs and says to me I believe it. How's the food?

Every time he comes he asks me how's the food. Like I'm gonna tell him It's been shit for a while but since the last time you asked they got a five star chef in the mess.

Then we just sorta sit there. I appreciate him comin out and everythin, on accounta he ain't got the same incentives like Daff or Janis got, but his heart don't seem in it, like I said. I ain't even sure why does he keep comin. What's he gettin outta this?

I ask him as much and he says It's what pals do for each other.

And yeah, Wally's a pal ain't got an asterisk like some of my other pals got, on accounta I sorted out a while back he was just as fuckin clueless about the whole goose chase as I was. Ha, ha. Still funny, goose chase. I sorted it by I asked did he know about the whole fuckin mess of misunderstandin and he told me he didn't. Most times I wouldn't believe that kinda thing, somebody just sayin to me they didn't know somethin I think they mighta, but what reason's he got for leadin me on? I got so many life sentences, I ain't gettin outta here without I got his help. He don't wanna see me in a room ain't got a guard might be too attentive, he's only gotta stop tryna help. He ain't done that yet, from what Janis says.

I tell him I really appreciate him sayin such a thing, then I ask him You know how's Daff doin?

He says Trial's still going.

I ask him *Still?*

He shrugs and says They're really trying to pin her as an accomplice, but you guys did a good… He looks at the corners of the little window like he's gonna spot a microphone and he says There's still not a lot of evidence she knew anything.

I nod on accounta that's how'd we fuckin plan it, and ain't neither of us're fuckin stupid. Specially not her.

I ask him Agnes dead yet?

He says I don't think so.

I says Hmph.

Then we just sit there real quiet for a while. I try to get Wally talkin a few more times, askin him real sly How's your job treatin ya or You got a new job you're workin or Some new gags on the horizon or what? Only he just kinda screws up his mouth around the corners and shrugs. He says Oh, you know or I dunno or he waves his hands like an airplane hit turbulence and makes an Eeeeh noise.

See, here's a skill I never picked up. Makin Wally talk. I always been so focused on the reverse, I never figured I'd need to learn to reverse that reverse. But it's alright. I got time to learn. Long as he keeps comin to visit, I got all the time in the world. I mean that literal-wise. You add up all the time I'm servin, it'd wrap ten times round the fuckin planet itself. Does time wrap? I don't fuckin know. I got a long sentence, that's the thing.

Only I'm hopin I ain't gotta learn that skill anyway. I'm hopin I'm gettin out prior to I been in here long enough to learn. No, hope ain't got nothin to do with it. I'm gettin out. Only question is, am I gettin out on acc-ounta my pals helped me...or on accounta I figured how'm I gonna do it myself?

Now we're both just sittin here, nobody runnin their mouth or even walkin it, til it's time Wally's gotta go.

GO FIGURE

ALL the guys in the group figured I'm real clever for callin it Paci-FIST. Now I never *said* to em I came up with it, but I ain't about to set em straight if they wanna figure I did. Somebody knows about the real Paci-FIST shows up here, which is maybe pretty fuckin likely, then maybe they're gonna have a slip on the stairs, then crawl back up and have the same slip a second time.

Ha, ha. Just kiddin. That ain't done. But humor sure ain't against the fuckin rules.

We meet in the mess once a week and have a nice chat. Just a buncha fuckin locked-up bruisers talkin about resolvin our differences non-violently. We yak on about copin strategies for when're we feelin angry or sad or confused. We talk about how maybe it ain't always right, holdin on to grudges like we worked hard for

351

em.

And then when the guards are outta earshot we talk about ways we might get the fuck outta here. We talk about how's Greg tryin to start his own group like ours, and maybe we wanna see him gettin clumsy around somethin pointy on accounta two groups're just gonna muddy the water and probably blow it for everybody. We talk about how're we gonna play it when we get out, where're we gonna go, who're we gonna see. Who do we wanna see ain't gonna see us comin.

We're gonna help each other out, is the thing. That's what fuckin pals do. Even if you're a bruiser, ain't nothin wrong with askin for help. That's a fuckin lesson I learned.

Talkin about the getout, prison riot's everybody's go-to. Only that's played. I says to em Ya wanna bring in the boys with the billy clubs, you go right on ahead. But it ain't the distraction it used to be. Besides, this place's probably got some kinda fuckin laughin gas they can pump in. Don't forget fellas, it's the future now. We gotta assume they got some future shit.

Jordan says to me It can't be the future now, Sammy.

I says to him Whaddyamean with that, can't be the future?

Al says It's always *becoming* the future, but it can't ever *be* the future on accounta if it was then it'd be the present.

I says to Al First off, I'm not gonna tell ya again, ya gotta stop sayin *on accounta*, on accounta that's what I say. You keep just takin shit other people say and pretendin you came up with it.

He says No I don't.

Everybody says Yeah, you kinda do.

He folds his arms and says No I *don't*.

Then we all ignore him.

I says I ain't lookin to get in a whole fuckin discussion about it. It's the future, and anybody wants to say it's the present or otherwise's gonna wind up on my naughty list. See what kinda presents you got *then*.

They all agree that's fair enough on accounta I spent some time here in solitary on accounta you ain't supposedta break guys' arms or stab em with chipped off bits of concrete. But like I said, a lotta stuff happens here ain't supposedta. And the guys in the group don't want nothin to happen to em ain't supposedta. So they all agree that's fair enough.

So yeah, I know, that sorta stuff ain't done. But how about when it's self-defense, huh? That's alright, I figure, even for a guy's been through the Ring. And same for if it's self-defense in advance. On accounta it's all down to the contextuals, the way I see it. Rings're for Resolutionizin sometimes…but you put a bruiser in any Ring and he'll square up with *somethin* in time.

Listen, outside's got a set of lessons ya wanna learn. The hoosegow's got a different set. I'm just tryna figure how'm I gonna square the circle.

Like I tell em in Paci-FIST, we're all a fuckin work in progress.

Speakin of, presently a guard comes back in earshot and I says to the other guys How'd that make ya feel,

Leland?

Leland comes back from outer space and he says to me Huh?

I glance at the guard and I ask Leland How'd it feel to resolve your fuckin differences with Walter usin words and sensitivities and shit?

Leland looks at Walter all confused, then he looks at the guard and remembers about how oh yeah he did have some differences he resolved in the manner I just fuckin mentioned. He says to me Oh, it felt real nice.

I says to him That's right. Violence oughta be a last fuckin resort, on accounta it ain't fair to people what're weak that we can just lean on em and then they do what we want em to. Hurtin people ain't nice, no matter how much're you gettin paid. It ain't easy bein a good person, but we gotta keep the ethics right where we can see em on accounta that's the only howsit what'll mean we're a buncha swell fuckin fellas.

They all agree that's fair enough about how violence ain't fair. Funny thing is, I don't figure they're just noddin on accounta the guard's stalkin past. I figure they just plain old agree. And funnier thing is, I figure I believe every fuckin word what'd I just say too.

Why the fuck not? I figure it'd be real fuckin swell if folks hear the name Samuzzo D'Amato and figure Oh, that guy? He's a swell fuckin fella. That's my fuckin resolution ain't gotta wait for a new year. I'm gonna be a swell fuckin fella.

Then the guard goes outta earshot again.

Samuzzo D'Amato will return in

THE WHOLE

BRANZINO

Also by Jud Widing

Novels
The Little King of Crooked Things
A Middling Sort
Westmore and More!
The Year of Uh

Stories
Identical Pigs

Made in the USA
Middletown, DE
12 May 2019